BOU

'Please, James, untie .... pleaded. 'We have guests and –'

'And it is time, my little love, for you to learn the first lesson of your married life!'

With that, James spun her around so that her breasts were pressing into the wall.

'James, please . . .' Caroline's voice was husky with her rising passion.

In answer, James pressed one hand firmly over her mouth, while his other found the hidden zip at the back of her dress and pulled it down, revealing her defenceless buttocks. 'I demand several things from my slave,' James announced. 'Total obedience and absolute silence unless I permit speech. You have already broken two of those rules, for which you will be punished.'

By the same author:

BOUND TO OBEY
BOUND TO SERVE

BOUND TO SUBMIT

Amanda Ware

This book is a work of fiction.
In real life, make sure you practise safe sex.

First published in 1997 by
Nexus
332 Ladbroke Grove
London W10 5AH

Typeset by TW Typesetting, Plymouth, Devon

Printed and bound by
Caledonian Books Ltd, Glasgow

ISBN 0 352 33194 1

Again for John –
as always in control!

One

'Fuigi! You are a genius!'

The compact Japanese man bowed his dark head. As usual, he remained unsmiling, but his eyes could not conceal a glow of triumph as he looked at the golden-haired girl standing before him. With just a touch of fussiness, he smoothed a fold in the white latex dress which the girl was wearing.

'Caroline, you look wonderful!'

The speaker who had complimented both Fuigi and Caroline had moved to stand before the girl and was now running his hands appreciatively over her rubber-clad breasts. The bodice of the latex dress was skin-tight to the tightly cinched waist, from which looser folds of material fell seductively to the floor, creating a sensuous shimmer of whiteness. The golden-haired girl looked into the eyes of her Master and husband-to-be and smiled shyly. She raised her arms to smooth the soft nap of the form-fitting black leather of the suit that James wore. As she did so, his eyes watched the swell of her breasts, tightly confined but clearly visible to the nipples within the low-cut neckline of the dress. James caught his breath as he looked at her. This wonderful girl was really his: the girl who he had waited such a long time for and the sex slave who made his life complete. He felt his penis harden within its leather confines as he reached into the pocket of his jacket and produced a white suede collar.

1

'My wedding gift to you, my darling,' he said, slipping the wide collar around her slim neck.

'I shall wear it with pride,' Caroline whispered softly, as she felt James buckling the collar around her neck.

'And until I decide to remove it,' James said with mock irony, producing a small gold padlock. 'Fuigi, if you would be so kind . . .?'

The little Japanese man moved forward.

'It will be my pleasure,' he said, taking the padlock from James and snapping it closed around the collar's buckle.

James moved to a table at the side of the huge floor-to-ceiling window that was a feature of the lounge in his Malibu beach-front home. To the accompaniment of the pounding surf, just audible through the thickened glass of the window, he walked back to Caroline. She felt a shiver of excitement and arousal run through her as she saw the white silken ropes that he held. As she felt him gently drawing her arms behind her, her clitoris pulsed a signal to her. The ropes were drawn around her wrists and firmly tied and when he had completed his task, James stood in front of Caroline, his eyes full of the admiration and desire that he felt for this girl. Was it really less than a year since he had first seen her? As if it were only yesterday, he recalled the picture that she had presented: she had been wearing a pair of tight black rubber trousers, the crotch being invitingly unzipped as she lay on a bed waiting for him. She had been offered to him for a night's entertainment by her then Master. Momentarily, James' face darkened as he recalled the face of the man who had offered him such a prize: Clive Craigen, the man with the darkly mesmeric eyes; the man who had lost his one-time slave to James. That first night with Caroline had made James determined to keep the lovely, submissive girl for himself. Reciprocating his desires in full measure, Caroline had been only too ready to be released from her bondage to Clive and to enter her new life of legal and loving servitude with James. Now, James hoped, Clive Craigen was history.

'There, my darling, you look exactly like a dutiful slave,' he said, his eyes lingering on the small, beautifully shaped breasts. He bent his head and kissed each one, before raising his lips to hers, feeling her excitement which matched his own.

'Not quite right! There is something missing!'

Caroline and James turned to look in the direction from which the sensuously commanding voice had emanated. Fuigi, who had also turned to look, gasped at the tailoring skill he saw displayed in the white PVC catsuit which literally seemed to flow over the incredible shape of the body confined within its shiny lustrousness. Tucked into the belt at the slim waist, a white leather whip dangled innocently, awaiting the decree of its Mistress. Holding out her arms in greeting, Lynne walked into the room, the spiked heels of her white PVC boots clicking on the polished teak of the floor tiles.

'Lynne! It's wonderful to see you!' Caroline exclaimed as she was embraced by the woman in whose household she had experienced her first taste of slavery. 'Is Francis with you?' she asked, referring to the man who had first dominated and owned her shapely body.

'Try keeping me away,' came a familiar deep voice, as strong arms wrapped both Caroline and Lynne in a warm hug.

'You said something was not quite right?' James asked, kissing Caroline in a warmly admiring manner.

3

'Oh, yes,' Lynne said, flipping her long, dark ponytail over her shoulder in impatience at her own forgetfulness. 'Caroline, I have something for you to remind you of your place!'

Smilingly, she unfolded a long, white leather lead from the package that Francis had passed to her. Clipping the lead to Caroline's collar, she ran her hand through the soft blonde waves that fell over the girl's shoulders. Lynne's eyes were moist with admiration and sexual desire. There was also the hint of times remembered as she looked at the beautiful girl standing before her. Lynne was no doubt remembering how she and Francis had interviewed Caroline for the position of their slave; thinking back to how Caroline's nervous excitability as she adapted herself to her new rôle, and how keen she had been to learn.

'You've come a long way, Caroline,' Lynne said, brushing her lips across those of her one-time slave. 'Both Francis and I are very proud of you.'

Now it was the turn of Francis, her first Master, to stand before Caroline. He was as handsome as she remembered him, especially since he had returned his hair to its normal dark colouring. When she had last seen him in England, she had been too confused to ask him why he had changed his hair colour to blonde. At that time, all she had been able to think about was James and how much she was missing him. Knowing of her deep attraction to the American, Clive had kept her closely confined, unable to make contact with anyone in the outside world. She remembered how she had persuaded Clive's housekeeper, Mrs Davies, to contact James on her behalf. Now she smiled as she looked at Francis, remembering the part he had played in rescuing her from Clive's clutches; how she had stayed with Lynne and Francis while Clive was away on business and how they had encouraged the reunion between the soon-to-be married pair. Caroline's eyes moistened as she studied Francis. He and Lynne had become good friends. She admired his now dark hair, which definitely matched the strength of his personality. He was wearing a cleverly worked suit in white and black leather, the white top seeming to meld seamlessly into the black trousers. Caroline would have thrown her arms around him, had not the pressure of the silken cords reminded her of her bound state.

'Francis! It's so good to see you,' Caroline said.

'I wouldn't have missed this for anything. It's another kind of ceremonial, you know. Passing the slave from one Master to another.'

There was a pause while Caroline searched James' face. In an unspoken communication, James understood that look and nodded imperceptibly. Caroline smiled her thanks and looked at Francis.

'Liam,' she said. 'How is Liam?'

Francis smiled. 'Liam is very well and, you will be pleased to hear, very happy. His businesses were saved from bankruptcy – Clive kept his promise as he didn't have much choice – and he's doing well. He apologises for not being here. He has another slave and he's ... um ... breaking her in!'

Caroline's smile was one of genuine pleasure. 'I'm very glad. He's a good Master and deserves the best.'

Caroline felt a wave of relief. Liam had succeeded Francis as her Master and she had been happy with him for a while until that happiness had been shattered by the man who had tricked her into living as his slave while Liam was out of the country, desperately trying to salvage his businesses. Clive had coerced Caroline into believing that he could save Liam from ruin by providing certain information that he had in his possession: the proviso had been that

5

Caroline was to live with him and be his willing sex slave, from which humiliating position she had been rescued by Lynne and Francis. Caroline looked across at James and smiled at him. She was marrying the only man she really cared about and the only one she was truly happy to love and serve for as long as he wanted; Caroline hoped that that would be for a very long time.

'I am neglecting my duties as Mistress-of-Honour,' Lynne said, approaching Caroline. 'As you obviously cannot hold a bouquet, you must allow me to have something to do.' As she spoke, Lynne tied a white silk scarf across Caroline's mouth, knotting it securely behind the bride's head. Standing back, she nodded her approval at her own work and took up the leash of the white leather lead she would use to take Caroline to her Master. 'That's better. You don't need to speak until the service begins. I will remove your gag at the appropriate time.'

Fuigi, James and Francis had already left to take up their positions at the edge of the white leather carpeting that had been laid across a section of the beach in front of the house. Lynne led Caroline down the stairs and stood with her at the beginning of the wide strip of white leather as they waited for the music to begin. As Madonna's breathy voice competed with the sounds of the ocean in her *Erotica* number, Lynne tugged gently at the lead, indicating to Caroline that she should begin her walk: it was a walk that would lead Caroline into a series of sexual adventures that would be darkly exciting and ultimately life-changing.

Two

James had met Judge Eric Fullman at a fetish party
in Los Angeles. The two men had become friends and
Eric had seemed the natural choice when James had
been looking for someone to officiate at his marriage
to Caroline. As Caroline proceeded towards them,
James smiled, not only at the vision that his bride
presented, but also at the undoubted excitement and
appreciation he sensed emanating from Eric. He was
also aware of the ripple of excitement which Caroline
and Lynne's appearance evoked from the seated
assemblage of guests. Caroline's head was bowed
submissively as she followed her Mistress-of-Honour.
Naturally shy, she was glad not to have to look at the
faces she passed. She was aware of only two things:
the knowledge that she was about to marry the man
she loved and the undeniable fact that she was
sexually aroused. The silken cords that bound her
wrists reminded her of her position as her Master's
slave, a position in which she gloried.

Reaching James and Eric, Caroline stopped and
stood looking at James as Lynne removed the gag
from her mouth. When this had been done, James
bent his head and parted her lips with his insistent
tongue. The kiss was passionately received by his
bride, and it was only the noise as Eric cleared his
throat that separated them. More than one person in
the watching ranks of people moved uncomfortably

in their seats, impossibly aroused by the scene they had just witnessed. Two of the watchers observed the scene with extreme and differing interests, one professionally and one obsessively.

Patrick Clelland was only twenty-six, but was already a renowned and respected photographer. Extremely interested in the SM scene, he had started to use his lovers of both sexes as models. He had had several very successful exhibitions of photographs, mostly in areas frequented by sub-culture aficionados. As he specialised in bondage photographs, he had become something of an expert in the use of ropes. There was no shortage of people who wanted to pose for him and he spent many happily sensual hours artistically tying his willing victims.

In his desire to be famous as a photographer, Patrick had included some more conventional pictures which had led to him being able to reach a wider audience. It was quite usual for him to have exhibitions running in tandem: one featuring his erotic pictures and the other normal portraiture and other studies. Patrick was now not only able to sell his work effortlessly, he was also much in demand as a commissioned photographer.

The words of the wedding ceremony faded into the background as Patrick looked at Caroline's latex-clad form and that of her Mistress-of-Honour demurely standing behind the couple. In his mind, Patrick was remembering the picture that the two of them had presented as they walked past him. This was definitely one for the *Los Angeles Times*! He was grateful for the white leather jeans that he wore. Had he been attired in his usual skin-tight trousers, his erection would have been very noticeable. Excited both by the erotic scenario he had witnessed and by professional interest, Patrick began to plan how he would compose the pictures for maximum controversial effect. He would make the usually staid readers of the *Times* come in their nicely tailored pants as they studied his pictures!

Another guest was watching the scene with a similar intensity. Leyla Dubois, known to her friends and slaves as Mistress Leyla, could not take her eyes off the shapely and impossibly sensuous figure of the bride. Leyla had known James for some time and, in the past, had supplied girls to cater to his needs. She had met his previous girlfriends and, with professional interest, had observed that they were unlikely to stay the course. She had always been right and now she knew why. If James had been waiting for someone like Caroline . . . Well, no wonder it had been a long wait! Surely there were not too many girls who looked like his bride, and this one was submissive as well! Mistress Leyla had to concede that the feelings she was experiencing were something akin to jealousy. If only she had met Caroline first. Leyla stroked a lock of her own jet-black hair with a smile. If they had met, would Caroline have been able to resist? Justifiably proud of her perfect figure, Leyla accepted – as nothing but her due – the homage paid to her by the people she met. She found it easy to obtain slaves of both sexes and enjoyed the training of each one. Leaning forward, Leyla rested her classically perfect chin on the back of one hand. The gesture which, performed by a more ordinary person, might have seemed affected, suited the black rubber-clad figure. Out of the corner of her slanting black eyes, she observed several of the guests looking at her with open admiration. Almost purring with satisfaction, Leyla returned her attention to Caroline. Yes, she decided, she would have that girl for her next slave. James would not be a problem. She could handle him.

Knowing that she was the focus of attention, yet unaware of the special interest felt by two of the guests, Caroline turned to James at the conclusion of the ceremony. For a moment he looked at her, before crushing her slight body within a powerful embrace. He parted her eager lips and probed her mouth with his tongue, feeling her response. She was still tied, but that was how James liked his new bride. She was his wife, but she was also his slave. Drawing back and looking into the blue-grey eyes that glowed with her love for him, James knew that Caroline was very happy with her new situation.

'Fuigi, you are going to have to help me,' James called out to the little Japanese. 'I want you to design a whole new wardrobe for my wife . . . All in rubber, of course.'

Pleased with his commission and with the prospect of designing for Caroline, Fuigi bowed to them both.

'It will be my pleasure. The garments will be for purely visual purposes, or . . .?' Fuigi raised an eyebrow, whilst exhibiting what for him almost constituted a smile.

'For visual and practical purposes,' James answered, smiling at Caroline.

Eminently satisfied, Fuigi bowed again. Almost immediately, his mind began to construct a gorgeous array of restrictive clothing for his client; clothing that would sensuously adorn the young bride while keeping her well controlled.

Accepting congratulations, Caroline and James hurried into the house. Pushing her into a cupboard in the entry hall-way, James pressed his new bride against the back wall.

'I've been remarkably patient,' James said, gripping her tightly above the elbows. 'Now it's time for that patience to be rewarded!'

10

'James . . . Our guests . . .' Caroline protested half-heartedly.

'They'll wait!' James declared triumphantly. 'You're really mine at last! I can do exactly what I want. Any objections?'

'Please, James, untie me,' Caroline pleaded. 'We have guests and –'

'And it is time, my little love, for you to learn the first lesson of your married life!'

With that, James spun her around so that her breasts were pressing into the wall.

'James, please . . .' Caroline's voice was husky with her rising passion.

In answer, James pressed one hand firmly over her mouth, while his other found the hidden zip at the back of her dress and pulled it down, revealing her defenceless buttocks.

'I demand several things from my slave,' James continued. 'Total obedience and absolute silence unless I permit speech. You have already broken two of those rules, for which you will be punished.'

Caroline struggled against him, anger at this injustice coursing through her. Her hands were still tied, making her struggles futile, struggles which were, in any event, part of the game they both loved to play. She yelped beneath the hand that gagged her as the first hard slap landed on her bottom. The slap was immediately followed by another, even harder blow. Caroline writhed as the pain flared within her. Fuelled with excitement at her resistance, James continued the rhythmic slaps, alternating between the creamy cheeks of her buttocks until they were both reddened and marked with the force of the blows. As he knew it would, gradually Caroline's struggling became sensuous wriggling as the pain from the beating turned to extreme pleasure and James felt her body straining

11

back against him. He ceased his blows long enough to free the zip on his trousers, releasing his straining penis which was already lubricated with pre-come fluid. Removing his hand from her mouth, James parted the glowing buttocks and pushed his cock into the tight bud of her anus. Caroline gasped her pleasure as she felt James sliding into her. She felt his hands cupping her rubber-clad breasts and, as his fingers twisted the hard nipples, succumbed to the full force of her orgasm. Her scream of pleasure was stifled as James' hand again covered her mouth, but there was nothing to stifle her husband's savage grunt of pleasure as he emptied himself into her willing body.

'Caroline, I'd like you to meet Patrick Clelland,' James said, holding Caroline's elbow in a firmly possessive grip. 'Patrick's a photographer and is interested in taking some shots of you and Lynne for the newspaper.'

Her stinging buttocks once again demurely covered by the latex of her dress, Caroline smiled and extended a hand, which was warmly clasped by Patrick. 'What sort of photographs do you want, Mr Clelland?' Caroline asked.

'You and Lynne made a pretty spectacular appearance just now. I'd like to recreate that, and also show Lynne congratulating you,' Patrick answered, his eyes alight with admiration.

'Congratulating me?' Caroline asked, turning and using her eyes to elicit James' approval.

'Patrick specialises in erotic photography, my darling. As well as the *Times*, he wants to sell the pictures to other publications. I think it's an excellent idea.' James' voice denoted his excitement at the proposed project.

'I sell pictures to some specialist magazines,' explained Patrick. 'I think you and Lynne would enjoy the experience.' Patrick's glance took in Lynne's PVC-clad form, noting her excitement.

'It's OK with me,' Lynne said, favouring Patrick with a sensual glance.

Patrick arranged Caroline and Lynne in their earlier poses at the edge of the white leather carpet. Caroline was again gagged and Lynne clipped the lead into her collar. Patrick photographed them for the newspaper and then took them inside for the other pictures that he wanted.

'Lynne, why don't you congratulate Caroline?' Patrick asked. Lynne and Patrick exchanged glances and then she stepped to Caroline and removed her gag. Caroline was more than a little surprised when Lynne grabbed a handful of her hair and sharply pulled her head back, covering the bride's mouth with her own. There was a murmur of approval from the watching guests as Lynne forced her tongue into the surprised Caroline's mouth. Lynne's free hand cruelly twisted one of Caroline's nipples, making the girl moan with pain beneath the imprisoning mouth. Both thoroughly excited, the watching James and Francis strode forward and each grabbed one of Caroline's arms, forcing her to the floor. Before Caroline could protest, Lynne was kneeling beside her and again forcing her tongue between the surprised, but excited, girl's lips. James and Francis expertly stripped the wedding dress from the far from reluctant bride and stood back, their cocks straining against the confines of their trousers as Lynne crouched down, her knees on either side of Caroline's head. Staring at Caroline, her eyes blazing with passion, she unzipped the front of her PVC catsuit, offering her wet bush for Caroline's probing tongue.

13

Unaware of the pain as she lay on her bound wrists, Caroline eagerly applied herself to her one-time Mistress' bush, lapping at the moisture. She was also unaware of the constant noise from Patrick's motor-driven camera as he moved around, constantly taking the shots that would earn him a fortune. Francis and James were both furiously masturbating as they watched the scene: James revelling in the sight of his new bride's submission; Francis enjoying his wife and one-time sex slave cavorting with each other while the other guests watched the show lasciviously. As Caroline and Lynne came together, one woman watched with passionate jealousy. Mistress Leyla masturbated herself to an excited climax as she gazed at the two women. As her breath came in short gasps, she determined that she was going to have Caroline as her own slave, to be kept tied up and waiting for Mistress Leyla's pleasure.

'Now, Caroline, you are to undergo your first test,' James said, stroking her long, blonde hair. He bent down and placed his lips close to Caroline's ear. 'I don't want you to disappoint me, my dear, or your punishment will indeed be severe. Do you understand?'

The blonde head nodded. Satisfied, James straightened and stood back to admire the picture that Caroline presented. She was naked except for her white leather collar, the shining padlock reflecting the candlelight that glowed from fifty white candles placed around the large chamber. Caroline was blindfolded and gagged with a large white rubber ball placed between her lips and secured with white leather straps behind her head. Her breasts were bound with white silken cords and her elbows and wrists were securely tethered behind her. White cords

14

bound her knees and ankles, making her kneeling position more than a little uncomfortable. James looked at Francis, Patrick and Eric, who stood beside him. All the men were naked, their cocks straining with excitement.

'Gentlemen, you see before you the lovely girl who is now my wife. She has sworn love and obedience to me. However, I need to put that to the test and you, my friends –' James gestured to the watching wedding guests '– are my witnesses.' The smell of sexual excitement was very noticeable in the air as James again knelt beside Caroline. 'Now, my dear, myself and three of our guests are each going to beat you. Pay particular attention, my darling, because I am going to ask you to identify your Master. To help you, your test will include tasting the cocks of the four of us. You will then be asked to identify your Master. If you get it wrong, my dear, I am afraid I will have to give permission for each of the guests here assembled to punish you as they each see fit. There will be no restrictions. Do I make myself clear?'

Filled with sexual excitement and not a little fear, Caroline nodded. 'Good,' James said, rising to his feet. 'Gentlemen, you may proceed.' Silently, James moved behind Caroline and began to whip her already abused buttocks. He placed the strokes carefully, trying to avoid the worst of the reddened area of her backside. Caroline was grateful for her gag. Without it, she would have been calling for mercy, even though she could already feel the stirrings of pleasure as the pain underwent its usual transformation. James finished the whipping and stood back, allowing Francis to take the whip from him. As agreed between the four men, the changeover was undertaken in complete silence, leaving Caroline uncertain as to whether the new assault on her was

15

performed by the same antagonist or a different one. In any event, it did not seem to matter. She was now experiencing pure pleasure. Her bottom glowed with warmth and her clitoris pulsed its need. She wished that her hands were untied and she could reach herself. It was with a sense of shock that she heard her new husband's voice and became aware that the beating had stopped.

'You have borne that very well, my dear, as I knew you would. Now for the second part of the test,' James said, reaching down to gently caress the nipples that strained so invitingly beneath the ropes. He reached behind her head and removed the restricting gag. Before she could thank him, James' hand closed over her mouth. 'No noise now, my darling. I want your total concentration on the task ahead.'

Caroline nodded, although she wanted to beg James for some sexual relief. She could have told him that, by his very concern for her already abused flesh, he had identified himself as the first of the beaters. Instead, she attempted to compose herself for the ordeal that she faced. She would have to try to concentrate on making the correct choice, rather than give in to the sexual pleading of her body. Her own pleasure would have to wait. She did not want to risk her Master's displeasure by failing this, the first task of her married life. With growing anticipation, she waited, aware of the palpable tension in the room. Silently, James motioned for Francis to step forward and it was not long before she felt the hardness of a penis as it pushed at her lips. Eagerly, she opened her mouth, letting the unknown cock slide into her mouth. Unable to control his excitement, Francis gripped Caroline by the hair, forcing more of his cock into her willing mouth. The others watched and waited their turn. By the time that Caroline was

16

swallowing her fourth mouthful of semen, she was almost in a state of frenzied excitement. She must get some relief soon, or she would go mad. James, the last of the pleasure seekers, took pity on her and gently pushed her so that she lay sideways on the floor. She felt fingers gently stroking her clitoris and that was all it took. With inexorable force, the wave of her orgasm swept her into blissful semi-consciousness as she gave way to the exhausted pleasure that she felt.

'Well, my darling, the guests are waiting. Are you going to disappoint them?' James whispered in her ear. 'Or are you going to disappoint me?'

James gently removed her blindfold and smiled at her as she half-opened her eyes and stared lovingly at her husband. 'I'm sorry to be rude to our guests, Master, but I know when it was you beating me and I know when your cock was in my mouth.' She didn't add that, on both occasions, it was his kindness that had given him away. She didn't have the energy to say any more and, in any event, she didn't have to as James' mouth closed over hers and he gave her his own personal thanks.

Three

'Come on, lazy bones, up you get!'

Caroline groaned as Lynne's words were accompanied by a sharp slap across her exposed buttocks. In need of some support, Caroline groped across the bed, hoping to locate James. She opened one surprised eye as her fingers explored only empty space. 'James . . .?'

'James and Francis have been up for hours. They're in the study discussing business,' Lynne said, wrinkling her nose in disgust. 'On a beautiful day like today. What a waste! Anyway, Miss –' she continued, pulling off the sheet that had only partially covered Caroline '– that gives us the opportunity to go shopping, so I want you up, showered and breakfasted within the next half an hour!'

Caroline groaned again. She felt that she needed a lot more sleep and Lynne was sounding just like she always used to when Caroline was her slave and could be ordered about in that fashion. 'I just want to sleep . . .,' she began, but Lynne forestalled any further protest by bodily hauling her off the bed and half-dragging her reluctant charge into the bathroom.

'You can sleep later,' Lynne promised. 'Francis and I are only here for a week and I want to see everything. Now shower!' With that admonition, Lynne retreated, slamming the bathroom door shut behind her one-time slave and feeling that, really, it was just like old times.

* * *

Dressed in clinging white PVC, her blonde hair brushed and gleaming, Caroline stared admiringly at the window display of a boutique called *Chained To Love*. The shop was a fetishist's dream, with skimpy black leather outfits vying with red PVC and rubber garments for their attention. Clad in dark blue rubber, Lynne was similarly fascinated.

'Perhaps you ladies would care to step inside and look around,' a sensual American female voice offered. Feeling identical sexual stirrings, Lynne and Caroline looked at the voice's owner. She was five feet six inches of pure sexuality.

'Hi, don't I know you?' the speaker continued, frowning as she tried to place the two girls. The frown disappeared as recognition dawned. 'You're Caroline and Lynne, aren't you?' The two girls exchanged amazed looks. 'I saw your pictures in the paper. Very, very nice. I'm sorry, I should introduce myself. I'm Laurie Selbourne and I own this pleasure palace.'

Lynne smiled and extended her hand. 'You have a great place here, Miss Selbourne.'

'Laurie, please. Come on in. I think you'll like it!'

Without further hesitation, Caroline and Lynne walked into the shop, still admiring the American woman and her incredible outfit. Laurie Selbourne had waist-length platinum blonde hair and a pair of cobalt blue eyes. Her figure was beautifully proportioned, squeezed into a form-hugging white rubber catsuit. Her feet were encased in a pair of black PVC ankle boots with the highest heels that Caroline had ever seen, yet Laurie walked in front of them with total confidence.

Once inside the shop, Laurie turned to Caroline. 'You are a very beautiful girl,' Laurie said, winking at Lynne. 'I must admit to being really turned on when I saw your picture in this morning's paper.' She reached out and stroked Caroline's hair. 'So beautiful and so very submissive. Just the combination I like.' She moved to a rack of shiny black clothing. 'I think that you'd look just fine in this.' Taking down one of the hangers, she smiled at Lynne. 'Mistress Lynne, perhaps you would be so kind as to help me . . .?'

Lynne and Laurie exchanged glances and knew that they were both on the same wavelength. Smiling, Lynne moved behind Caroline and unzipped the white PVC. Undeniably aroused but still a little unsure, Caroline looked at the other two women. 'I don't know . . .,' she began, but, shaking her head, Laurie pushed a black rubber ball gag between the girl's lips.

'Slaves shouldn't speak without first obtaining permission, isn't that right, Mistress Lynne?'

'You and I think alike, Mistress Laurie,' Lynne responded. 'Shall we tie the slave?'

'There is no need, Mistress Lynne, as I think you will shortly see,' Laurie said, slipping over Caroline's head the black rubber folds of the garment she was holding. 'This bondage cape is one of my specialities.'

Once it was draped over Caroline, Laurie demonstrated the cape's interesting possibilities. Concealed within its folds were several rubber belts of varying lengths. Caroline's wrists were quickly imprisoned within one of these as Laurie fastened them behind her, tightening the buckle on the belt to ensure a secure fit. Another belt went around the arms and a third cinched the waist to a pleasurably hour-glass shape. Pushing Caroline into a chair, Laurie demonstrated further belts which fitted snugly around the girl's ankles. 'You will see that these have rings fitted to them,' Laurie explained to Lynne. 'Just in case you feel the need to secure your slave with her legs conveniently apart.' Tightly buckling the ankle belts,

Laurie pulled Caroline to her feet. 'There,' she said triumphantly. 'To an outsider, she is merely dressed in a rather sexy cape. No one would know that the girl is in very tight bondage.'

Admiringly, Lynne walked around the now helpless Caroline. 'Mistress Laurie, I am most impressed. However . . .' She paused and tilted her head to one side, almost as if she were considering something.

'However?' Laurie questioned, enjoying the game.

'However, I'd like to put those ankle restraints to the test,' Lynne finished.

Now thoroughly aroused, Caroline joined the fun by struggling and making pleading sounds into her gag. 'You must excuse the slave,' Lynne said. 'Being married, she sometimes forgets that she is still just a slave.'

'Perhaps you would care to bring the slave into the back room. There is nothing I like better than disciplining the wayward ones!'

Laurie led the way into a room which was amply provided with items of discipline. Whips and canes lined the walls and there were shelves stocked with leather hoods, ropes and handcuffs. Holding her captive firmly by the arms, Lynne followed Laurie. Caroline whimpered into her gag, more through sexual pleading than protest. Laurie indicated a black leather couch and helped Lynne to push Caroline on to the couch. Swiftly, Laurie spread the prone girl's legs and buckled the couch's leather restraining straps on to the rings on the cape's ankle belts. A thick leather belt was strapped around Caroline's tightly cinched waist and a further strap ensured that she could not move her head. Now totally helpless, Caroline could only look to her captors for mercy.

Laurie selected a thin, whippy cane from the wall rack and approached the girl. Pushing up the folds of the voluminous cape, she demonstrated to Lynne how the garment could hold a prisoner securely, yet allow unobstructed access to the important pleasure zones. 'I think we should start with some marks across those nice white thighs,' Laurie said, moistening her lips in anticipation of the punishment to come.

Lynne stood to one side, admiring the sight that Caroline provided. She could see that the girl was wet and could smell the scent of sexual arousal – which was not just coming from Caroline. Her own excited fingers played with the wetness that the rubber of her outfit concealed. The cane struck the insides of Caroline's thighs, as Laurie expertly marked her captive. Caroline could only shout into her gag; firstly with pain and then with exquisite pleasure as an orgasm shook her. In her excitement, Laurie threw down the cane and turned to Lynne. Before long, the two of them were struggling together on the floor, breathing hard at the exertion of trying to remove tight-fitting clothing as quickly as possible.

Bound as she was, Caroline could only listen in extreme frustration to the sounds that the two women made as they pleasured each other; Lynne licking and sucking at Laurie's slit as probing fingers slid into her own moistness and stroked at the hard little nubbin that they encountered. Both women came at the same time, Lynne's scream of pleasure muffled by the increase of juices that filled her mouth as Laurie provided the evidence of her own gratification.

'You two are really something,' Laurie said admiringly, as she and Lynne unstrapped Caroline from the couch. 'I have an idea. It's something you could both help me with.'

'Name it,' Lynne said.

'I am planning a new catalogue for the boutique.

You and Caroline would be perfect as the models. You would be paid, plus you'd get to wear some very exciting outfits. What do you say?'

Lynne looked at Caroline, who nodded eagerly. 'When would you like to do this? Francis and I are going home shortly.'

'How about tomorrow? Patrick Clelland is a good friend of mine. He's already agreed to do the shoot if I can get suitable models. You two are certainly that!' Laurie enthused. 'I could ring him and check on his availability . . .'

'Do that,' Lynne said. 'I think it could be very exciting. Will we be modelling everything?'

Laurie caught her meaning and smiled. 'I think you will find that everyone will be well satisfied,' she said. 'Do I make myself clear?'

Lynne smiled and nodded. Caroline looked at the restrictive hoods and harnesses, shivering delightedly at the prospect. Looking at Laurie, she smiled her agreement.

Desperately trying to ignore the hardness within his jeans that distracted his concentration from his work, Patrick Clelland again bent over the viewfinder. 'Give me that sultry sneer, Melanie,' he instructed the beautiful ebony-coloured girl. Sensually coiling herself around her 'captive', Melanie complied. 'Great! Brilliant!' Patrick shouted excitedly as he reeled off shot after shot of the two girls. Melanie's chain-bound prisoner, nipples erect, joined in enthusiastically, watching Melanie yearningly, pleading with her eyes for the sexual release that her stern Mistress seemed to promise.

Leaving his camera, Patrick moved into the pool of light and crouched down beside the two girls. 'Melanie, why don't you stroke Clara with your whip?' he suggested, gently squeezing Clara's nipples and smiling at the blonde girl's frustrated moan. 'Shut up, darling,' Patrick said, smiling at her. 'If you keep that up, perhaps you had better be gagged.'

Melanie laughed as Clara moved restlessly, her chains making a delicious clinking sound. Looking pointedly at Patrick's bulging erection, Melanie ran a moist tongue across her lips. 'Perhaps we should gag her with something . . .?'

'Enough!' Patrick said, slapping Melanie's beautifully rounded bottom. 'However, that's not a bad idea.' Moving to Clara, Patrick eased the blonde girl's chain-bound limbs into a kneeling position. 'Now, Clara, you have been a naughty girl, haven't you?' Clara bowed her head submissively and nodded. 'Hold that look!' Patrick yelled, running back to his camera and reeling off a few shots. Looking up, he smiled. 'Now Melanie, why don't you kneel down with your back to Clara?'

'What do you have in mind?' Melanie asked, enjoying the situation hugely. She had been a little concerned when her agent had asked her to do this shoot. She had posed nude on numerous occasions and, although she was excited at the idea of being photographed by Patrick, she was not sure about his raunchier requirements. She had to admit, though, that she had enjoyed the first part of the job incredibly. Patrick wanted the two girls to have fun on this shoot. It was for a glossily produced bondage section in a superior photography book. Patrick had told Melanie that she was to play the part of the Mistress to Clara's prisoner and suggested that her first task was to bind Clara's voluptuous body in layers of shining chains. Melanie had become increasingly aroused as she performed this task and rightly suspected that such was Patrick's intention. Of her own

24

volition, she had caressed and kissed Clara as she had bound the girl and had been gratified by Clara's immediate response. Both girls had become so involved in what they were doing that they were unaware of Patrick's presence behind the camera. He was getting some unbelievable shots and that was just what he had intended.

After Melanie had knelt in front of Clara, she turned her head and looked challengingly at Clara. Without being told, the two girls were playing a game of their own. 'Lick me, slave!' Melanie commanded. 'If you do not obey, you will taste my whip!' Totally involved, Clara leant forward and bathed Melanie's backside with the wetness of her tongue. Melanie sucked in her breath and arched her back. 'Oh, yes. Do it for me, baby!'

Clara needed no further encouragement and used her tongue to greater effect, slipping it inside Melanie's appealingly presented rosebud opening. Melanie screamed her pleasure as Clara's exciting tongue pushed her towards an orgasm.

Behind the lens, Patrick tried to control his own excitement. The shoot was going brilliantly, better than he could have hoped. It was only his professionalism that reminded him to keep shooting and not rush to join the two girls, particularly when Melanie picked up her whip and thrust the handle into her own slit. She screamed out her pleasure and then fell upon the helplessly chained girl. She was soon lying on top of Clara, sucking and chewing at Clara's engorged nipples. While his assistant reloaded the camera, Patrick stood to one side, massaging his erection as he watched the two girls. Melanie pressed a firm hand over Clara's mouth, stifling the girl's cries, as she again used the whip handle to good effect. 'Be quiet, little girl, or I will have to punish you severely,' Melanie said, her voice deep and low. 'Would you like that, baby?' she asked. 'Shall I whip you and mark those beautiful thighs?'

With a muffled scream, Clara came swiftly and strongly. The excited contortions of her face were faithfully captured by Patrick's all-seeing lens.

Exhausted by the intensity of the shoot, Patrick took the phone that his assistant handed to him.

'Hi, Laurie,' Patrick said, unable to keep the exhaustion from his voice.

'Patrick, you sound *very* tired!' Laurie said.

'I am indeed, my darling, but it was worth it!'

'I'll bet,' Laurie said affectionately. She and Patrick had known each other for a very long time. 'I hope you're not too tired to consider doing me a favour?'

'It depends,' Patrick said.

'You'll love it *and* you get paid!' Laurie informed him.

'I'm listening.'

'I saw your photo of Lynne and Caroline,' Laurie said. 'I loved it and I want you to do some more photos of them for my new catalogue.'

'Sounds good. When and where?'

'Here of course and –,' Laurie hesitated, '– tomorrow. Please, Patrick. Lynne and Francis won't be here for very much longer. I've got some new stuff from England . . .'

'What sort of stuff?' Patrick asked, flicking through his diary.

'One of the outfits I'd like to see on Caroline is a very sexy see-through rubber number . . .'

Mentally rearranging his appointments, Patrick laughed. 'You do it to me every time, Laurie! What time do you want me there?'

* * *

Wearing a transparent pair of rubber directoire knickers and a matching peep-hole bra top, Caroline stood patiently while Laurie and Lynne considered row upon row of erotic bondage equipment.

'I want some photographs of Caroline in one of my new soft leather bondage hoods,' Laurie explained to Lynne. 'However, that won't be practicable with this outfit.'

Both women turned to look appraisingly at Caroline. Already aroused by the whole situation, Caroline shivered with anticipation. As befitted a Mistress, Lynne was attired in skin-tight black rubber which disappeared into tall rubber riding boots. A wicked looking whip was tucked into the top of one of those boots and Lynne had already expressed her intention of trying it out before the shoot was over. Laurie walked over to Caroline, tilting the girl's chin consideringly. 'A nice wide collar, I think,' she said, her five feet six inch frame managing to look imposing in black PVC.

Holding a suitable collar, Lynne joined them. 'I don't think James will mind,' she said, removing the white leather collar from around Caroline's neck. 'After all, it is in a good cause!' As Lynne fitted the new collar around Caroline's neck, Patrick arrived.

'Hello, Patrick,' Laurie welcomed him. 'You are looking very sharp this morning. No assistant?'

Patrick bent his brown leather-clad body and carefully deposited his camera equipment on the floor. Turning to Laurie, he smiled. 'I thought it would be better if there were no ... unnecessary people around. You did say that this was to be a no restrictions assignment?'

Laurie smiled approvingly. 'Quite correct,' she said, gently smoothing Caroline's hair. 'James and Francis are in complete agreement and only regret that they are unable to attend, but business needs have, I'm afraid, had to take priority. Patrick, I think you are already acquainted with Caroline and Lynne . . .?'

Patrick smiled at the two women. 'How could I forget?' Turning back to Laurie, he found it difficult to conceal the excitement he was feeling. 'I hope you realise, Laurie, that I have had to re-schedule a very important Senator in order to be here.'

Laurie ran her hands suggestively over the bulge in Patrick's trousers. 'Oh, I think you will find this assignment to be very . . . satisfactory,' she said. 'Where would you like to start?'

Patrick walked into the back room of the shop. Knowing Laurie well, he was aware of the existence of her black-painted punishment room. Laurie followed him.

'This will do fine. You want the first picture with Caroline in that outfit?' Patrick asked, gesturing towards Caroline who, with Lynne, had followed them into the dark room.

'It will certainly do for a start, don't you think?' Laurie asked, her own excitement growing. 'Lynne is going to be taking the part of the Mistress and will act accordingly during the shoot.'

'Excellent. Perhaps, ladies, you would like to make yourselves comfortable while I set up my lights,' Patrick offered, returning to pick up his camera case. 'I think we can look forward to a stimulating session!'

As Lynne tied her wrists together behind her back, Caroline felt a wetness between her legs which was not totally due to the stickiness of the rubber knickers that already adhered to her skin with the warmth she was generating.

'Do you want her gagged?' Lynne queried, looking at Laurie.

'Yes, I think so,' Laurie said, selecting a leather and chain gag from one of the shelves. Roughly, she tilted Caroline's face towards her. Chuckling at Caroline's look of surprise, Laurie bound the thick leather strap across the girl's mouth, securing it in place with an interlocking length of chain. 'I'm sorry, my dear, but you must be treated as befits your station in order for the session to be a true success,' Laurie said, bending her head so that her lips were close to Caroline's ear. 'You see, my dear, you are nothing but a slave and I intend that you shall be treated as such.' Blue-grey eyes met cobalt blue, and Caroline realised that Laurie could see how she responded with even greater excitement to this sort of treatment.

Laughing, Laurie squeezed one of the nipples so invitingly presented. 'Later, my dear,' she whispered. 'We are all going to be satisfied.'

Lynne joined them, removing the whip from her boot. 'If she gives you any trouble, Mistress Laurie, I will ensure that she regrets it,' she said, gently stroking Caroline's exposed breasts with the supple leather thongs. Caroline whimpered into her gag. She wanted to feel those fingers that held the whip stroking her swollen clitoris. It would not take much to make her come and she did not know how much more of this frustration she could take.

Caroline knelt on the floor. She was wearing a leather and chain body harness and one of the chains rubbed uncomfortably against her clitoris – uncomfortable because, even after a succession of orgasms during the prolonged shoot, she was still sexually excited and ready for more. The insistent rubbing of the chain did nothing to ease her sense of frustration at being left alone, illuminated only by Patrick's lights. She was gagged with a thick leather strip which had three buckled straps in front of her mouth, all of which were pulled tight and securely strapped. Caroline could only moan her frustration. Her arms were strapped into a leather single arm glove which ended in a fingerless mitten. Struggling was futile, but she writhed uncomfortably until she toppled over on to her side. The chain tightened even more against her clitoris and she gasped into her gag as another orgasm shook her. A slight chuckle made her eyes open and she saw Patrick's leather-clad form squatting beside her.

'What a naughty little girl you are, Caroline. Girls! What are we to do with her?' Patrick asked and Lynne and Laurie came into Caroline's field of vision.

'Naughty little girls must be punished,' Lynne said, smiling with anticipation. 'I think she should be whipped, don't you, Mistress Laurie?'

Laurie smiled. 'I think you're right, Mistress Lynne. I suggest that we take it in turns.'

'Before you start, ladies, I think the slave should be suitably presented, don't you?' Patrick suggested with an innocent smile.

Caroline could not know that the three of them had been planning for a suitable climax to a very successful session. After three exhausting hours, during which Caroline and Lynne had been attired in many varied outfits of leather, rubber and PVC and Caroline had also been bound and gagged in many different ways, Patrick knew that they had an unbelievably exciting series of pictures for the catalogue. Now he wanted some for selective publication and for his own private album. He had enlisted the assistance of both Lynne and Laurie in achieving just the kind of look that he wanted.

'We will position the slave suitably for her punishment,' said Laurie and, together with Lynne, she dragged Caroline back on to her knees and forced her bound arms up at an oblique angle, fastening a length of chain that dangled from a hook in the ceiling through the ring into which Caroline's mittens culminated. Caroline moaned as her arms were pulled upward as the slack in the chain was tautened before it was padlocked into position. Lynne forced Caroline's legs apart with a leg spreader, buckling the leather straps firmly at each end.

Another moan from Caroline resulted in a sharp tap from Lynne's whip. 'Silence! You have been very naughty and you are to be punished,' Lynne informed the helpless girl, using the handle of the whip to stroke against the tight little rosebud in Caroline's now appealingly presented buttocks. 'Who knows, you might even enjoy it,' she continued, squeezing the nipples that were visible between the taut chains of the harness.

Caroline was helplessly forced forward by the way that her arms were drawn up behind her. She was bending at the waist and the leg spreader caused her extreme difficulty in standing. It was the combination of these problems, together with the stimulation that Lynne was providing, which truly excited the girl. She had always liked rough treatment. She liked to feel totally helpless and she liked the feeling that she could not question what was happening to her and could therefore only give herself up to the pleasure of a situation that she so utterly enjoyed.

'Don't make her climax yet,' Patrick said as he positioned himself behind the camera. 'I want to catch that expression on her face when she comes . . . but only after you have punished her.'

Only too happy to comply, Lynne stationed herself in her familiar dominant position. She stood behind Caroline and raised her whip, a threatening figure clad in tight black rubber.

'Get ready, my darling.' Patrick's sensual voice abjured Caroline. 'This is for real and this is going to hurt!'

As the whip fell, Patrick's shutter went into operation, capturing picture after picture of Caroline's face as she ran the gamut of pain and pleasure. Lynne constantly paused in the whipping to admire the red weals she was laying across Caroline's white skin and to force the chain aside to thrust her fingers into Caroline's wetness.

For a voyeur like Patrick, the shoot was a dream. He knew he was getting excellent shots and he knew that, before Caroline was unbound, he would have to find some release by thrusting his erect penis into that deliciously tight hole between the helpless girl's buttocks. He was not aware of Laurie, who had slumped to the floor, her fingers furiously busy at her own slit as she watched Lynne punish Caroline. She had been so right about these two, Patrick thought. Laurie gasped as an orgasm overwhelmed her and, for some moments, remained helplessly writhing on the floor as her orgasm seemed to go on and on in seemingly endless spasms. She was forced into consciousness by Patrick's insistent shaking of her shoulder. He was naked and his erect penis dripped pre-come as he urgently gestured towards his camera. She nodded and, as agreed, got to her feet and staggered over to the camera.

Patrick went behind Caroline and clasped her chain-covered breasts as he fitted his body to hers. Lynne dropped to her knees in front of Caroline and started to gently whip the girl on her exposed thighs. Patrick lubricated the entry to Caroline's anus, making the girl struggle wildly, but they both knew that it was part of the game, a means to excite them further. Laurie did her best with the camera. The whole scene was tremendously erotic and photographer and subjects were caught up in a pulsating sexual excitement.

Unable to speak or usefully struggle, Caroline gave herself up to sheer pleasure and, as Patrick's cock pounded so excitingly into her, she surrendered to wave after wave of a multiple orgasm, her cries muffled by the thick leather of her gag. Laurie ran out of film and left the camera. Throwing herself down beside Lynne, she took the whip from her and the two women fell on each other, fitting themselves together so that they were able to lick and suck at each other until they were totally oblivious to everything but their mutual pleasure.

After his own hugely satisfying orgasm, Patrick clung to the bound and helpless girl, grateful to her for the way she had satisfied him totally – both professionally and so very, very personally.

Four

The script sailed cleanly through the air, landing on the leather-covered desk top and sending a glass ashtray to a shattered demise on the tiled floor. Lee Esslyn released another string of expletives as he surveyed the mess. That was just the way his day had been going! First, the call from the intended star of his forthcoming picture to say that she had decided not to do the film, then the almost immediate call from one of his backers to say that he would no longer be taking part in the finance package. Running a frustrated hand through his dirty blond hair, Lee wondered at the coincidental timing of the second call. Of course, it couldn't be anything to do with the fact that his erstwhile star and backer were sleeping together. His desperate musings as to what he could possibly do next were interrupted by the shrill of the telephone. Angrily, he snatched up the receiver.

'Yes!'

'My, someone got out of bed on the wrong side this morning!' the laughing voice of one of his closest friends admonished him.

'Leyla! I'm sorry. I've had one bitch of a day. I've lost my star and one of my financial backers. How does that grab you for starters?'

There was a fractional pause.

'Don't move! I'll be right over. I think I have the answers to your little problems!'

* * *

34

Leyla Dubois entered Lee's office and was immediately enfolded in a bear-hug embrace.

'Thanks for coming over, Leyla. I don't see how you can help, but . . .'

'Darling, I have every intention of helping you to get *Love's Obsession* back on the rails. I think we can help each other.'

Puzzled but interested, Lee narrowed his slate-coloured eyes and watched Leyla's purple rubber-clad form drape itself into a chair opposite his own. Admiring the curves that were a definite added attraction to his office, Lee smiled.

'Leyla, it's always a pleasure to see you, but how can you help me?'

Leyla crossed elegantly booted legs, showing even more delicious thigh, before replying. 'What would you think if I offered to supply you with another backer and another star?'

Lee laughed. 'I am not doubting your abilities, Leyla, but this is the movie business and . . .'

'Check this out!' Leyla said, extracting a book with a glossy cover from the envelope she was carrying. 'Hot off the presses and all yours . . . for a price!'

Lee looked at the book that had been pushed across his desk. It was a fetish catalogue, like many he had seen before, but it was the cover picture that riveted his attention. A blonde girl dressed in clinging black rubber with her hands placed behind her back looked out from the cover. She was beautiful, and the intimation from her pose that her hands were tied produced an immediate erection for Lee, which Leyla was quick to notice.

Smiling with satisfaction, she settled back in her chair. The quarry had taken the bait. Now it was time to reel him in! She had been very excited when she had learned of Laurie's proposal to use Lynne and

Caroline for her new catalogue shoot and she had begged to see the finished product. She and Laurie had been friends ever since Leyla had first entered the boutique as a potential customer. She had received her copy of the new catalogue as promised and, once she had seen how very well Caroline photographed, had immediately thought of approaching Lee to see if he was interested in using the girl for his new film. Once she had spoken to Lee and heard of his problems, she had realised the possibility that, instead of a small rôle, Caroline could be his new star. Leyla knew about Lee's project: it was a film containing erotic sexual bondage. Now she watched as Lee flicked through the book she had given him. He was aroused all right. Perhaps she could do something about that later.

'Leyla, who is she and where can I find her?' Lee asked excitedly. 'She's perfect and if she can't act, we'll get a coach for her. The main thing is that she photographs like an angel!'

'I will tell you all you need to know . . . on one condition,' Leyla said.

Ever the businessman, Lee frowned at this intimation of terms. 'What condition and how much will it cost me?'

Leyla laughed and shook her head. 'Oh, Lee. I thought we knew each other better than that. I'm only too pleased to help. It won't cost you a penny, just –' Lee looked at Leyla and raised his eyebrows questioningly '– an appointment before filming begins. I want to be given total charge of little Caroline the week before you start filming, to . . . introduce and prepare her for the rigours of her new rôle.' Leyla smiled as she finished.

'You want to be on the payroll . . .?'

'No. I don't want to be paid. I'll do the job for the

sheer satisfaction of helping out my old friend.' Leyla grinned. She felt a wetness between her legs at the thought of taking control of Caroline. She would teach her the art of real discipline. She would need to keep the girl in constant bondage, of course, to prepare her as she had told Lee. She had another sweetener up her sleeve. Before she had left her home, she had spoken to a potential replacement backer for the film, whose identity she would reveal once Lee had agreed to her terms.

Carefully replacing the catalogue on his desk, Lee looked at Leyla.

'OK, Leyla. You've got yourself a deal! I'll have my lawyers draw up the contract for you to sign. Can you come back in an hour?'

Contentedly, Leyla smiled. She rose to go. 'In an hour, then. I'll bring the backer I mentioned when I return. It's good doing business with you, Lee. You won't regret it. I'll keep your little star all safely tied up for you!'

Caroline added the finishing touches to the meal she was preparing. Her Master would soon be home. She wished that she could look out of the window and watch for his arrival, but the chains would not reach that far. She looked at the broad leather belt at her waist from which the imprisoning chain ran to its securing bolt in the wall. It was long enough for her to walk around and visit each of the rooms on the ground floor, but not quite long enough for her to be able to reach any of the doors to the outside world or the shuttered windows. Even if she could, she knew that the doors and windows were securely locked. She didn't mind. She found it as exciting as her Master did for her to be locked up while he was away on business. She revelled in the knowledge that he spent his working day enjoying the thought of his helpless prisoner safe at home. They had reached this mutual agreement in the early days of their relationship. She enjoyed the discomfort of the chains and other restrictions she was forced to wear, although forced was not really the right word. One word from her and she would instantly be released. That, too, was part of their agreement.

California was hot, which enabled her to wear nothing other than her restraints. She enjoyed the feel of walking around naked, secure in the knowledge that no unauthorised eyes would be able to catch so much as a glimpse. Caroline reached up to her very erect nipples and lovingly squeezed them. Very soon the Master would be doing that. Caroline shivered at the thought, making the chains clink together excitingly. During her Master's absence it was the only pleasure she was allowed. The tightly strapped leather chastity belt she wore only allowed her to go to the toilet. She was not able to touch herself. She knew that the Master's first task would be to check the padlock at the back of the belt. The leather wrist cuffs she wore were joined to her waist belt by means of chains just long enough to allow touching of her nipples but, even if she were in possession of the key to the chastity belt, her restraints would not allow her to reach behind and use it. Her Master had thought of everything. Even though he knew she would not want to call for help, he had designed and had tailor-made a leather gag which would prevent her from doing so should anyone come to the house in the Master's absence. Before he left each morning, her Master summoned her to his side and fitted her restraints. First, the gag. It was of thick black leather, form-fitting from just below her nose to the base of her neck, so that it seemed almost moulded to her. The gag was secured behind her head with a series of straps. Her Master enjoyed closing these straps firmly before securing them with tiny, but very efficient, padlocks. 'Can't have you screaming for help now, can I?' he would ask, further exciting them both. After the gag was in place, the belt was strapped and padlocked to her waist. He always secured her wrists into the leather cuffs before fitting the chastity belt around her hips. 'I don't want you struggling while I make sure that no other man can have you!'

Thinking of all this, Caroline smiled, or at least as much as she was able. The gag allowed very little in the way of movement. When it was in place, she was unable to move her head independently and could only do so if she also turned her body in the required direction. She heard the key in the lock. She had been too engrossed in her reverie to hear the sound of the car engine. She ran to the door as it opened and then waited patiently while her Master closed and re-locked the door. He smiled at her and walked around behind her to check on the padlock of her chastity belt. She heard the sound of a key turning in the small lock and then tensed herself for the expected and welcome probing finger which, as usual, was inserted into her wetness.

'What's this?' a stern voice demanded. 'You are a very wet little girl! You know what that means, don't you?' Her Master came to stand in front of her and gripped her tightly by the arms. 'Well?' Unable to answer, Caroline could only lower her eyes. 'Ashamed, eh? You'll be sorry, too, after I've finished with you!'

Deftly, he removed the restraints. As the gag fell away from her lips, she began to plead, knowing it to be useless. 'Please, Master. I'm so sorry. Please don't hurt me. I'll try to behave myself, I promise! Please!'

Ignoring her cries, her Master dragged her upstairs

and into their bedroom. He threw her on the bed, face down, and stood breathing heavily from his exertions.

'Get into position!' She lay whimpering with fear, unable to move. 'Don't waste my time or it will be the worse for you!' Daring no further delay, Caroline stretched her arms and legs out, placing them into leather cuffs that were opened and waiting. She felt the cuffs being tightly strapped to her wrists and ankles, effectively spreadeagling her on the bed. She was now totally helpless and very aware of her Master's righteous anger as he stood beside the bed. She knew that she deserved this punishment and she knew it would be harsh. Her Master was already inserting a finger into her vagina, checking the undoubted signs of her sexual excitement. The finger was removed and again the stern voice questioned her. 'Do you want a gag?'

Caroline thought of the punishment to come and of her Master's extreme displeasure when she cried out during any chastisement. 'Yes, please, Master,' she mumbled into the bed-cover.

'What did you say? Speak up, girl!'

Caroline moved her head. 'Yes please, Master.'

Satisfied, her Master ripped off a piece of adhesive tape and sat beside her. 'You agree that you deserve this punishment?' he asked her.

'Yes, Master.'

His hand closed over her face, sealing her lips closed. He smoothed down the tape and then she felt him rise from the bed. 'I'm going to shower. While I'm gone, you can consider the punishment to come and how well you deserve it!' With that he went into their en suite bathroom and closed the door. Caroline heard the water running in the shower and pulled desperately at her bindings. The cuffs were secured by lengths of chain which were bolted into the walls. There was no escape, but even so the helpless girl struggled. She knew what was to come and her excitement built as she contemplated her punishment. She was now very wet, her clitoris swollen by its need. She moaned into the tape that covered her mouth. Her Master liked the fact that only the most muffled of noises were possible through the adhesive fabric and he knew that was why his slave also liked it.

By the fourth stroke of the whip, Caroline was struggling so much that her Master threw down the implement. 'You are a very naughty girl and must be taught a lesson!' he cried. He moved to the top of the bed and operated a hidden switch beside the anchor point of one of her wrist chains. By operating the switch, he tautened the chain, pulling Caroline's arm straight until she moaned with the discomfort in her arm muscles. Ignoring her whimpered protests, her Master repeated the procedure on the other wrist chain, then both ankle chains, until the four leather cuffs were pulled taut with the strain. Smiling his satisfaction, the Master retrieved the whip. He was pleasurably aware that Caroline could no longer struggle and that her wrists and ankles would be pleasingly marked by the cuffs, marks which would remain for a couple of days. The Master stroked the strands of the whip across his slave's reddened buttocks, smiling as she shuddered beneath his sensual ministrations. 'Easy, my little slave. You will only hurt yourself if you do not remain perfectly still,' he reminded her. 'I am sorry that I have to be so cruel, but you do not seem to be able to learn without the infliction of pain.' The Master slipped two fingers inside the girl. She was satisfactorily wet. It proved to him that she was still enjoying the punishment. He loved disciplining her, but wanted to be assured that her pleasure needs were also met. Using his thumb to massage the swollen clitoris, he smiled as she again shuddered and pulled at her fastenings. Removing his fingers, he straightened. 'No, my darling. There are other means of torture which are not necessarily painful, but which are just as effective.'

Caroline moaned with frustration. She had been so close to an orgasm and now she knew that she would have to await her Master's pleasure before she could obtain release. She knew from experience that she might indeed have a long wait. She whimpered again as she felt another stinging stroke across her buttocks. Her Master was an expert and would continue with this pain and pleasure treatment, keeping her on the verge of an orgasm, for as long as it pleased him. She felt the movement of the mattress as he sat on the bed. She sensed his lips brush against her shoulder and then the wetness of his tongue as it slipped down her right arm. When he reached her cuffed wrist, he kissed the already marked skin.

'Such beautiful marks, my little slut, and you will wear them with pride, will you not?'

She groaned as she acknowledged that he was right. After one of these sessions she was always marked and she willed the marks to remain on her body as long as possible. They were the proof of her Master's ownership and she *did* wear them with pride.

'Have you had enough, my darling? Shall I release you?'

Caroline tensed. Part of her wanted to have the cuffs removed, but another part said no. She felt another movement of the mattress and then another line of fire erupted across her buttocks.

'Little slut!' shouted her Master, and there was anger in his voice. She heard the whip as it clattered to the floor and, unexpectedly, the tension in her arms and legs was released as the chains were loosened and the cuffs removed. Gently, she was turned on to her back and her Master stared lovingly into her eyes. He had not removed the tape from her mouth, but she raised her arms to wind them around his neck. 'Slut!' he yelled and grabbed her wrists, holding them painfully together in a rough grip. He forced her from the bed and on to her knees. 'Hands behind your back, slut!' he ordered and, as he released his grip, she hurried to obey. He moved behind her and she felt rope binding her wrists tightly together. Her Master moved in front of her and yanked the tape from her mouth. Without another word, he grabbed her hair, forcing her head back. She cried out and he clamped his free hand over her mouth. 'Shut up! I want you to suck my cock and you had better do a good job, otherwise I will whip you until you are begging for mercy!' He was still holding her hair but had released his grip on her mouth. 'Do you hear me, slut? Not a sound from you other than the noise of your lovely lips and tongue as they pleasure me! I want to come in your mouth and I want every drop swallowed! Understand?'

Her head was pushed downwards until she felt his cock against her lips. Very willingly, she took it into her mouth. In spite of the painful way her hair was gripped, she sucked and licked her Master's cock, tasting his saltiness. With satisfaction, she heard his groans of pleasure. This was their favourite game. She liked his threatening roughness while they played their games. It was so different from his usual loving demeanour, a difference that thrilled and excited her. His groans were becoming more insistent and his grip in her hair increasingly painful, but she revelled in the discomfort. She knew that he would allow her satisfaction and she knew that it would be incredibly good. She greedily swallowed the saltiness as it flooded into her mouth, mixing with her own saliva. She writhed against the ropes that tied her, feeling the near orgasmic excitement as her Master spent himself into her mouth. He crushed her against him at the culmination of his orgasm, holding her still against his hard body until she felt him slip from her mouth. She knew enough not to make a sound as he recovered himself. When eventually he got to his feet, she kept her eyes lowered and remained kneeling on the floor until he returned to her and gently urged her to her feet. She was folded into his embrace and felt his tongue probing her mouth. She returned his kiss, feeling the slipperiness of his sweat-drenched body as it moulded to hers. He twined a hand in her hair, but more gently this time. She looked up at him with eyes full of naked adoration.

'My little darling slave. You know how I adore you and you know how I like you to be my dutiful slave, don't you?' She nodded. 'Open your mouth, my darling,' he said. 'I want to gag you and then I will pleasure you.' She complied and, as he thrust a wad of cloth between her lips, he pushed three fingers into her wetness. In total contrast to his earlier roughness, he gently picked her up and laid her on her back on the bed. Because she knew that he expected it of her, she tried to spit out the cloth. Shaking his head, he produced a length of rope and, replacing the cloth even more firmly in her mouth, tied it tightly in place, knotting the rope over the cloth. 'Silly, disobedient little girl,' her Master said, but his eyes belied his words. Her excitement mounted, as she knew she had pleased him. He moved down the bed and used his tongue and fingers to edge her to an orgasm, constantly looking up as she twisted and writhed, moaning into her gag. 'That's right, my little slave, your Master knows what you like, doesn't he?'

Caroline bucked as her orgasm thrilled through her. The feeling was incredible and the orgasm seemed to continue for a long time. Her Master continued sucking at her slit, drinking her juices, until she quietened. They lay together, both satiated with pleasure. Eventually, it was her Master who moved first, untying her and slapping her reddened buttocks. 'Up, slave! I want my dinner!'

They enjoyed their dinner and spent a loving evening in each other's arms until they retired to bed. First, they stripped and showered together, massaging each other as the warm water cascaded over them. When they emerged from the shower, they towelled each other dry and her Master pulled her to him and kissed her savagely. 'Slut! What is it that you do to me? I want you all the time and I'm aroused all day, even when I'm not with you.'

Caroline nuzzled his neck. 'That's because you know that I am suitably tethered until you return, unable to escape and run away,' she murmured.

'Do you want to run away?' her Master asked.

She shook her head. 'No, Master. I've never been happier!'

He laughed and reached down to slap her arse. 'Move it, slave! Bring me your night-time attire!'

Obediently, she opened a cupboard and extracted some items, returning and offering them to her Master. He pulled back the bed covers and patted the mattress. She sat on the bed and, turning her back, offered him her crossed wrists. She felt the usual surge of sexual excitement as she felt the cords slipping around her wrists. The ropes were tied loosely enough for comfort but securely enough for her to be unable to struggle free. Kissing her again, he gently pushed her back on to the bed and tied some rope around her knees and then around her ankles. 'I don't want you running off in the night,' her Master said as he finished tying the knots.

Obligingly, Caroline struggled. 'I cannot get free, Master,' she said. Bending his head, her Master kissed her, feeling her mounting passion, which matched his own.

'One more thing,' her Master said, raising his head. 'I can't run the risk of you screaming for help, now can I?' Saying that, he sealed another strip of adhesive across her mouth, then lay beside her as his eyes devoured her. His beautiful slave, bound and gagged and awaiting his pleasure. 'I will never let you go, slut, you know that don't you?' he asked, holding his erect cock and stroking himself as he stared at her. She looked at him with eyes full of love and he knew that she would never try and escape. She would never want to leave him.

The insistent buzzing startled Lee back to reality. Hastily wiping himself, he pushed his cock back inside his trousers and zipped himself up. He tried to collect himself, as he pressed the intercom on his desk.

'Yes?' he queried, somewhat shakily.

'Mr Esslyn,' came his secretary's anxious voice. 'Are you all right?'

'Of course I'm all right,' Lee snapped, then in a slightly calmer voice. 'Sorry, Karen, I was busy with something.' Lee shifted uncomfortably in his seat. And how! he commented mentally.

'I have Miss Dubois in reception, Mr Esslyn. I also have the contract that you wanted.'

'Oh, yes, Karen. Let Miss Dubois have the contract and send her in,' Lee said, then sat back and waited. He took some deep breaths and hoped that he looked less flustered than he felt. The door opened and Leyla stood there.

'Well!' she said as she closed the door and entered the office. 'What have you been thinking about?'

Lee smiled. Leyla saw everything. 'Just thinking about my future star,' Lee said.

'She's married, you know,' Leyla said, sitting across from him.

'Where's your mystery backer?' Lee asked, changing the subject.

'He's meeting me here in –' Leyla consulted her watch '– ten minutes. I wanted to see you first. He and Caroline know each other. Apparently, they had some sort of relationship – I don't know the details – but he doesn't want Caroline or James to know that he is even in the country.'

Lee nodded. 'Fine with me. I just want his money. Does he know what the film is about?'

'Oh, yes. In fact, that's one of the reasons that he's so keen to be involved,' Leyla said, glancing at the contract in her hand.

Following her glance, Lee smiled. 'I hope that that is in order. You will have the exclusive use of our little star for the week before filming begins.'

'Unrestricted use?' Leyla asked.

Lee laughed. 'No, Leyla, I know you. I do not want her to be marked. She will be nude for a lot of the film so I don't want her returned to me covered in whip marks.'

Leyla smiled. 'Agreed. There are other delicious things I can do to little Caroline which won't leave any marks, but which will have the same effect. I will deliver her to you, suitably disciplined and very used

47

to spending long periods of time in bondage, but totally unmarked.'

'Good, because that is part of the contract.'

Leyla smiled and extracted a pen from her bag. She signed the contract with a flourish and handed it to Lee.

'You obviously know that this contract is invalid if Caroline does not sign to do the film?' Lee asked.

'Oh, she'll sign,' Leyla said. 'I am holding an SM party tomorrow to which I have invited our little Caroline and her husband. She is his slave and it is his permission that needs to be obtained.' Leyla smiled. 'No problem, Lee, that I can promise you. Your little star is as good as signed!'

There was a further buzzing sound and Lee leant forward and spoke into the intercom.

'Yes?'

There was a slight pause and then the unusually flustered tones of his normally efficient secretary. 'There . . . there's a gentleman to see you, Mr Esslyn. He says that you are expecting him.'

Raising an eyebrow in Leyla's direction, Lee laughed. 'Send him in, Karen.'

Lee waited expectantly as the door opened. He stared at the dark, well groomed man who entered his office. From his elegantly polished shoes to the top of his sleekly combed black hair, the man was impressive. He was tall and his dark eyes held Lee's with an intensity that was hard to resist.

Lee rose from his chair as Leyla also stood and moved to lay a possessive hand on the stranger's arm. She turned to Lee, smiling as she stood aside to allow him to shake hands with the visitor.

'Lee, I'd like you to meet Clive Craigen, your new backer.'

Five

A particularly interesting group of people had assembled at Leyla Dubois' luxurious home high in the Hollywood hills. Unlike the majority of fashionable parties, no one was attempting to outdo anyone else by being seen in the most expensive designer outfits. Leyla had included a strict dress code on her invitations: rubber, leather or PVC. All the guests had adhered to this injunction and the main concern appeared to be to dress more outrageously than your neighbour.

Leyla stood at the top of the white marble steps leading up to the front door. From the top of her shining upswept black hair to the tips of her impossibly high-heeled boots, she was dressed in form-fitting black leather. The material clung to her breasts and clearly defined her narrow waist and perfectly shaped bottom. A concealed zip caused many a guess as to how she had managed to fit her perfect body into the leather, speculation in which Leyla revelled. She knew that she looked good as she stood at the top of the steps receiving her guests, her eyes constantly alert for any transgression of her dress code and also for the first sign of her guest of honour. Of course, Caroline did not know that she was to be so honoured, but it was Leyla's intention that the girl would be the centre of attention. It was her firm desire

49

to have Caroline as her house guest. She wanted to exercise the authority given her in the contract she had signed with Lee and she wanted to use it to the full. Leyla knew that Lee was fantasising about the girl after seeing her in Laurie's catalogue, and she had promised that she would ensure Caroline spent the coming night in his company. It was the price she had agreed for her own supervision of Caroline before and during filming. She gave only a small amount of consideration to James. If he had known her real intentions toward his wife, Leyla was well aware that he would never agree to let Caroline out of his sight!

James adjusted the folds of his full-length black leather cape and admired the effect in the mirror. Not bad for an old bloke! He smiled as he looked at the effect of the cape over his black leather suit, feeling pleased with himself. When he had first met Caroline, he had known she would be good for him, but things were going even better than he could have hoped. He loved and treasured her. She was his partner and his very willing slave: in fact, she was everything that he had ever wanted in a woman. Since the appearance of the infamous catalogue, he knew he had become the envy of everyone who saw it. Caroline had been deluged with offers of further modelling work, but James had advised her to decline them all. Living in Los Angeles had made him very aware of how to play the fame game and he had told Caroline that, in making herself unavailable, she was becoming even more desirable. Now Leyla had intimated that if Caroline and James attended her party, they would certainly learn something to their advantage.

'Master, do I look all right?' a small voice behind him asked. James turned towards his wife and immediately glowed with pleasure. Caroline was wearing the chains that he had had made especially for her. His eyes alighted on the shining metal bands around her throat, waist, ankles and wrists, from which heavy interlocking chains draped. They dwarfed her slight figure, enhancing the vulnerability that, from the first, had so entranced him.

'My darling, you are adorable,' James enthused, running appreciative hands across her chain-wrapped breasts, pausing to squeeze the pert nipples that peeped through the heavy metal bindings. His eyes caressed her, from the thick steel collar at her neck, over the wide metal band at her slim waist and the shining metal of the chastity belt, to the narrower bands at her wrists and ankles.

'Can you walk, my darling?' James asked.

'Just about, Master. I find these chains very restricting,' Caroline answered, her eyes downcast.

James considered her a moment longer. 'Turn around, my darling,' he instructed, unable to conceal the pleasure he felt as he looked at his chain-wrapped slave. 'I want to make sure that your chastity belt is properly in place.'

Obediently, she turned, the chains making a satisfying sound as she moved. She sighed with pleasure as she felt James' hands on the cheeks of her arse, knowing what his intention was. Gently, James slipped one hand over her mouth. 'We have a little time before we leave, my darling, and you do look so very fuckable,' he whispered, massaging the entry to her anus. Beneath his hand, she murmured her pleasure. James pushed a finger between her lips, at which she eagerly sucked and licked, before it was removed and the pressure across her mouth was relieved. Holding her tightly, James pushed the wet finger between her arse cheeks and felt her bear down to receive him. 'Ah, you little bitch. You want it, don't you?'

'Please, Master,' Caroline begged. 'Please.'

James pushed his finger further into her, making her moan with pleasure. His other hand captured one of the chained breasts and squeezed the nipple painfully. She groaned and pushed back against him, making James instantly remove his finger and replace it with his hard cock. Caroline was making small whimpering noises and, as he slipped inside her, he used his free hand to clamp over her mouth firmly.

'Not too much noise, my darling. Remember, you are my slave and you must do everything that I want without demur.' James' thrusts were becoming more urgent and his free hand slid down to Caroline's engorged clitoris, making her moan beneath his restraining hand. She was very wet and very ready for him. James cried out as his orgasm shook through him and he felt the increased wetness on his fingers as Caroline reached her climax. It seemed to take a long time before he finished pumping his semen into her backside. Spent, he released her mouth and hugged her tightly as the flow ebbed, to be replaced by a feeling of satisfied exhaustion which he knew to be well reciprocated by his wonderful slave.

'James and Caroline! Welcome!' Leyla hugged them both in greeting. She kept her arms around Caroline for a little longer than was absolutely necessary, revelling in the sight of the chained girl. 'Mm, you look delicious,' she purred, brushing Caroline's nipples.

'You have a lovely house, Leyla,' Caroline managed, as always feeling a little in awe of her hostess.

'You must come and stay,' Leyla said as she released her. 'There is plenty here to keep you amused. It would really be a pleasure to have you,' she added, with a meaningful glance.

James thoughtfully slipped an arm around his wife's shoulders. 'We might take you up on that, Leyla. I have to go to England for a week on business and it would certainly ease my mind if I knew that Caroline was safely in your care.'

Leyla smiled. Because of their shared love of fetish clothing and the whole SM scene, the two had been friends for some time. Now Leyla put her arm through that of James. Things were working out even better than she could have hoped. Leyla was well aware that her proposed activities with Caroline might cause the ending of her friendship with James, but her desire for his wife had become obsessional, to the exclusion of all other feelings.

'James, I want you both to meet a man who has become a fan of your lovely wife,' Leyla said, propelling them on to the patio, where a luscious buffet was being served.

Caroline frowned as she looked questioningly at Leyla. 'A fan? I don't . . .'

'He's seen Laurie's new catalogue, my dear. He wants to talk to you and James about a film project,' Leyla said, looking around until she caught sight of Lee. 'Lee!' she called, gesturing for him to join them. Dressed in white leather, Lee strolled over to them. His eyes assessed Caroline and his cock hardened in instant acknowledgement of the way she was attired. Silently thanking the covering capabilities of the supple hide he wore, Lee extended a hand to Caroline.

'I know who this is. You have already given me a great deal of pleasure, Caroline. You photograph like a dream.'

Caroline smiled and gently extracted her hand from Lee's imprisoning grasp. She had been drawn to the handsome stranger but, as a new bride, was very conscious of her husband's watchful presence. 'Thank you, Mr . . .?'

'Caroline, this is Lee Esslyn,' Leyla said, taking control of the situation. 'He wanted to meet you and James, because he has a proposition for you.'

'Proposition?' James queried, his businessman's attention immediately caught.

'Caroline, you are even more beautiful in the flesh,' Lee enthused, his eyes travelling over the girl's chained body. 'I am about to begin shooting a new film and I would very much like you to consider testing for the main female lead.'

'What does the part involve?' James asked, interested but cautious.

'The heroine is the object of obsessional love by an admirer,' Lee answered, looking straight at James. 'I will be frank with you. The rôle requires that the heroine be tied up fairly frequently. The girl who was originally cast for the film got cold feet and when I saw Laurie's catalogue and how beautiful Caroline looked in those great clothes, not to mention the bondage items, well . . .' Lee's voice trailed off; he knew that he more than had James' interest.

There was a pause, broken by Leyla. 'Let's go inside and we can all talk about this,' she said. Agreeably, James, Caroline and Lee followed her. Leyla could hardly contain her excitement. James was hooked, she knew he was! All she had to do now was to put the second part of her plan into operation. She knew exactly what she needed to do and Caroline would indeed spend the night as Lee's very willing prisoner.

Her chains clinking, Caroline took the proffered pen and signed her name to the document that Lee had presented.

'You're taking a risk, aren't you, Lee?' James asked.

'Risk? In what way?' Lee replied.

'You haven't even tested Caroline. She may not meet your requirements.'

Smiling, Lee looked at the picture that Caroline presented, curled on the floor, with the exciting chains proclaiming her status. 'I have no doubt that she will meet all my requirements,' he answered. 'I know she photographs superbly and I can see how very submissive she really is. Those are just the qualities my heroine requires.'

Settling himself more comfortably in the deep, beige-coloured leather of the impressive sofa on which he was seated, James watched Caroline initialling the contract pages. 'This film of yours sounds interesting and I understand that you plan to shoot it in England. Are you not worried about the censors?'

Lee smiled at James. 'All covered. The film is based on a best-selling book and the sex and bondage sequences have been suitably tailored to side-step all censorship requirements. The fact that Caroline will play a submissive character opens the door for some interesting rôle-playing sexual games. My main backer has offered me the use of his newly acquired studios in the English countryside and has guaranteed me a closed set during filming. He also enjoys considerable influence within the film community.'

'Oh, yes, your mysterious backer,' James said. 'What was he called again?'

Lee laughed. 'James, James. I didn't tell you his name because, as I've already mentioned, he has asked to remain anonymous for administration purposes. Something to do with the English tax rules regarding recent company acquisitions, I believe.'

'Nothing illegal, I trust?'

Again, Lee laughed. 'My dear James, I have a reputation to consider. There is nothing remotely illegal connected with this film.'

Satisfied, James beckoned to Caroline, who had completed the necessary signatory work on the contract. Gladly, she came to him. 'How will you like being a film star, my darling?' James asked, stroking her shining golden hair.

'If it pleases you, Master, then I am well content,' Caroline answered, lowering her eyes. She felt excited and aroused. She adored James, and fulfilling his wishes in this respect was very enjoyable. Pleased with her answer, James tweaked one of her nipples and, bending his head, kissed her with a fierceness that spoke of his pride in her and his desire for them to be at home as soon as possible. Lee and Leyla watched, their indulgent smiles concealing the jealousy they both felt.

Leyla suddenly jumped up. 'I have an idea . . . a way to celebrate our new star and demonstrate her extreme submissiveness!'

'What are you talking about, Leyla?' James asked, but she was already moving away from the secluded corner in which they had been sitting and into the main area of her enormous lounge.

'Listen, everyone!' she shouted, clapping her hands for attention. There was an immediate hush as all faces turned to look at Leyla. 'Lee Esslyn, whom you all know, has just signed his newest star. Let me introduce you to her.' Leyla turned and beckoned to James and Caroline. 'Caroline is here with her Master, who has very kindly given his permission for her to appear in Lee's film.'

Uncertainly, Caroline looked at James. With only a momentary hesitation, James rose and urged Caroline to stand. Together, they walked to where Leyla was holding court. Lee followed, curious as to Leyla's intentions. When they had all reached the centre of the room, Leyla turned to James, her face flushed with triumph. 'Master James, I offer you a unique chance to prove your slave's submissiveness.' She turned to take in the assembled guests, who watched with interest. 'Ladies and gentlemen, Lee has waived the usual director's right to a screen test for his new star. As the film will require certain bondage scenes, I think it would be only fair to request Caroline and her Master to consider the right of the director to hold his new star overnight and to personally test her out!'

'Leyla,' James said warningly. 'What are you playing at?'

'Simply this, darling James,' Leyla replied, turning to face him. 'I think that Lee should have the opportunity to see for himself how well Caroline responds to being in bondage.' She stopped and looked challengingly at James. 'Unless, of course, you do not think Caroline would agree to such a request.'

James looked around at the expectant faces and then at Caroline's wide-eyed and questioning face. All the people here knew him as a firm and strong Master. He could not back down from Leyla's challenge. He was annoyed with her, but they both knew that he could do nothing but accept. He moved to Caroline and spoke gently to her. 'You know that I have no choice?' he whispered.

She looked at him adoringly. She realised that he had to acquiesce and she knew she could not let him down. 'I accept, Master,' she said quietly.

James bent down and kissed her gently. 'I won't let him hurt you, my darling. You may rest assured that he won't hurt you,' her husband said, hugging her tightly. Turning to Leyla, he narrowed his eyes and Leyla knew that she had lost a friend.

'Very well. As it is my wish, Caroline has agreed to go with Lee Esslyn for one night!'

There was a round of applause from the other Masters and Mistresses as they acknowledged such a deep gift of submission. Lee was aware of his insistent erection as he contemplated the coming night. He would have Caroline at his mercy and he would make her submissive to him, enabling him to live out some of his fantasies. Observing the proprieties, he turned to James and held out his hand. 'My dear James, this is as much of a surprise to me as it has obviously been to you. I promise that I will look after her.'

James accepted the proffered hand but, as they publicly showed their friendship, he spoke in low and measured tones. 'Be sure that you do, Lee. If you don't, I can assure you that I make an impressive enemy.'

As she watched, Caroline shivered. Seeing this, Leyla smiled and put her arm around the girl. 'Don't worry, Caroline. It will be all right.'

Caroline looked at Leyla, no doubt wishing they had never met, but Leyla was certain that the girl was shivering more from anticipation than fear. Lee was a very attractive man and the idea that she was virtually to be his prisoner for the night would fill any true submissive with excitement. Her clitoris was probably already pulsating at the prospect of what was to come.

'Well done, Leyla,' Lee said. 'I applaud your initiative. Now, there is one more thing you can do for me.' Leyla looked at him, satisfied with the way things had gone, but wary. 'I want you to phone Clive Craigen for me. Tell him that I have Caroline and he should meet us at my house in about an hour,' Lee instructed.

Leyla looked suspicious. 'What's this all about, Lee?'

'Just as you earned your contract tonight, princess,' Lee said, smiling, 'I have to earn my backing. Clive is still prevaricating on signing. Once he knows that Caroline has contracted to do the film and I have offered him a little sweetener, I think my worries will be over!'

Leyla looked over her shoulder. Caroline and James were saying their farewells and were too occupied to take any notice of anything else that was happening.

'What sort of sweetener, Lee? You promised James that she wouldn't be hurt.'

'Nor will she be, my love. After all, I don't want a damaged star, now do I? I will offer Clive a little time with Caroline, but she won't know anything about it. I have plans for her and I will make sure that Clive knows she is to be returned unharmed or the deal is off!' Lee kissed her on the forehead. 'Don't worry, my love. Just speak to Clive and tell him I have a present for him.'

Six

Lee watched the lovely girl as she wandered around his house, touching and examining items of interest. She had signed to do his film and she was here. James had given permission for her to stay the whole night with him. He had made no preconditions, just his assurance that any harm to Caroline would result in his extreme disfavour, and Lee was in no doubt that he would not enjoy the outcome. Besides which, he had no intention or desire to hurt Caroline. He merely wanted to explain and demonstrate her rôle in *Love's Obsession*. He glanced at his watch and realised that Clive could be expected in less than an hour. He walked up to Caroline and gently touched her shoulder. She had changed into a clinging black PVC bolero top and micro skirt. She also wore thigh length PVC boots. Lee had been in a constant state of arousal since Caroline had climbed into his car.

'Why don't we sit down and talk about the movie?' He guided her to the luxurious white leather sofa, and Caroline could not help wondering how on earth Lee was able to keep it so clean. As they sat down, Lee gently held her hands. 'Caroline, you are a very beautiful woman and I am very pleased that you have agreed to be in the film. I think you'll be sensational. I would like to photograph you in some of the outfits you will be wearing, or I should say, have you photographed. I have an excellent cameraman who works with me and he will need some still shots so that he can judge the best way to photograph you when filming starts. Now, before he arrives, I suggest that you take a shower which will relax you. How does that sound?'

Caroline looked at her director, and he realised that she was drawn undeniably to his almost untidy sexuality. Lee knew that James had given her no instructions other than to do as she was told and she was to tell him about everything that happened. As she looked into Lee's slate-grey eyes, he could see that she shivered with anticipation.

'Are you cold?' Lee asked.

'No, I'm fine,' Caroline said.'I'm just anticipating what is to come . . . the film and everything.'

Lee smiled in understanding. 'Don't be afraid. I'll be with you and I won't let you come to any harm. We'll make a great film.'

Caroline nodded. They both knew that Lee had not been talking about the film. As Lee helped her to her feet, he knew that she had given him her permission for whatever he had in mind.

Caroline stood in the shower cubicle, revelling in the feel of the warm water on her excited body. She wanted to touch herself, but she resisted the urge. It was better to wait for Lee. She had the feeling that it might be a long night. The warm water was helping to ease the tension in her back and shoulders and she moved sensuously, accommodating the flow of water. It came as no surprise when she heard the door of the cubicle opening and then closing. She arched her back as strong arms entwined her upper body and she felt Lee's hardness against her. Gently, he stroked her breasts, fondling the erect nipples as he nuzzled her neck. She loved the feel of his nakedness against her

61

own and moaned softly as his fingers slipped inside her slit, wet from more than just the shower.

'I want you to put your arms up for me, Caroline,' Lee whispered. Obediently, she did so and felt a thrill of arousal as cold steel snapped around each wrist. Looking up, she saw that her hands had been manacled around the shower head. 'Now you really are my prisoner.' Lee's voice caressed her. 'Will you do everything that I say?'

'Yes.'

'Yes what?'

'Yes, Master,' Caroline whispered.

Triumphantly, Lee replaced his probing fingers with the hardness of his cock. He cupped her breasts in his strong hands, deftly manipulating and stroking, driving Caroline to a peak of desire. She gasped with pleasure as Lee moved within her. She felt no guilt. James had ordered her to do as she was told and she knew that, being something of a voyeur, he would obtain pleasure from hearing of her exploits. Lee was an expert at pleasuring women, the more so when he was aroused to the pitch that his close proximity to Caroline engendered. He was approaching his own climax and redoubled his efforts to ensure that it would be mutual. He was rewarded with Caroline's incoherent cries and desperate struggles to free her hands as her orgasm overwhelmed her. It was her passionate helplessness that pushed him over the edge of his own climax. As he pumped his semen into that gorgeous body, he thought of the night to come and of all the things he would do to his beautiful slave.

Caroline and Lee had dried each other in big fluffy towels and now sat on Lee's bed. It was almost with reluctance that he had released her from her shower bondage. His director's eye told him that such a scene would look very good on film. Time was getting on, however, and he knew that Clive's arrival was imminent.

'Caroline, there will be more than one cameraman on this film and the one who is coming tonight does not want you to know who he is.'

Caroline laughed. 'Why? Is he the nervous sort?'

'No, it's for your benefit that he would prefer to remain anonymous. He is going to see you in intimate detail and, because you're new to filming, he wants to spare your embarrassment. If you don't know which cameraman sees you tonight, there will be no problem.'

Caroline shrugged. 'OK. I don't think there would be such a problem, but if it makes him feel better . . .'

'Thank you,' Lee said. 'Now, don't be frightened, but I am going to put a hood over your head. It's also one of the things you will be wearing on film, so it serves two purposes. You won't be able to see or hear him and we'll both see what you look like in the hood.'

Caroline nodded her acquiescence, feeling it was not necessary for him to know that James liked her in a hood and used one fairly frequently. She felt a pulsing in her clitoris as Lee opened the back of the black leather hood that he produced and turned her to facilitate its placement. She felt her nipples harden as the soft leather closed over her face and knew that Lee could hardly fail to see her arousal.

'I'm going to tie you as well, Caroline. Is that all right?'

She nodded, unable to speak as the hood was being closed with black leather ties. When Lee had finished, she could no longer speak, see or hear, as she discovered that the hood had padded areas over her mouth and ears. The only openings in the hood were small air holes positioned over her nostrils so that she could breathe.

'Can you hear me, Caroline?' Lee asked and was satisfied at the lack of response. He could not resist squeezing the nipples that were so invitingly erect. He had not been wrong about her. With her obvious love of bondage, she was so right for the part. Gently and caressingly, he ran his hands down her arms until he grasped her wrists and guided them behind her back. As he bound her hands with soft white rope, the doorbell rang. Tying off the knots securely, Lee kissed Caroline's bare shoulder and arose from the bed. Momentarily, he stood looking at the helpless girl and felt a twinge of jealousy as he reflected on the vagaries of business which pressured him to give such a beautiful present to Clive Craigen.

Clive stood beside the bed looking down at Caroline. He felt a mixture of emotions: passion and desire; love and a hatred for what she had put him through; renewal of the desire he had always had to possess her body and her mind. Clive examined the way she was hooded and tied with an almost professional interest. He tested the bonds at her wrists and nodded approvingly. He rubbed one of her breasts and watched the almost immediate response in her hardening nipples. He moved lower and slipped an enquiring finger into her slit, smiling with satisfaction at the resultant wetness. 'Oh, Caroline.' He almost purred. 'You haven't changed.'

Lee watched the scene unfolding before him with an extreme curiosity. All he knew of Clive's history was that he and Caroline had in the past been acquainted. He didn't know of Clive's long-held obsession with Caroline and his attempts to prise her away from previous Masters; most importantly, as far as Clive was concerned, Lee did not know of Clive's determination to own and mark Caroline as his slave.

'I want her hood taken off.'

Lee was taken aback. 'I got her ready for you just as you asked. I've explained to her that you want to remain anonymous . . .'

'I've changed my mind! I want her to see me!' Clive's tone allowed for no further argument. As Lee unlaced the hood, Clive found that he was trembling with excited arousal. His original plan to remain unknown to Caroline had dissipated the minute he had again set eyes on her. She had to know he was back and she had to realise that she was in his power. Otherwise, his plan would become meaningless.

Caroline had been Clive's slave when she and James had first met. Despite their obviously mutual attraction, Clive had taken no sensible precautions and had allowed his greed for money and power to make him careless. He had lost Caroline to James and he did not intend to repeat that mistake. His own stupidity in signing a much-needed business contract with the man, which included the proviso that James was free to come and see Caroline whenever he so required, had led to him losing her. Now it was his intention to turn that hard lesson to his own advantage, by using the same control over Lee Esslyn. He clamped his hand over one of Lee's wrists, thereby stopping him in his task. Surprised, Lee turned questioning eyes on him.

'You need my financial backing, is that right?' Clive asked. Lee nodded affirmation. 'I will sign your contract provided you back me up on whatever I may say to Caroline. Is it a deal?'

'Now, wait a minute,' Lee began. 'It depends on what . . .'

'Do we have a deal?' Clive insisted, tightening the pressure around Lee's wrists. Startled, Lee looked at Clive and found himself unable to tear his gaze away from the darkness of those mesmeric eyes. What had he let himself in for? Lee's mind worked frantically, desperate for an answer, even as he felt his will draining away. He needed Clive's backing and Clive's offer of the use of his English studios meant a tremendous saving. He tried to think of Caroline.

'I need time to think. I . . . Of course we have a deal,' Lee said, his own words surprising him.

'Then I suggest that you go and prepare the contract,' Clive said, releasing his grip. 'Caroline and I have much to discuss.'

Caroline felt fingers again working at the back of her head. She assumed the cameraman had arrived as the loosening of the hood had enabled her to hear muted sounds, enough to tell her that there were now two people in the room. She had been unable to hear what was being said and was very surprised that the hood was being removed. Perhaps they would replace it with a blindfold so that she could not identify the cameraman. She hoped that, whatever happened, those wonderfully strong fingers she had felt would continue their exploration of her breasts and clitoris. The hood fell free of her face and she was again able to see and hear. Should she turn around or would they rather she waited to be told what she must do?

'Caroline, you are lovelier than ever,' said a voice she thought she recognised, but she dismissed the idea as impossible. Her hands were still tied, but she pulled experimentally at the bindings, which held firm. Clive smiled at the small movement.

'Have you missed me, my dear?'

The question made her freeze. There could be no

doubting the identity of the owner of that voice. The hint of a Scottish burr; the seductive tones that reminded her of this man's ability to control and dominate. She tried to twist around on the bed, but he moved further behind her.

'Lee?' she ventured, her voice rising in panic.

'Mr Esslyn had to leave us. He's gone to prepare the contract that he wants me to sign. Caroline, I am the financial backer you've been told about. My darling, I am your new boss!'

Finding a measure of bravado in the fact that she could not see Clive's eyes, Caroline forced herself to remain calm.

'Clive, if you don't leave this room immediately, I am going to scream for help . . .'

'To whom, my dear?' Clive asked, moving in front of her and smiling at her swiftly lowered eyes. Gripping her chin, he forced her head up until she was looking at him. 'I repeat, to whom?'

'To Lee,' Caroline faltered, trembling as she felt the full force of that powerful gaze. 'Lee doesn't know about you, but I'll tell him . . .'

'Do you think Mr Esslyn is going to be interested in what you have to say? Without my financial backing, he won't be able to do his film. I think you'll find your pleas for help will fall on deaf ears,' Clive said, sitting beside her and again sliding his finger into her moistness.

'James . . .'

'James will only want to hear about how you asked Lee to contact me and ask me to come here,' Clive continued smoothly, rubbing his finger across her swollen clitoris. 'Mr Esslyn will say whatever I tell him to say.'

Caroline could only stare at him as the full force of the threat sank in. She knew Clive and he would not

67

speak like this without the surety of the truth of what he was saying. She wished he would stop stroking her clitoris in such a way: it prevented her from thinking straight. Clive had lost none of his power to control and arouse her. She tried to fight against her own helplessness, but knew it to be a pointless battle. Clive extracted his finger and traced it around her lips smilingly, pushing it into her mouth and nodding his approval as she sucked on the intruder.

'That's my girl. I knew you'd see sense. Mr Esslyn says that I may audition you tonight.'

Clive got off the bed and Caroline struggled to stop herself from begging him to come back and touch her clitoris, to satisfy the huge craving within her. Clive returned quickly, holding something in his hands. Caroline could not prevent her eyes from roaming over his black-clad body. As always, he was impeccably dressed, the thin material of his sweater doing little to conceal the muscled hardness of his body.

'Before we start, I had better make sure that you are properly gagged and restrained. I don't want your screams irritating Mr Esslyn's tender conscience; besides which, I remember how well you like to be tied, don't you my darling?'

Caroline could only stare at him. She felt frightened, but in a way that only exacerbated the sexual feelings she had always had for this man. She wanted to open her mouth and scream for Lee to come, needing help to resist this man who had once more entered her life and yet again was taking control. Clive smiled as he watched her inner struggles.

'Can't do it, can you, Caroline?' he asked, as though reading her mind. 'We always had something good together and we will do again.' As he spoke, Clive unfolded a wide piece of transparent plastic material. Moving behind her, he placed the plastic over her mouth and tied it firmly, before returning to kneel on the bed in front of her and bringing the ends forward, fastening them beneath her chin. Caroline was puzzled as there was quite a lot of the plastic lying in loose folds across her mouth. Surely she could easily scream through such a loose gag?

Spotting her baffled expression, Clive chuckled. 'Go ahead and try it, my darling. Open that lovely mouth and scream for your director.'

Caroline looked at him uncertainly, wondering what he was up to. Clive reached for both her nipples and twisted them. 'I said scream, my darling!'

As the pain hit her, Caroline opened her mouth to scream, only to find that she sucked in the plastic material which very effectively muted her attempt to cry out, reducing it to nothing more than a murmur. The squeezing of her nipples became a caressing motion and the only sounds she was capable of making were moans of pleasure. Clive pushed her back until she was lying on her tethered wrists. Bending his head, he began to lick and suck at her clitoris until she was writhing with sexual excitement. Her ineffectual strugglings with her bound wrists were only adding to her arousal and it was not long before Clive tasted the increase in her juices which told of her satisfaction.

Lips wetly gleaming, Clive smiled as he raised his head and looked at her.

'The first of many, my darling. Now I think I will really tie you up before I begin your punishment.' His smile grew broader as her eyes widened. 'You didn't think I would let you get away with it, did you, darling? Running off and leaving me was not a very nice thing to do, you know, and for that you must be punished. I intend to make it a punishment you will always remember!'

69

Seven

Caroline was quivering with anticipation as Clive untied her wrists. She was unsure as to her feelings. The man she had never expected to see again was back and he seemed just as capable as he ever had been of controlling her emotionally and physically. She had tried to block out her memories of the time before she had met James, but one look from Clive's darkly fascinating eyes and she seemed to be lost. Everything that had happened between her and Clive seemed as if it had only occurred yesterday. She remembered how she had lived in his house and how she had done everything he asked of her. Ironically, that was how she had met her husband. Clive, anxious to land a large business contract with James, had invited him over for dinner and something special. Caroline had been that something special and she and James had become hopelessly attracted. After that, it was only a question of when she would leave Clive. Now she was married to the man she loved, yet here she was obediently waiting for her previous Master's instructions. She tried to tell herself that it was because she did not want James to think she had asked Clive to come to America, but the pulsating of her clitoris told her the truth. She still wanted Clive – as she always had. When he was with her, he had the power to make her do whatever he wished. The prospect of her punishment at his hands merely made her feel aroused in the way she remembered so well. It was as though she had no choice, although she knew that was not really the case. If the door was opened and she was offered her freedom right now, she knew that she would stay. It was not disloyalty to James; it was something she could not and would not attempt to explain.

Still gagged, Caroline remained immobile with her back to Clive. She knew that he would tell her of his requirements when he was ready. Idly, she wondered about Lee. Had he planned this? She shuddered as she felt a movement, Clive had come to sit on the bed beside her. He stroked her shoulders and, had she been able, she would have begged him to fondle her breasts; those small, beautifully shaped breasts with the large nipples he liked so much. As if aware of her needs, his hands slipped along her arms and down to her waist, gently stroking and smoothing her tanned thighs.

'California agrees with you, my darling,' he whispered. 'You are truly adorable.' There was a light chuckle as he continued to stroke her inner thighs, so desperately close to her swollen bud. 'You didn't really think that you had got away from me, did you? Surely you knew that I would come after you, my darling. We have unfinished business and you know I don't like to be in that position.'

His stroking fingers moved up to circle her breasts and she pushed them out for his caress. Chuckling again, he bent his head and sucked gently at both nipples. 'Oh, Caroline, I can read you like a book,' he continued, raising his head and looking at her intently. 'I want you to understand, my dear, that you are mine. You have been – shall we say – loaned out, and now I want you back.' Bending his head, he bit her shoulder, making her suck in

71

her breath with surprise. Clive laughed as he saw that she had also sucked in folds of the plastic that covered her mouth. Smiling, he ran a finger across the top of the gag. 'Yes, I thought this would really keep you quiet. You see, my dear, I have been planning this for some time. I am not telling you everything yet; it is too soon, but I will tell you that you are coming back to England. I have offered Lee the use of my newly acquired studios in Hertfordshire and, when filming has been completed, you are going to say goodbye to James and you are going to come back to live with me.'

Caroline's eyes opened wide and she moaned a protest. Ignoring her reaction, Clive retrieved the roll of thick black masking tape he had brought into the room. Seeing her look, he kissed the area that he had so recently bitten. 'I told you, my dear, that I have been planning this. Do you remember the last time I put this sort of tape on you?' Vigorously, Caroline shook her head. 'Oh, but I think you do, my darling. I taped your eyes and your mouth and your struggling limbs because I wanted to make you permanently mine. I'm sure you remember how Liam rescued you, don't you? And then I had to go to all those devious lengths to get you back. Surely you remember that?'

Clive peeled off a piece of tape and cut it neatly to the required length. Silently, he taped the strip over the top of the gag, sealing it even more firmly in place. 'Now, I tell you what, my darling. I am going to get the implement with which I intend to punish you.' Firmly gripping her plastic covered chin, Clive stared into her eyes. 'I am going to hurt you, Caroline, and it is no more than you deserve for running out on me. I am not going to tie you before I leave, although you may rest assured that on my return you will be very securely bound. I have put the tape on

72

your gag, because I know that it cannot be removed without temporarily leaving a mark.

'Now listen to me very carefully, Caroline. On my return I am going to punish you as you deserve, but in the meantime, I am going to trust you. The door will not be locked and you will not be tied, so you have the choice before I return to take off your gag and run away. There is a robe that you can wear hanging in the wardrobe. If you stay, it will be an acknowledgement that you deserve your punishment and that you are willing to accept it. It will also be an acknowledgement that I am your true Master and that you are my slave. You will be accepting that your return to England will be permanent.'

Releasing her chin, he bent his head and sucked at her nipples, slipping his fingers inside her warm moistness. Almost involuntarily, she arched her body towards him, urging him to go on. She moaned with disappointment as he removed his fingers and raised his head.

'I am going to leave you now and I expect total obedience,' Clive said, his eyes boring into hers. 'You will not attempt to remove your gag and you will not attempt to leave.' He sucked his fingers, tasting her, and rose from the bed. 'After the punishment, if you have been a very good girl, I will fuck you.' Smiling as if he had just bestowed a treasured gift, Clive walked to the door. He turned and remarked pleasantly, 'Oh, I almost forgot, Mrs Davies sends her love.'

Having delivered his parting shot, Clive went in search of Lee. He found the young director in his black and white study. The furniture was all in white leather, the walls were panelled in shining black leather. As he entered, Clive could not withhold an admiring whistle. Lee looked up from the papers on his desk and looked grudgingly at the visitor. He did not like Clive but he could not ignore him, either. Clive prowled around the room like a slinky black panther, every movement a testament to subtle but undoubted power.

'Where's Caroline?' Lee asked as Clive draped himself across the white leather sofa with an elegant economy of movement that had to be admired.

Clive smiled as he extracted a long cigarette from a black monogrammed case. 'The lovely Caroline is at this moment fighting a mental battle that only I can win,' he said, lighting his cigarette with an elegant movement.

Lee frowned and rose to get himself a drink from the well stocked corner bar. As he filled his glass with a ruby red liquid, he tried to assert a little authority. 'I hope she is all right and that she will remain so,' he began, turning to survey his languid guest.

'What is your interest?' Clive asked in brittle tones.

'She is soon to be the star of my next picture. Obviously, that makes her very important to me, and . . .'

'And you fancy her,' Clive remarked baldly.

'I . . . well, yes, I like her, but even if I did fancy her, as you put it, ours is a purely business relationship.'

Very carefully, Clive stubbed out his cigarette in a black marble ashtray before moving to stand beside Lee. He put his hand on the younger man's shoulder, not threateningly, but in an assertion of his control. 'I like you, Lee, and so I will be perfectly straight with you. Caroline used to belong to me and now I want her back. I am perfectly prepared to allow her to do your film, but after that she will return to my complete and absolute control.'

74

Lee looked at his backer, startled. He needed this man and his money and he was prepared to go along with Clive's duplicitous treatment of others, but there were limits. 'Clive, I will agree to your terms regarding the contract and I will go along with whatever you may want me to say to James, but kidnapping . . .'

Quite suddenly, Clive bent forward and gently kissed Lee on the lips. Raising his head, he looked at the director. 'My dear Lee, whoever said anything about kidnapping? Caroline will come to me of her own free will. At this very moment, she is sitting in an unlocked room with the knowledge that she is free to leave. Shortly, we will join her and you will see that, although she is untied, she will have made no attempt to remove her gag. She awaits me in the full knowledge that I am going to punish her, yet still she will not attempt to leave.'

Clive's kiss had taken Lee completely by surprise. He was shaken by it and unsure of how to deal with the mixed emotions that were surging through him. Before now, he had never had the least homosexual urging, and yet as he looked at Clive, he could appreciate the man's magnetism. He realised he had no doubt as to the veracity of Clive's words. Breaking away in a desperate attempt to regain his normally cool attitude, Lee walked to the window.

'I don't want her marked. She appears naked in the film and it would not be suitable for continuity purposes if she had whip marks . . .'

'My dear Lee, who said anything about a whip?' Clive said, once again settling himself on the sofa. 'Expertly applied, the cane is a much fiercer implement, but the marks will have faded prior to the commencement of filming.'

'What about James? What will he say when he sees her?'

'You will just have to confess that the tests involved a little punishment. He will understand that,' Clive assured him.

'What about Caroline? She will tell . . .'

'She will tell him nothing other than that which I order her to say,' Clive said, rising from the sofa and walking over to Lee. 'I can see that you still have doubts about the efficacy of my control. Do you have the financial contract?'

Flustered at Clive's closeness, Lee moved quickly to his desk and picked up the document. Silently, he handed it to Clive and watched as the other man quickly perused its contents. Without a word, Clive sat at the desk and signed and initialled the contract before returning it to Lee.

'Now we are partners in this endeavour, which I am sure will be very successful. Why don't we go and see our star?' Clive asked. As he spoke, Lee noticed that he held in his hands a thin willow cane. 'I've been wanting to test out this little item for some time. I selected it with Caroline in mind and I would be very pleased if you were present to witness her punishment. You will be able to see for yourself how very easily I can control her.'

Lee followed Clive to the door. His heart was beating unnaturally fast as he contemplated Clive's words and the punishment the man intended to mete out to his newest star. At the door, Clive turned to Lee. 'Who knows? You may develop a taste for this sort of activity and if it transpires that you would prefer to be on the receiving end –' he paused '– that can also be arranged.'

In the bedroom, Caroline was pacing the floor. So many times, her hands had risen to her face, ready to peel off the tape and remove the gag. Now that Clive was out of the room, she was able to think more clearly. Why should she stay? What was preventing her from simply removing the gag, putting on the robe and fleeing from the house? She could phone James and he would come and get her. He would know how to deal with Clive! Her hand moved to the phone, but she let it rest there, looking at herself in the mirrored doors of the wardrobes. She raised her hand to her face and touched the gag, running her fingers over the thick black tape holding it so firmly in place. Why didn't she just remove it?

Angry with herself, she dropped her hand to her lap and looked around. She rose quickly, crossed to the door and tried the handle. It opened easily, as she had known it would. Clive had no need to lie. He believed in his power over her, which was a better prevention to any disobedience that she might try than any lock could ever be. Frustrated, she closed the door and ran to the wardrobes. Opening one of the doors, she saw the towelling robe hanging there, just waiting for her to pull out and slip over her nakedness. She knew the hopelessness of the situation even before she closed the wardrobe door.

Caroline returned to the bed and sat down, wishing that Clive had tied her and made it impossible for her to leave. By doing things this way, he was making it her choice. She would stay because she wanted to and she had no doubt that Clive would know how she was feeling and what she would do. She picked up the roll of tape and looked at it, imagining the feel of it around her wrists and ankles. How would he restrain her? She looked at the bed. There was an ornate brass headboard with matching corner posts at the end of the bed. She lay on her back and spread her arms and legs. Of course he would do it like that. She would be spreadeagled, her arms and legs firmly taped into

77

position so that he could punish her in the way she knew he would choose. She shivered as she brought her hands down to her nipples, taking the erect teats in her hands and squeezing them. He would beat her inner thighs. That was where it would hurt the most. She moaned as she moved one hand down to her clitoris. She was gloriously wet and, as she ran her fingers over her slippery bud, she knew that she was submitting herself voluntarily to her punishment; Clive's very willing little prisoner.

Flexing the cane in his strong hands, Clive stood in the open doorway and surveyed the prone girl. Turning triumphantly to Lee, he smiled. 'You see. Just as I told you. Do you need any further proof?'

Startled at his words, Caroline struggled upright into a sitting position. She whimpered as she saw Lee. Had he come to help her, and was that something she wanted? She watched as Lee walked over to the bed and sat beside her. His fingers went to her gagged mouth, smoothing the soft plastic before rubbing gently on the black tape. Caroline was startled by his words as his hands slipped to her breasts. 'A very clever way of gagging her, Clive. I applaud your choice. I trust she is to be restrained for the punishment?'

'Of course,' Clive agreed, walking over to the bed. 'I can't quite decide between the tape or ropes. Perhaps you would like to choose, Lee?'

Caroline could not believe this show of gentlemanly politeness. They were both acting as if it were the most normal thing in the world to survey a helplessly gagged girl, whilst discussing how she was to be presented for her punishment. Her hands moved to her face in annoyance, intending to rip off the gag and berate the two men. Swiftly, Clive bent over her, strong hands gripping her wrists.

'Now, now, my darling,' he chided her. 'You have been very good. We don't want you spoiling it, now do we?'

Now very much involved in what was going on, Lee helped Clive to push Caroline back down on the bed and held her while she struggled.

'Rope, I think, Clive,' Lee said, storing the scene before him away in his memory for possible later utilisation in his movie. 'You'll find plenty in that drawer over there,' he said, indicating a small cabinet. 'I'll hold her for you.'

Lee smiled at Caroline as he gripped her wrists in one hand whilst he kept her pinned to the bed with the other. She struggled desperately, making ineffectual sounds behind her gag. She wanted Lee's hands to grip her breasts; wanted again to feel the hardness of his cock sliding into her vagina. Her frustration kept her struggling until Clive returned, holding several lengths of white silk rope.

Sitting on the bed, he spoke sharply to her, saying the words he knew she wanted to hear. 'Caroline! Stop struggling! You know it will only make matters worse. You are not going to escape because we are going to keep you here for as long as we choose.' As he fixed her with his mesmeric gaze, his voice became gentler, but no less authoritative. 'You will relax and let me tie you up. You will only hurt yourself if you do not. Your punishment will soon be over and then perhaps Lee and I will allow you a little pleasure. But first you have to be a very good girl, do you understand?'

Lee marvelled at the instantaneous quiet which resulted from Clive's words. He watched as Caroline allowed her wrists to be pulled outwards and securely tied to the headboard. Clive was very thorough, taking endless turns of rope around the intricate scrollwork of the headboard, pulling each turn tightly and securing the rope in a complicated series of knots. The same procedure was repeated at her ankles before Clive bound several lengths of rope around the girl's waist, securing each turn of rope around the mattress. When he was finished Caroline was only able to move her head but, not satisfied with this, Clive instructed her to close her eyes before sealing them shut with strips of tape. Standing back to admire Clive's handiwork, Lee wished he had a camera to record the picture that Caroline presented. She was very securely bound, gagged and blindfolded and at the mercy of two men, one of whom had the avowed intention of punishing her very severely. As he contemplated this, Lee glanced a little uncertainly at Clive, who measured the look and smiled.

'I appreciate your concern, Lee, but why don't you feel her cunt and gauge her reaction to all this bondage?'

Lee sat on the bed and slipped two fingers inside Caroline, only to find that she was dripping wet. Smiling in relief, he stood up.

'Let me demonstrate the advantage of having her blindfold,' Clive said as he tapped Caroline's thighs with the cane. She moaned and tried to move. As she discovered that she was truly helpless, her nipples hardened visibly and she moved her head from side to side. Clive bent down and squeezed her nipples, chuckling as he did so. 'You see, she doesn't know who it is that is touching her. If we remain silent during the punishment, she will not know which one of us gives her the pain and which the pleasure.'

Caroline whimpered and again tried unsuccessfully to ease her position. Clive bent his head and whispered in her ear. 'I would advise you not to struggle, my dear. You will only hurt yourself. The more you pull, the tighter the ropes will become.' He watched with pleasure as she opened her mouth to say something, but only succeeded in taking in a mouthful of plastic. 'Now don't be a silly girl. You must realise the helplessness of your position. You are our prisoner and there is no escape.'

As he said this, Clive probed her slit with three of his fingers, feeling her desperate attempts to writhe beneath him. He could not stop himself from taking one of her nipples into his mouth, while stroking and fondling the other. He was impossibly aroused and desired satisfaction just as much as Caroline. Almost impatiently he stood up, retrieving the cane. Without a word, he brought it down hard on Caroline's inner thighs, repeating the strokes without hesitation until a network of raised weals became apparent on the girl's skin. In between strokes, Clive was fondling her clitoris, feeling the increase in juices which told of her approaching climax.

Caroline pulled futilely at the ropes that bound her so securely. Each tug delineated her complete helplessness. The pain, at first intense and burning across the delicate skin of her inner thighs, changed inexorably to intense pleasure as she once again slipped easily into her role of Clive's slave. She knew she was where she wanted to be, fully aware that she could expect no mercy from her former Master. She acknowledged the delicious justice of her punishment and surrendered completely to Clive's dominance. She did not think about what was to happen and how she was going to deal with her new situation. All she could do was give herself up to the almost continuous orgasms that racked her body. In fact, she was reaching the stage of pleading mentally with Clive to finish the punishment and let her relax, but she knew that was all a part of the way he chose to exercise his control and mastery over her.

81

She tried to subdue her excitement by letting Clive's earlier words echo and re-echo around her brain: 'Mrs Davies sends her love. Mrs Davies sends her love'. The exhausting pleasure of yet another orgasm thrilling through her merged with images of Mrs Davies, Clive's housekeeper and the woman who had so enthusiastically kept Caroline a prisoner at his behest. She remembered the beatings she had suffered at the woman's hands and also the pleasure she had enjoyed as those same skilful hands had manipulated her often bound body. Mrs Davies' features seemed to fill her mind; she opened her mouth to scream as yet another orgasm shook her. The plastic, now wet with her saliva, entered her mouth and she tried ineffectually to push it away with her tongue. Her head tossed and turned on the pillow as her body begged to be allowed some relaxation.

Seeing her exhaustion, Lee looked at Clive, who only shook his head and redoubled his efforts with the cane. She had not suffered enough. Grimly, Clive reflected on his own desperate attempts to find Caroline after she had left his house and not returned. How he had suffered when he thought he had lost her forever. Now she was back in his clutches and, when she had been punished enough, he would relent and let her body relax, but he would not let her go. First, she had to satisfy the raging need within him and then – temporarily at least – he would release her. In England, she would return to him and, when he needed to be absent on business, he would allow Mrs Davies to have the care and control of his little slave. He knew he could rely on his devoted housekeeper to impose a rigidly disciplined regime which would remind the girl of what being a slave was all about. He could hardly wait.

Eight

'Perfect!'

Clive walked towards Lee and grasped the proffered handcuffs. Returning to the bed, he looked down at Caroline. She was still gagged and bound, her thighs marked with cross-crossing stripes. Her head was turned to one side and he assumed that, in her exhausted state, she was probably asleep. He resisted the urge to peel the tape from her eyes, but it was too soon. He had not yet finished with her. Sitting on the bed, he gently rubbed a finger over her face, causing her merely to moan softly in her sleep. He traced the outline of her gag, noting with satisfaction the way the plastic now clung to her face, against skin wet with saliva and sweat. Reluctantly, he turned from his contemplation of the helpless girl and started to untie the knots at her wrists. With a start, Caroline awoke and turned her head frantically.

'Easy, my darling,' Clive said. 'I'm just going to untie you. The evening is still young and we haven't yet finished testing you.' He smiled as Caroline moaned. He knew she was tired and only wanted to sleep, but his desire for satisfaction was paramount. He released her ankles and then moved to sit beside her again. 'I'm going to remove your gag now, my darling, so I want you to be a very good girl. The punishment is over and now we shall have some fun.'

As he spoke, Clive unpeeled the tape before

untying the gag. When her mouth was free, Caroline sucked in a gulp of air, relieved to feel a cool breeze on her face.

'Please, will you remove the tape from my eyes?' she asked in a small voice.

Clive considered the request before shaking his head. 'I think not, my darling. I want your pleasure to be considerable and I think being blindfold will only increase that pleasure.'

Knowing better than to argue with Clive, Caroline lay still, luxuriating in the freedom from her restrictions. Clive bent down and kissed her, pushing his tongue between her unresisting lips. She lay still, accepting his kiss, and unbelievably, feeling faint stirrings of desire within her sated body. Almost involuntarily, her arms went around him. Her nipples were hardening with arousal once more as Clive continued to probe her mouth with his tongue, gently slipping his fingers into the moistness that told him she was again ready for him. Gently, he urged her into a kneeling position and, turning to Lee who had now removed his clothes, gestured for him to stand beside the bed.

Disengaging himself from Caroline's arms, Clive moved behind Lee. 'I want you to put your arms straight out in front of you, my darling,' he instructed, pleased at the instant obedience his voice was able to evoke. As instructed, Caroline stretched her arms out and Clive pushed Lee towards her. Putting his finger to his lips, he indicated that Lee should not speak. Clive gently grasped her hands and pulled them around Lee before snapping closed the handcuffs upon each of her wrists.

'Clive?' Caroline asked, a note of uncertainty in her voice.

'I'm here, my love,' Clive assured her, hurriedly

divesting himself of his clothes. He felt relief as his erect cock was freed from any restraint, and gently pushed Caroline's head lower until Lee's hardness brushed her lips. 'You know what I like, my darling,' Clive said and, without further hesitation, Caroline opened her mouth, enabling Lee's cock to slide between her lips. With a gasp, Lee tangled one hand in her hair, holding her in position. With his free hand, he played with her small breasts, twisting the hard nipples alternately as she used her lips and tongue to suck and lick at him as his excitement grew. Satisfied, Clive moved behind Caroline and knelt on the bed. He had lubricated his cock and now tested it against the tiny rosebud entry to the girl's anus. To his delight, he instantly slid inside, feeling her bear down to accommodate him. He grabbed her buttocks as he quickly climbed towards his orgasm, fuelled by the sight of that lovely blonde head bobbing up and down as she pleasured Lee.

Caroline knew she was approaching yet another climax and she welcomed it. The whole scene in which she was involved was tremendously exciting. Her hands were cuffed behind the naked male body of the man she was so enthusiastically pleasuring. Effectively gagged by the cock that filled her mouth, she could only guess as to which of the two men was in front of her and which behind. She arched her back and pushed her buttocks out as the thrusts deep within her rectum became stronger and more urgent. She tasted saltiness in her mouth as her efforts were rewarded, and she swallowed the offered semen. At the same time as the hand in her hair tightened, another stroked across her engorged clitoris, sending her into the paroxysms of orgasm. She did not know who it was that had so pleasured her. She only knew that, for the moment at least, she was content to stay where she was, a very happy and willing prisoner.

Leaving Caroline lying on the bed, Clive escorted Lee to the door. Lee turned, his clothes in his hand.

'What are you going to do?'

Clive smiled and reached out to tweak one of Lee's nipples. 'Why? Are you jealous?'

Again flustered by the confusion of feelings this man engendered, Lee shook his head. 'No, of course not,' he said, doubting the truth of his words. 'I just have a natural concern for the safety of my star.'

'I share your concerns,' Clive responded. 'She will not be harmed. Caroline and I have a lot of history and I want to take up your kind offer and stay the night. With Caroline of course.' Lee looked surprised as he could not recall making such an offer. He had no objection to Clive staying, but could not decide in whose bed he would prefer him to spend the night. 'Of course. Well, I'll say goodnight then.'

'The first of many such,' Clive said, closing the door on his host. For a moment, Lee stood irresolutely on the landing before shrugging his shoulders and turning away.

Caroline was awakened by a soft touch on her shoulder. She could not remember much about what had happened, apart from the sexual enjoyment she had received and knew she had given.

'Stay perfectly still, my darling. I am just going to take the tape off.' She was aware of growing brightness of light as Clive gradually removed the strips from her eyes. After the session with the two men, one of them had unlocked one of the handcuffs and pulled her hands away from the body around which her arms had been imprisoned. Her hands had been brought together in front of her and the open handcuff re-locked on to her wrist.

'You are taking no chances with me,' she had said very softly, feeling lips brush her forehead.

'You got away from me once before, my darling. I do not intend to repeat my mistake,' Clive's voice had responded and, accepting the inevitable, she had settled back on the bed.

Now, as the remaining tape was peeled from her eyes, she blinked in the unaccustomed light. Clive bent over her. 'I think we had better get you showered, my love. You smell disgustingly of sex!' Laughing, he pulled her off the bed. She held her hands out in mute appeal; he shook his head firmly. 'I'm sorry, Caroline, you are my prisoner and until I have to let you go that remains the position and don't tell me that you don't enjoy it!'

Caroline looked at Clive and knew that he spoke the truth. Was there a part of this evening that she had not enjoyed? Tremulously, she smiled at him, confirming his assumption.

'Come on then. Into the shower with you!' Clive ordered.

Once in the shower, Clive was gentleness itself, soaping her and allowing her to do the same to him. As his fingers curled around her breasts, she responded to his touch with a growing sexual need. 'Tomorrow, we are going to spend the day together . . .'

'No!' Caroline was as startled by her reaction as Clive. He stared intently at her, his black eyes seeming to fill her vision as they both stood immobile under the warm water.

'I . . . I mean, I can't . . .' Caroline faltered. 'James . . .'

Clive ignored all her protestations subsequent to that one word which had lodged in his brain. Now,

87

he reached out and gripped her by the arms. 'No? You dare to use that word to me! Have you learnt nothing? Was your punishment not sufficient? Listen to me, my dear, and listen well. You are my slave and as such there is no room in your vocabulary for that word!'

Suddenly, he bent his head and kissed her fiercely, forcing her lips apart as he jammed his tongue into her mouth. Caroline made a small sound of protest and struggled against him, causing him to grab the chain between her cuffed wrists and wrap an arm firmly across her shoulders, immobilising her. She could not help moving against him as her arousal grew. The kiss was so intense that she could hardly breathe, but she returned it with a passion which almost equalled his own. Suddenly he released her and grabbed a flannel from the side of the soap dish.

'If you can't say what I want to hear you say, you had better be quiet!' Clive growled, pushing the cloth into her open mouth. Grabbing her again, he roughly massaged her clitoris as the water continued to cascade over them both. He forced her cuffed hands over his head and stared at her. 'You are mine, Caroline, as you have always been since the first day I set eyes on you. Tell me that you're mine!'

She whimpered into her makeshift gag and tried to shake her head. Clive redoubled his efforts with her clitoris and she felt her knees weaken at the approaching orgasm. As she reached the peak, Clive pulled her hands roughly from around his neck and pushed her against the wall of the shower cubicle. She felt him behind her, penetrating her anus again and pounding into her as she climaxed. His fingers gripped her nipples, intensifying the strength of her orgasm. At the height of his fury, Clive pumped his semen into her rectum. His fingers clawed at the gag in her mouth.'You are my slave, Caroline! Say it! Say it!'

Weakly, she nodded. 'Yes, Clive, I am your slave.'

'And you always have been?' he gasped.

'Yes, I always have been,' she whispered, wondering in her confusion what on earth she was going to do now.

Having achieved his aim, Clive dried her gently. As he removed the cuffs, he bent his head and gently kissed both of her wrists.

'Caroline, I have missed you so very much,' he said, cradling her head.

Caroline felt a surge of confusion. She loved James, she was sure of that, but how was it that Clive was able to make her feel as he did? Clive dried her hair and she was amazed at his gentleness. This man was capable of such contrasting emotions. After the violence of their scene in the shower, he was now behaving with such gentleness. As she watched him, Caroline felt a sexual awareness that could not be denied. She decided to forget her confusion and just enjoy the moment. She watched as Clive rolled a black stocking over her foot and smoothed it up her leg, before repeating the process on her other leg. He produced a black leather suspender belt, which he clipped around her waist before fastening the stockings to the belt. Caroline shivered with anticipatory sexual excitement as Clive pushed her feet into black high-heeled shoes. Smiling at her, he got to his feet and stood back to admire her. Turning, he retrieved some white silk rope from the bedside table and knelt before Caroline.

'We have to get you ready for bed, my love,' Clive said. 'I do not want you trying to escape while I am asleep.'

Both of them knew she was not about to try any such thing, but Caroline surrendered to pleasurable feelings as Clive placed her feet together. Running a caressing hand across her shoes, he tied her ankles tightly. When he had bound her knees together, he helped her to stand. His expression as his eyes travelled over her made her clitoris pulse, her wetness telling her that she was yet again very aroused. Crossing to the wardrobe, Clive extracted a garment and returned to her. He held out a floor-length transparent plastic coat and helped her to slip her arms into the sleeves. Once she had done that, he buttoned the coat and she realised that it fitted her exactly. She shivered as the cold plastic enfolded her body. Clive put his arms around her.

'I had it specially made for you, Caroline. I knew I would get you back.' Caroline relaxed as his embrace warmed the plastic, which was already beginning to adhere to her body. 'Do you like it, my darling?'

Caroline nodded. She hoped that this was the prelude to another session. She was a little disappointed when Clive released her and eased her hands behind her back. As he tied her wrists tightly together, he whispered to her, 'Patience, my darling, patience.'

Caroline smiled. Yet again he knew exactly what she was thinking. Clive bound her elbows together, before tying more rope around her arms, allowing her erect nipples to remain visible through the turns of hemp. He paused in his work to squeeze those nipples, making her knees buckle so that she almost fell. Laughing softly, Clive eased her on to the bed. With a rustle of plastic, he pushed the coat apart where the buttons ended and slipped a finger into her wetness. Caroline groaned and leant back on her bound arms.

90

'You are such a delicious little slave,' Clive said, his cock dripping with the fluid of his own excitement. 'How could I ever have let you go?' He bent his head as he removed his finger. Caroline screamed with delight as his tongue probed into her. Making small tutting noises, Clive raised his head. 'Too much noise, I think.'

'No, please! Clive, I'll be quiet!' Caroline pleaded as Clive moved to the bedside table and returned with two squares of matching plastic.

'My dear, what did I tell you about that word?'

Before Caroline could say anything further, one of the squares had been folded and tied across her mouth. She made protesting noises as the gag was knotted behind her head. The second square of material was similarly folded and tied across her eyes. Clive stood back to survey the effect, stroking his cock as he did so. This was everything he had waited and planned for ever since she had left him. She writhed on the bed, fighting her bonds more as a means to give herself added pleasure than from a genuine desire to escape.

He fell on her and pushed her roughly over on to her side. She moaned with pleasure as she felt the hardness of his cock against her buttocks. The coat was pulled up and that hardness probed her anus yet again as she bore down to help him ease his cock further into her. He gripped her plastic-covered breasts as his climax mounted, feeling the ropes that bound her and ensured her helplessness. Suddenly, he was pumping his semen into her bound body as she struggled against him. Putting one hand between her legs, he felt the hard little bud, triggering an almost instantaneous orgasm. He felt the increase in her juices and hugged her closely, revelling in the feel of her plastic-covered body, so helplessly bound. Whatever it took, he knew that he would do everything in his power to keep her with him and to carry through his original plan to make her his permanent slave.

Caroline lay in bed beside Clive. The way she was dressed and her bondage made sleep impossible. She felt incredibly aroused. Every movement reminded her of the plastic which covered her bound body. Before climbing into bed, Clive had pretended to consider removing the coat and ropes, but Caroline knew that he did not seriously intend to let her sleep in anything other than the sure knowledge of her slavery. Twisting her wrists, she again felt the tug of her bonds. Clive had loosened them a little, which allowed her to lie comfortably but offered no prospect of escape. She thought about James and of what she could say to him once they were reunited. Certainly, she could not be entirely truthful. She could not tell him that Clive had held her prisoner. In any event, she knew that she was a very willing captive. She thought again about the story that she had been instructed to relate to James: that she had been tested for the film and Lee was delighted with her; that she had agreed to all the nude and bondage scenes; that, while James was away, she was to stay with Leyla Dubois, who had offered to train her for the rôle and that, during filming, she was to live in Leyla's English home. Caroline moved uncomfortably. She was, in fact, going to be staying at Clive's Hertfordshire home. Clive had delighted in informing her that the house was very isolated and that she would be in the joint custody of Leyla and Mrs Davies.

Caroline shivered as she thought of her reunion with Mrs Davies. The housekeeper had looked after her in the past, if such whipping and restraining could be so called. Guiltily, Caroline recalled the many orgasms she had experienced when under those strict but caring hands. She felt a pulsing in her clitoris as she wondered what delights could be anticipated. As her nipples hardened, Caroline moved again, this time awakening Clive. Without a word, he turned and put his arm around her, squeezing one nipple and moving against her. She felt his hardness and wriggled within her bonds, whimpering her longing into her gag. She was rewarded as her coat was pulled up over her buttocks and a sharp slap stung across them; a reprimand, she knew, for disturbing the Master. The probing finger inserted in her labia resulted in enough moisture to smear across the entry to her anus. She was already bearing down as Clive entered her, his iron-like embrace further imprisoning her firmly bound arms. She felt fingers at her clitoris, fuelling her excitement. Words were not required, as both bodies mounted to their climax and Caroline's gag stifled her scream of pleasure. She moved her head in frantic movements as she tried to dislodge her blindfold. She wanted to tell him with her eyes how she was feeling, but Clive had no need for this sentiment. She felt her blindfold being secured as his fingers told her that he was in control and he would decide when and if she was to gain any sort of freedom.

Nine

Caroline crumpled the note and threw herself into a deep leather couch in the lounge of James' palatial Malibu house. Restlessly, she got up and wandered to the full-length picture window, gazing unseeingly at the ocean. As he had promised, Clive had kept her for most of the day, only allowing Lee to drive her back to the house in the evening. Desperately wanting to see James, Caroline had run upstairs, calling his name. The house was empty. Flinging open his wardrobe door, Caroline saw that some of James' clothes were missing. He had already left. She had wandered downstairs and found a note informing her that he had had to leave and could not wait for her return. The note said that James had spoken to Lee and been satisfied to learn that the tests were going well but that further time had been needed. James had given his permission.

As Caroline stared through the window, she suddenly saw Clive's mesmeric eyes, seeming to obscure the view. Clive! Somehow, Caroline felt he must have known at what time James would have to leave for the airport to catch his flight to England. He had deliberately kept her until he knew that her husband would have left. Another example of his control! Caroline shivered. She already felt that she was in Clive's power and that he was tightening the net. Inexorably, the sure knowledge crept over her. Once she was in his house in Hertfordshire, Clive had no intention of allowing her to leave. She had no idea how this would be achieved. Of course he would allow the filming to conclude before he made his move, but then he would show his hand and she would not be allowed to return to James.

Caroline poured herself a drink and wished that Lee was still with her. There were so many gaps in her knowledge. Most of all, she wanted to know just how far Lee was involved and how far would he go to carry out Clive's wishes. Sipping her drink, Caroline wondered at herself. How did she really feel? She still loved James, but Clive was back and, as usual, exerting his considerable influence over her so that she felt helpless, unable to do anything other than let events carry her on their relentless tide. Clive excited her. She was also afraid of him, a fact of which she knew he was well aware. He enjoyed exercising his control over her in this manner and she herself knew that the fear he aroused in her was an added excitement which merely served to exacerbate her sexual fascination with this man.

Thinking of him, she was aware that she was becoming wet and longed to give herself some relief, but Clive had forbidden her to masturbate and she knew that, however many lies she was prepared to tell, if she gave herself satisfaction, somehow he would know and would punish her for her disobedience. She asked herself why it was that such a prospect only served to excite her further.

Turning from the window, she decided to busy herself with the packing she had to do. Leyla was calling for her in the morning and would expect her to be ready. Caroline felt a surge of excitement. What could she expect from her training? She wondered if James would have given his permission for such training had he known the identity of Lee's financial backer.

Caroline struggled as Clive snapped shut the cold steel handcuffs on her wrists. She opened her mouth to tell him to stop; tell him that James would not be pleased. Something was taped over her mouth, silencing all her protests. Rough hands were dragging her from her bed. Deciding that the dream was actually becoming painful, Caroline forced herself into wakefulness. She wanted to turn to James. He would comfort her and tell her it was just a dream. Instead, she stared into a hard, coarse face. The owner of that face was responsible for pulling her out of bed. She tried to strike out at the stranger, but the short chain between her cuffed wrists would not allow it. Now fully awake, Caroline realised that this was certainly no product of her imagination. Hard hands gripped her arms and forced her to stand absolutely still. She mumbled furiously beneath the wide strip of tape that had been adhered to her face. She heard the click of heels and, in enforced silence and immobility, she waited for the identities of her captors to be revealed. A perfectly groomed and smiling Leyla Dubois strolled into view. Dressed in knee-length black rubber, Leyla twirled a whip between her hands.

'Caroline, my dear. I thought you were told to be ready at nine a.m.' Consulting a Cartier wristwatch, Leyla smiled. 'It is now ten past. Really, Caroline. This will not do at all.'

Ineffectually, Caroline struggled. The coarse-faced woman who held her merely reached around and slapped her hard.

'Oh, I'm sorry, you haven't met Rudetska, have you?' Leyla said. 'Rudetska has been with me for many years. She is totally loyal and cannot be bought. You will be staying in her quarters where she can keep an eye on you.'

Caroline felt a fury rise within her. How dare this woman have her servant gag and handcuff her and pull her from her own bed?

Reading her mind, Leyla held up a piece of paper. 'James is fully aware of my intentions, Caroline. If you care to look at this paper, you will see that he has signed his confirmation of the fact that while he is away I am to have complete control over you and train you for your rôle. That training is to include a high level of discipline of which, James acknowledges, you are in great need. Rudetska will help me. She is well used to disciplining my ... guests. We knew it would come as a surprise to you and so we have taken precautions to avoid a scene.' Still smiling, Leyla ran the tip of her whip over Caroline's gagged mouth and then continued down, circling the girl's breasts. In spite of herself, Caroline felt her nipples harden. 'You have beautiful breasts, my dear. I think we should begin our lessons with a little painful reminder of what disobedience can bring.'

She snapped her fingers at Rudetska and the woman threw Caroline on to the bed. 'It is in your best interests not to move, Caroline,' Leyla warned. 'Rudetska was raised in the eastern way and she has little compassion.'

Caroline lay still. Her arms still felt as if they were in the servant's grip and she had no wish to further antagonise her. Her hands were cuffed in front. She knew that she could bring them up to try and remove the tape, but one glance at Leyla and she knew that that would be a mistake. So distracted, she was momentarily unaware of the other woman, until a sharp pain in her left breast made her give a muffled scream. Looking down, she saw the glint of the steel nipple clamp, just as her other nipple was similarly abused. Leyla smiled as she watched Caroline struggle with the sensation. 'Hush, my dear. The pain will ease,' Leyla said, sliding the thin handle of the whip into the girl's slit.

Caroline brought her hands up to remove the clamps and instantly she felt her wrists seized in an iron grip. Rudetska unlocked one of her wrist cuffs and forced Caroline's arms behind her back, firmly re-locking the cuff.

'Now be a good girl,' Leyla said. 'You are only following your Master's wishes and, if you *are* a good girl, it won't be all bad.'

Leyla sat on the bed and began to manipulate the whip within her slit, causing Caroline to arch her back as the pain in her nipples became pleasure and she felt a strong desire to begin the climb toward orgasm. 'Yes, my dear, I can be very kind when I want to be and I can make you feel so good,' Leyla crooned, smiling as her prisoner writhed in pleasurable anguish. 'Now, however, I think we must arrange your transportation,' Leyla said, abruptly withdrawing the whip and getting to her feet. 'Once I have you safely locked away, I will feel much happier and we shall have all the time in the world for our little game playing.'

Turning to Rudetska, Leyla gave her orders and Caroline found herself dressed in a loose-fitting long PVC cape. The cape had an integral matching scarf which Rudetska tied over Caroline's face, in a way which appeared casual but effectively concealed the fact that she was gagged. When she had finished dressing her charge, Rudetska held her firmly by the arm while Leyla concealed her whip by sliding it inside one of her PVC boots.

Leyla turned to Caroline. 'Let's go downstairs. One

false move, my dear, one effort to escape or call attention to yourself will be very severely punished. Do you understand?'

Caroline nodded, again wondering at herself as her clitoris pulsed its excitement.

'Good,' Leyla said, taking one final look at Caroline. 'No one would guess that you are gagged and handcuffed, besides which, this is California. You know its reputation as the state where anything goes!'

The room into which Caroline was dragged had been designed as a cell. The windows were shuttered with heavy wooden planks and were heavily padlocked. The door of the cell was double locked and could also be bolted from the outside. The room contained a small bed, a cabinet, table and two chairs. Rudetska threw Caroline on to the bed and awaited orders. Caroline looked up at the older woman. Her unsmiling features were framed by iron grey curls and the woman's stocky stature reminded Caroline of Mrs Davies. She could not begin to guess her age, but even if she had been able to vocalise the question, Rudetska's grimly harsh features did not invite enquiry.

'I hope your cell is to your liking, my dear,' Leyla said, walking into the small room. 'I had it renovated especially for you. You will be kept just as your character in the film is kept and you will also be similarly treated. You will at all times be regarded as a prisoner. You will not be allowed any freedom. For most of the time you will be kept in restraints and you will certainly be gagged. At times, your character will attempt to escape and I will be just as watchful over you as is your captor in the film. I realise that you are here by consent but you will be treated as if you had really been captured and wanted to escape.

99

I will, therefore, be severe upon you if such attempts are made.'

While Leyla was speaking, Caroline was being divested of the cape and scarf. Rudetska unlocked the handcuffs, replacing them with firmly tied ropes. Caroline's knees and ankles were then bound and the tape peeled from her lips, immediately being replaced with a scarf, which was pushed between her lips and securely tied at the back of her head. Leyla stood watching the procedure, eyeing Caroline's naked body with lascivious enthusiasm.

'That will do, Rudetska,' she said and watched as the woman left, closing the door behind her. Leyla sat on the bed, her fingers circling Caroline's breasts. 'Those nipples will really hurt when the clamps are removed. Shall I do that now or shall I chain the clamps to your collar?' Leyla mused, moving to the cabinet and taking out a thick black leather collar. Moving back to Caroline, she studied the girl. 'I think you are in need of some good discipline, my dear, and perhaps a night wearing the clamps will be an excellent start.' So saying, Leyla strapped the collar around Caroline's neck and snapped the attached padlock shut. Producing a thin chain, she threaded this through the rings at the end of the clamps before taking it around behind the girl and fastening it to the collar. Caroline gasped into her gag as the chain was pulled taut.

Leyla chuckled. 'Just a reminder, my dear, that you must stay perfectly still. Any movement and you will pull on the clamps. It is in your interests to behave yourself or you will spend a very painful night.' Leyla stroked Caroline's hair. 'I'm so glad you are here, Caroline. I have looked forward to this and Lee has agreed that I can go with you to England, just in case further training is required.' Leyla ran her perfectly manicured hands over Caroline's clitoris, laughing at the wetness she discovered. 'Why, Caroline, you naughty girl. I think you are aroused and I don't recall that I gave you permission!' Leyla withdrew her fingers and got to her feet. 'Rudetska will have prepared my dinner so I will leave you now. You may or may not be allowed some food. I have yet to make up my mind, but I will return and when I do, you will be punished. After that, we shall see,' Leyla whispered softly. 'Maybe I will give you pleasure and maybe it will just be pain.'

Caroline sat immobile in the darkness. Leyla had switched off the light as she left the room and the shutters allowed no light from outside to enter. Caroline had experimentally tried to shift her position, only to be rewarded with sharp pain in both nipples as the chain tautened. Nevertheless, she felt a strong arousal. The promise that she would be kept restrained and gagged during her imprisonment merely exacerbated her sexual excitement. She wondered about the forthcoming punishment and felt an increase in the wetness between her legs. Who would deliver the punishment? Would it be Leyla, or would she order her servant to carry out the task? At least it was not cold in the room. Being California, the temperatures rarely dipped very low. Caroline reflected on her situation. James had sanctioned her imprisonment. How did that make her feel? Perhaps he didn't know how cruel Leyla could be. Immediately she dismissed that thought. Of course he knew. He and Leyla were old friends. Did it make any difference anyway? James knew that she would find the situation sexually arousing and being made a prisoner in the way that she had been only fuelled that arousal. She could not help wondering whether the whole week of her imprisonment would be like this and, if it were, could she possibly spend the time in such an aroused state? Just as she was thinking this, the bolts were withdrawn and she heard the keys in the double locks. Leyla came into the room. She was carrying a long-handled whip and Rudetska was standing behind her, her arms full of some heavy chains.

'Well, Caroline. I see you have decided to be sensible. That's a good girl. I have brought you a little present and Rudetska will put it on you. Stay very still while you are untied or you will only hurt yourself.'

Caroline stayed perfectly still while Rudetska unfastened the ropes from her ankles, knees and wrists. When her gag was removed, Leyla bent towards her with her finger to her lips. 'Ssh, my lovely girl,' she whispered, and Caroline did not attempt to speak. A thick leather gag was strapped over her mouth, its wide straps being buckled into position in front of her lips. The collar was not removed and neither were the nipple clamps. Some very thick and wide wrist and ankle straps were buckled into place; the chains between them were the heavy ones she had seen in Rudetska's arms. A wide leather belt was buckled on to her slim waist and the chains that fell from it were padlocked to the chain between her wrists. She could not move her arms above her waist.

Leyla stood back admiringly. 'Very nice indeed. Those chains will certainly deter any escape attempts and you will find that the gag will not allow anything other than the feeblest of moans. No one will hear you. It is a pity, but you must learn to behave, Caroline, really you must!' With this admonishment, Leyla moved to the bed. Sitting, she stroked Caroline's clitoris and brought her fingers to her mouth, tasting the resultant moisture. 'Oh, Caroline, so badly behaved. Shall I let Rudetska have you? She enjoys the punishments so much and she is such a devoted slave.'

Leyla bent her head and licked at Caroline's clitoris, making the girl gasp with shock into the leather gag as her involuntary movement caused stinging pains in her nipples. Tutting, Leyla raised her head and got off the bed. 'Oh, Caroline. I think I will give you to Rudetska. She will know how to deal with you.' Tossing the whip to the servant, Leyla blew Caroline a kiss and went out, bolting and locking the door behind her.

For several moments, Caroline and Rudetska looked at each other. Caroline wondered about the woman. She had seemed to enjoy herself as she had restrained the prisoner and now she stood watching, her eyes gleaming with the knowledge of what she was about to do. Caroline felt a thrill of fear – or was it excitement? She did not know. She hoped that the tenseness in the atmosphere would be dissipated when Rudetska made her move. At last, she had her wish. Rudetska sat on the bed and, unexpectedly, began stroking Caroline's breasts. The girl dared not move, not only because of the pain such movement would undoubtedly cause, but also because her curiosity was aroused as she tried to fathom the older woman's intentions. She yelped into her gag as, completely without warning, Rudetska released both nipple clamps and studied Caroline as the girl writhed in helpless agony. Suddenly, the pain of returning feeling in her abused nipples began to merge with increasing sexual excitement, as Rudetska stroked her clitoris and then bent her head to suck at Caroline's engorged bud. Now freed from the clamps, Caroline was able to arch her back to meet the probing tongue. The sound of Rudetska licking and sucking became lost in the noise of the clanking chains as Caroline struggled to find release from the urgent needs of her body.

Suddenly, Rudetska ceased her ministrations and Caroline's eyes flew open. The older woman was getting off the bed and advancing towards her with a black leather blindfold in her hands. Mutely, Caroline shook her head. She wanted to be aware. She wanted to see what was happening. Ignoring the girl's pleading eyes, Rudetska roughly pulled Caroline's head up from the pillow and quickly fastened the blindfold in place. There was some kind of soft fabric on the inside of the leather, which completely shut out any chink of light when the blindfold was strapped behind her head. Her face now practically obscured by the gag and blindfold, Caroline whimpered her protests. She knew that she was completely at the mercy of the unsmiling woman. She could not see where the woman was or what she might have in her hands. There was no clue as to what she might expect. Caroline knew that her very helplessness was increasing her desire to orgasm. She did not know that, at last, Rudetska was smiling as she turned around to face the hidden camera which was recording everything for her Mistress' pleasure.

Turning back to Caroline, Rudetska knelt on the bed and switched on the vibrator that she had previously concealed. Caroline heard the buzzing and thought that she was to be allowed to reach her climax. She felt the implement as it was stroked across her clitoris and made desperate but futile attempts to free herself, only to be rewarded with the cessation of the buzzing sound and the lifting of the exciting pressure on her clitoris. She felt the leather cuffs at her wrists and ankles being tightened inexorably as a warning against further escape attempts.

Still no word had been spoken. Caroline was twisting on the bed as her frustration increased. With relief, she heard the buzzing noise as the vibrator was again switched on. She felt the gentle stroking on her clitoris and a soft tongue slithered over her nipples. Now moaning into her gag, Caroline writhed helplessly on the bed as her climax approached. If this was her punishment, she wanted more of it! Then, just as suddenly as before, the vibrator was switched off and removed from her vicinity. There was the sound of a bolt being withdrawn and the grating of keys in locks. Still moaning her protestations, Caroline felt a gentle hand in her hair.

'There, my darling. Rest easy. You are not going to be allowed your pleasure today.' Caroline spat a protest into the gag, to be rewarded by Leyla's soft chuckle. 'No, my dear. You see, there are other ways to punish than just the administering of pain. Rudetska has brought you to the brink and, I am afraid, there you will remain until I decide that you have been punished enough.' Leyla bent and kissed the girl's forehead. 'Rudetska will prepare you for the night and I will see you tomorrow. I hope you have . . . pleasant dreams.' Caroline vented her frustration, but it was only a muffled sound.

Smiling, Leyla nodded at Rudetska and walked to the door. 'Once you have settled our guest for the night, Rudetska, perhaps you will come to my room. I feel somewhat excited and you can help me to relax. Good night, Caroline. Until tomorrow.'

Leyla could not disguise her satisfaction as she walked to the door. She knew that Caroline would be intensely frustrated, even more so by the knowledge that she and Rudetska were planning a very satisfying evening. Turning, she threw a bundle of clothes to Rudetska and left the room. Herself frustrated by the sexual activities of the evening, Rudetska smiled as she contemplated the evening to come. Bending to her work, she removed the chains and cuffs from Caroline's helpless body. Still without a word, she forced the girl's arms into the sleeves of one of the garments that Leyla had given her. Caroline felt the cold, slippery material and, smelling its unmistakeable aroma, knew it to be rubber. She tried to struggle as the garment was fitted, although all she really wanted to do was to luxuriate in the exciting feel of the material. Caroline knew that this mode of dressing her was intended to fuel her frustrated desire to orgasm. Grasping both her wrists in a cruel grip, Rudetska forced the girl to stop struggling. When this was achieved, she pulled Caroline's arms behind her and tied the girl's wrists firmly together. Next, she tied her elbows, securely but loosely enough for some comfort to be achieved. Rope imprisoned her arms and Caroline felt renewed arousal as the cord was bound over her breasts. Rudetska's fingers constantly brushed her nipples as she worked, though Caroline could have no way of knowing that this was because her Mistress would be watching and enjoying the scenario. Once Caroline's arms and breasts were bound, Rudetska pulled the rubber material of what was, in actuality, a black rubber negligée closely around the girl, before securing it in position by binding Caroline's thighs, knees and ankles. Pushing the girl back on to the bed, Rudetska finished off by tying some rope tautly across her prone body, securing her to the bed.

Standing back to survey her work, Rudetska grunted her satisfaction, before going to the door and opening it. Looking back at her helpless prisoner, Rudetska stroked her own nipples, smiling as she felt their immediate reaction. Her Mistress would be pleased with her and she would build on that pleasure by helping her to achieve the satisfaction that she had so cleverly denied the new prisoner. If she succeeded, Rudetska hoped that she might be allowed to whip the new girl and teach her to pleasure her wardresses.

Unable to see, Caroline lay helplessly tethered to the bed. She was unable to move. Her bonds, although tightly secure, were not uncomfortable. Her mind, at least, was able to roam freely as she surveyed her situation. As her tormentors knew it would, the black rubber of the negligée allowed her little rest. She had always been excited by the look and feel of rubber and now she lay wrapped in the fabric, the cords that restrained her lower limbs keeping the material sealed to her body in a far from restful manner. If only they had removed her blindfold, but she knew that this was part of the punishment. Deprived of sight, she could only dwell inwardly on the feelings engendered by her bondage. She could feel her nipples pressing against the soft rubber and was all too aware of the dampness between her legs. She was unable to wriggle about and give herself any hope of satisfaction. Her thoughts wandered to Rudetska and Leyla. They would not be feeling her frustration as they gave themselves mutual pleasure. She thought of Clive, who was responsible for her predicament, and of the week to come. Would Clive come and see her? Did she really want him to? As Caroline feebly struggled within her rubber bondage, she knew that she did want Clive. She wanted him as she had always wanted him and, as ever, he could do with her whatsoever he chose. Leyla had her body imprisoned but her mind, Caroline knew, was Clive's. The sexual excitement that such thoughts created made her struggle against the ropes which bound her so tightly. The long night stretched before her, fraught with her desperate frustration.

Ten

'Come in.'

Clive looked up as the door opened. Not for the first time, he thanked Lee silently for allowing him to be associated with his new film. Getting Caroline back into his power was worth every penny of the investment he had agreed to make. Now that Lee was becoming so attracted to him, Clive had started to request certain favours. This afternoon, for instance, he was 'auditioning' eager would-be starlets for some of the film's smaller rôles. Appreciatively, his black eyes studied the newcomer. Lee had allowed Clive the use of his office and secretary; he smiled as he recalled the secretary's open-mouthed fascination with her boss' new associate. Returning his full attention to the girl standing in front of his desk, Clive extended his hand, hoping that his erection was not too visible.

'Miss Soames?'

The auburn curls moved against her shoulders as Anthea Soames nodded her acknowledgement.

'Well, Miss Soames . . . or may I call you Anthea?'

Enthusiastically, Anthea nodded. Lee Esslyn's secretary had told her that Mr Craigen, the assistant director, would be auditioning her. What she had neglected to mention was how gorgeous Clive Craigen really was. Nervously, Anthea smoothed the soft leather of her blue mini-skirt and hoped that she didn't look as nervous as she felt.

'Please sit down,' Clive said, indicating the chair across from him. 'Now . . .' He flicked through some papers on his desk, noting that Anthea had already done some film work, although nothing very substantial. Her agent had assured Clive that Anthea was very keen to be involved in the film – very keen indeed.

'You've read the script?' Clive asked. Smiling prettily, Anthea shook her head. Clive settled back in his chair. 'Then I'd better fill you in on the background before we talk about your rôle.' Inwardly, Clive smiled at the way Anthea sat forward. He had deliberately intimated that the rôle was already hers, and indeed, it might be, he reflected, looking at the shapely legs revealed beneath the short skirt. 'The heroine becomes the object of an obsessive relationship. In fact, it becomes so obsessive that her boyfriend decides to keep her at his country house. At first, she is more than willing to stay until . . .'

'Until?' Anthea asked, caught up in the story.

'Until she becomes restless and wants to leave.'

'What does he do?' Anthea asked, almost breathlessly.

'He tells her that she cannot leave and that she is to stay with him so that he can play his sex games.'

'What sort of games?' Anthea asked, now impossibly excited.

'Bondage games,' Clive said, watching closely for her reaction.

'Oh!'

'Do you know what bondage games are, Anthea?' Clive asked, his voice softly sensual.

'Yes, Mr Craigen.'

Smiling, Clive stood up and walked around the desk. Standing beside Anthea, he touched her hair with gentle fingers.

'Call me Clive.'

'Yes, Mr . . . Clive.'

'Good. Now, your rôle will be that of the heroine's friend who becomes suspicious and calls on the boyfriend to look for her friend. Sensing her suspicions, the boyfriend cannot let her go and on some pretext invites her in. She soon finds herself a not unwilling participant in the games.'

'Not unwilling?' Anthea asked, tilting her chin flirtatiously to look at Clive. Gently, Clive ran a finger along her jawline.

'She finds that she likes the bondage games . . . likes being tied up. Do you think that you would enjoy being tied up, Anthea?'

'If the rôle called for it, Clive,' Anthea responded, her eyes liquid.

'Have you ever been tied up?'

'How do you mean?'

Clive walked behind her and began gently massaging her shoulders.

'During sex, has your boyfriend ever tied you up?'

Anthea blushed and Clive felt the muscles in her shoulders tighten.

'Not exactly . . .'

'Anthea, if we are to work together, we have to be honest with each other.'

'All right,' Anthea said but then fell silent. Crossing to the office door, Clive turned the key in the lock, before returning to stand in front of her.

'You can tell me anything, Anthea. I don't judge.'

'My . . . my girlfriend sometimes ties me up.'

'Better and better,' Clive enthused. 'There will be an element of lesbianism in your rôle.'

'Oh, I'm not exactly a lesbian,' Anthea said. 'I have boyfriends.'

'You swing both ways?'

'Yes. I hope that doesn't make a difference.'

'On the contrary, my dear,' Clive said. 'It only increases your suitability for the part.' Moving behind her, Clive let his hands slide down the front of Anthea's tight-fitting top and was rewarded when he came into contact with very erect nipples. 'There is only one remaining thing that I need to see . . .'

'What is it, Clive?' Anthea asked.

'I need to see how you look in ropes,' Clive said smoothly. 'Do you mind?'

'No, of course not,' Anthea said, by this time hopelessly attracted to Clive.

Smiling, Clive pulled out some white silk rope from his pocket. 'Will you also be prepared to let me gag you?'

There was no hesitation as Anthea nodded. She was trembling with excitement, the more so when Clive drew her arms behind the chair and secured her wrists. 'There. Perhaps you would struggle for me, my dear.' Obligingly, Anthea twisted in her chair, pulling at the securely tied ropes. 'Excellent,' Clive said, bending down and tying her ankles to the legs of the chair. He rose, and took out a large white pocket handkerchief. Moving behind her, he folded the cloth before lowering it in front of her face and tying it in place. 'Now, can you scream?'

Joining in the fun, Anthea made a muffled noise. Clive stroked his fingers across her gagged mouth, continuing down over her breasts before, seemingly hesitant, he allowed his fingers to slip beneath the leather skirt. He was delighted to find that she wore no underwear and his fingers were able to slide between her legs and into her wet slit. Bending, he kissed her hair. 'Anthea, you are perfect for the part. Would you like to come to my house tonight for further discussions, although –' Clive paused '– of

111

course you may not be able to make much of a vocal contribution.'

Removing his fingers, Clive pulled down the gag.

'What time would you like me to be there?' Anthea asked, smiling into the eyes of the man for whom she already knew she would do anything.

'Leyla?'

'Clive! Good to hear from you. How are things going?'

'Things, my dear Leyla, could not be better. Shall we dispense with the social niceties. Do you have her?'

Leyla laughed softly. 'Yes, Clive. I have her. Right now, she's contemplating a very frustrating night. I might alleviate some of that frustration later . . . or I might not. Does that answer your question?'

'Don't hurt her too much, Leyla. That is my prerogative,' Clive warned.

'I may not hurt her at all. She is rather delicious and there are plenty of things that I can think of which aren't necessarily painful,' Leyla said and then paused. When she resumed, her tone was flippant but with an underlying note of seriousness. 'I might even decide to keep her.'

'That would be an unwise move, my dear. She is mine.'

'I think you British have a saying,' Leyla said. 'Possession is nine-tenths of the law?'

'Forget it, Leyla! I agreed to let you have her for this short period, but . . .'

'Oh! You decided, did you?'

There was another pause, during which Clive made a heroic effort at control. 'Yes, Leyla. You seem to forget that I hold the purse strings and Lee will do whatever I tell him. Perhaps you would do well to remember that.'

112

Leyla's annoyingly assured laugh came over the wires. 'We shall see, Clive, we shall see.'

Suddenly, the line went dead. His mouth set in a firm line, Clive punched in Lee's telephone number. It was time to establish his authority.

There was silence in the darkened room, broken only by the soft rustling of rubber as Caroline moved as much as she was able. She tried to blank out her sense of frustration by concentrating her mind on James and what she could do about the situation now that Clive was back in the picture. Not for the first time, she wondered at herself. She who, more than anyone, knew Clive's capabilities and the lengths to which he would go in order to control her. Why was she so easily susceptible to his control again? Before his re-entry into her life, she had been supremely content: married to the man she loved and resident in a new and exciting country. Why wasn't it enough? Conscious of the ropes biting into her as she moved so restlessly, she resolved to remain still. Perhaps in the morning, Rudetska or Leyla would come and relieve her frustration. James had told her that Leyla was going to train her for her film rôle. Where was the training element in this incredibly frustrating situation? Perhaps James had lied to her. Perhaps he just wanted her safely tucked away while he conducted his business affairs. Didn't that seem to indicate that he did not trust her? Caroline shook her head, anguished at the direction her thoughts were taking. This was Clive's doing. She hoped that he had no intention of visiting her at Leyla's. Didn't she?

Lee opened the door to Anthea's knock. His eyes admired Clive's choice as he stood aside for the newcomer to enter. She wore a see-through tunic top

113

over a short skirt. The top amply demonstrated her lack of a bra and Lee felt his cock hardening as he preceded the way out to the pool area. Clive was already there, wearing the briefest scrap of material around his hips. Momentarily distracted from his perusal of Anthea's very inviting bottom, Lee went to the pool-side bar and offered drinks to his guests. Selina, another of the girls who Clive had invited for a more intimate audition, sidled over to the bar and sat down on one of the stools. Her ample breasts were minimally contained within a silver latex top. As she sat, the matching skirt rode up around her waist. 'Silly me,' she commented. 'I should have asked if a swim suit was required.'

Lee chuckled as he added ice to a tall glass already filled with topaz coloured liquid. 'Who said anything about a suit? Haven't you ever been skinny dipping?'

Arms linked, Clive and Anthea joined them. Clive assessed and approved Selina's charms. Compared to Caroline, she was a little heavy for his taste, but would provide suitable evening entertainment. Lounging at the bar, Clive almost negligently laid one of Anthea's arms across Selina's breasts. 'Now's your chance, Anthea. You told me that you swing both ways, so let's see how inventive you can be in providing us with some entertainment.'

Anthea did not hesitate. Selina was her type of woman and she was delighted to make the most of this opportunity. Slipping her hand between the other girl's legs, she decided to play the dominant. Moving her fingers into Selina's wet slit, she moved her other hand to grip the girl's upper arm in a painful clasp. 'You must be new here, my dear. You look a little warm. Why don't we strip off and sample the pool? Perhaps you can then show me how delighted you are to be here.'

Nothing loath, Selina stood and removed her skirt. Anthea released her hold on the girl and stripped off her top and skirt, conscious of the men's approving stares. She slipped into the warm water and then lay against the steps. Her legs were outstretched in an unmistakeable invitation. This was the sort of audition at which she excelled. Without hesitation, Selina joined her. Anthea rested her outstretched arms along the side of the pool and awaited the anticipated pleasure. Selina bobbed her head under the water and licked and sucked at Anthea's slit until the need for oxygen forced her up. Taking in great lungfuls of air, she smiled at her Mistress and reached out to stroke the erect nipples. Anthea smiled deceptively before reaching forward suddenly to grasp Selina's hair, smiling at the surprised girl's gasp of shock. She forced the girl's head down between her legs in determined fashion, only slightly relaxing her grip as the sucking motions heightened her pleasure. The men watched, leaning forward in their excitement. Lee slipped a hand on to Clive's erect penis and was gratified when that hand was not removed. Clive was breathing hard: Anthea was certainly providing a show. How long would she leave it before allowing Selina to come up for air? Clive watched the steady hand in Selina's dark hair and suddenly imagined himself doing that to someone with long blonde hair. He was glad of Lee's insistent hand as it rode up and down his hard stem. He had been tolerant of the man's obvious desire for some time, but had managed to keep him at arm's length; now, however, he could be useful. As Clive's excitement mounted, he needed the release that Lee could provide. Perhaps he should force the younger man on his knees so that he could perform the same service as Selina was providing for Anthea, but he knew he could not wait that long. As he saw Selina struggling to free herself from Anthea's hard grasp, his own evidence of excitement spurted over Lee's hand. Clive was suitably gratified when Lee bent his head and licked him clean.

With finely judged accuracy, Anthea pulled the dark head free of the water. Taking the girl in her arms, she probed the willing mouth with her tongue as, with excited fingers, Selina finished off her task. As Anthea reached her climax, Clive clicked his fingers, gesturing for both women to join him. Sated, Anthea climbed from the pool. Revelling in his control, Clive directed both women to pleasure the director. Lying by the bar, Lee welcomed Anthea's mouth on his cock and almost immediately climaxed as Selina stroked his anus with her tongue. It took only a few minutes of Anthea's delighted sucking at her clitoris before Selina joined the others in their mutual satisfaction. Surveying the scene with half-closed eyes, Clive lounged at the bar. It had been an eminently successful evening. Now, there was something else to be taken care of. Tomorrow, he was going to see Caroline and also Leyla. It was time that both women learnt who was really in control.

Eleven

'I hope you slept well, my dear,' Leyla said as she
entered the room. She looked approvingly at Caroline. Rudetska had performed her tasks well, untying
the girl and removing the rubber negligée before
taking the prisoner into the bathroom and assisting
her to shower and wash her hair. Now breakfasted,
Caroline had been tied to a chair, adhesive tape
replacing the leather gag. Leyla stroked her shining
blonde hair and smiled at the mutinous expression in
eyes that seemed to spark their frustration.

'Oh, I'm sorry, I forgot. You must have spent a
very difficult night,' Leyla said, moving her hand to
stroke the erect nipples framed by the rope with
which her arms were bound. 'I think that rubber is
such a very sensual material, don't you? It always
makes me feel very sexual and, of course, you
couldn't give yourself any satisfaction. However, that
can be seen as the start of your training. Lesson
number two is where you demonstrate how good you
can make me feel and maybe, just maybe, I will
return the pleasure.'

As she spoke, she was busy at the ropes and
Caroline felt the pressure ease as they slipped from
her arms and wrists. Automatically, she brought her
hands up to remove the tape. Quickly, Leyla caught
her hands. 'No, no, my dear. We can't have that. I
am not prepared to take the risk of you calling out. I

think a little insurance is called for.' Snapping a pair of handcuffs on Caroline's wrists, she attached a thin chain around the girl's waist to which the cuffs were padlocked, allowing her a small amount of movement, but not enough to raise her hands to her mouth. 'There, that's better. It's a nuisance, but I always find that new slaves need such careful watching and Rudetska is always scolding me for being too lax. Never mind, I am sure that you have fingers clever enough to please me, isn't that so, my dear?'

Mutely, Caroline kept her head still and her eyes downcast. Impatiently, Leyla gripped her chin and forced her head up until she could do nothing other than look straight at her tormentor. 'I said, isn't that so, my dear?' Leyla repeated unsmilingly, twisting Caroline's left nipple. With a moan of pain, Caroline nodded. 'That's better. You seem inclined towards disobedience this morning. I think we will have to deal with that before the pleasure, although you may find it otherwise.'

Leyla released her grip on Caroline and moved to the bed where Rudetska had so thoughtfully placed a riding crop. Picking up the black leather implement, Leyla returned to her captive. 'You English,' she said, stroking the crop. 'So imaginative. Once upon a time, it was believed that such things were only of interest to the riding fraternity. Now, of course, we know better don't we?' As she spoke, Leyla slid the crop down Caroline's body until she reached her slit. She paused. 'If I give way to my natural instincts, I will push the crop into your slit, but that would only give you pleasure, would it not? First, you must taste the pain!' Suddenly, the crop was brought down across Caroline's thighs with an intensity that sent a trail of fire across them. When the pain was at its height, Leyla bent her head and sucked at each of the girl's pert nipples until the captive was writhing in an ecstasy of pleasure/pain, her chains tinkling as she fought to contain the sexual arousal such treatment engendered. Another stroke across her thighs left Caroline gasping into her gag, but intensely alive to the hoped for prospect of pleasure to come.

Leyla did not disappoint. Sliding to her knees, she used her lips and tongue to bring the girl to the precipice of an orgasm, intending to withdraw and increase the frustration. That particular plan went unheeded as Leyla tasted Caroline's juices and knew that she wanted more. Licking and sucking, she dropped the riding crop, all else forgotten as she concentrated on giving her prisoner extremes of pleasure that she could not have expected. As Caroline bucked in the throes of her long awaited orgasm, Leyla looked up in satisfaction. Running her tongue around her wet lips, Leyla smiled. 'You taste very good, Caroline. I think you may now be allowed to give your Mistress just as much pleasure. I don't hold with the saying that it is always better to give than to receive!'

'Well, a real sight for sore eyes!'

Startled, Leyla's eyes flew open and she found herself staring straight into Clive's black gaze. Caroline had raised her head and was also looking at Clive. Behind him, Rudetska stood uncertainly, well aware of what she might expect from her Mistress. She was not looking forward to explaining how it was that Clive's insistent stare had almost been sufficient for such defiance. His assurance that Leyla would not welcome anything but an immediate admission had secured her co-operation.

Amused, Clive strolled further into the room, his gaze taking in Leyla's kneeling state and her wet lips before travelling to Caroline's chained nakedness and her spread legs.

'I'm sorry, ladies. Was I interrupting something? I just came to check up on my investment.'

Embarrassed at her inactivity, Rudetska moved to Caroline and gripped her arm, forcing the girl to her feet. Clive nodded approvingly. 'Excellent idea. Leyla, you are really very lucky in your staff.'

Frustrated, Leyla frowned at Clive, even while her clitoris throbbed at his presence. 'It's always nice to see you, Clive,' she said tightly, rising to her feet. 'As always, your timing is impeccable.'

Clive smiled pleasantly, sniffing the aroma of sexual arousal. He hoped that he had arrived before its consummation. Lazily, his eyes travelled over Leyla's shapely body. He thought how nice it would be to tame this particular dominatrix. Clive revelled in challenges and bringing a dominant person to heel was a very exciting one. Turning to Rudetska, he waved his hand in dismissal.

'Take the slave away,' he said in an imperious tone. Winking at Rudetska, he continued. 'Keep her safe and quiet for your mistress. She and I have much to discuss.'

Leyla tried to re-assert some authority. 'You can't come into my house and order my staff about!'

Smiling lazily, Clive walked over to her and placed his hands on both of her arms in a deceptively gentle restraining movement. 'That's where you're wrong, Leyla. I can do whatever I want and you will do as you are told.'

Leyla stared at him, anger outweighing fascination. 'How dare you! Get out of here, you English bastard!'

Laughing, Clive moved behind her, clamping one arm across her breasts in a hard grip, which effectively pinned both her arms. Still laughing, he placed his free hand over her mouth. 'Scottish, please!' He nodded at Rudetska, who was standing with her mouth open at seeing her mistress thus treated. Her hold on Caroline had become slack. 'Don't let your charge get away from you. Don't worry, everything is in order. Your mistress and I are old friends and I have long felt that she needs a lesson in humility. Why don't you take the slave and give her a good whipping? Leyla and I are going to be busy.' As if to underline his words, Clive tightened his grip on Leyla as she struggled wildly, trying desperately to bite his hand.

Caroline watched the scene in disbelief. Ever since Leyla had brought her off, she had begun to feel differently about her. She had even begun to think that a week in this woman's care would not be so bad after all. Now she was seeing that same woman, shamed and humiliated in front of her own servant, writhing and twisting in the grasp of the man who so fascinated and controlled her.

As if making a sudden decision, Rudetska pulled Caroline roughly towards the door. She did not like to see her mistress so treated, but she would more than compensate for her distress when she laid her whip across this slut's buttocks! Rudetska pulled Caroline through and slammed the door behind them, leaving a furious Leyla making muffled pleas for help beneath Clive's gagging hand.

As soon as the door had closed, Clive threw Leyla on to the bed. Almost spitting with fury, Leyla immediately rose up, glaring at Clive. 'How dare you! This is my house and . . .'

'And I am your guest and of course guests don't normally behave like this, do they? I'm sorry, Leyla,

121

but you asked for it. You have challenged my authority . . .'

'Your authority?'

'Yes, my dear, my authority! In case you have forgotten, I am financing this film and . . .'

'For which I am responsible. I introduced you to Lee.'

'I am most grateful for that introduction, but Lee has given me total control.'

Leyla laughed contemptuously. 'Only as long as the money keeps coming!'

'Which I will ensure that it does. I have total control over Caroline . . .'

'No! Lee knows that I want to have that. He wouldn't . . .'

'Money talks, my dear,' Clive said smoothly. 'Don't let that undoubted fact depress you, my dear. Caroline has simply gone to the highest bidder and, whilst I would welcome any assistance that you can offer, my word is law!'

There was a momentary silence as Leyla digested this information. She was desperately trying to think of an answer, and some way to deal with this man.

'Cheer up, my love. I will let you visit . . .'

That was too much for Leyla and she flew at Clive, spitting and scratching like an alley cat. Highly amused at this not unexpected response, Clive controlled her effortlessly, wrenching her arms behind her back. As she felt her wrists being drawn together and the unmistakeable bite of rope as it was tied securely, Leyla became even angrier, shouting at Clive and calling him every imaginable name she could think of, until she ran out of choices. Again throwing her on the bed, Clive smiled as he approached. As she saw the scarf in his hands and guessed his intention, Leyla desperately shook her head, straining against the bindings at her wrists. 'Don't you dare gag me! You can't do this!'

The only response was an amused chuckle as Clive knelt on the bed and effortlessly tied the scarf over her mouth. Unable to fight his strength, Leyla could only mutter helplessly into her gag. Clive stood back and folded his arms.

'That is much better. You can be a bit of a harridan, my dear. Oh, no you don't!' As Leyla desperately lunged off the bed and made a bolt for the door, Clive grabbed her and forced her into the chair to which Caroline had been bound. Now, it was Leyla who felt the bite of the ropes around her legs as Clive quickly subdued her kicking ankles. 'I can see you really do need to be taught a lesson,' Clive grunted as he tied rope around her breasts and arms, completely securing her to the chair.

Breathing hard with his exertions, Clive drew up a chair in front of Leyla. 'Now listen to me, my dear,' he began, only to be rewarded with a desperate shaking of the head and furious struggling which rocked the chair. Holding her firmly by the shoulders, Clive stared hard at his captive. 'I said listen!' Compelled into stillness by the steadiness of his gaze and the firm grasp on her shoulders, Leyla quieted. 'That's better. Now listen to me, my pet, as much because it is in your own interests to do so as because you really have no choice in the matter.'

He raised a quieting hand as she renewed her struggles. 'We have a conflict of interests here. You want Caroline and so do I. I have a proposition which you may find interesting. I will never give you Caroline. I have wanted her for a very long time and through my own stupidity I once lost her. That is a mistake which will not be repeated. Caroline will be staying with me in England, during filming and after.' Clive smiled at the surprise in Leyla's eyes. 'Oh, yes, my dear. I am not letting her go a second time, but I

123

am going to need a great deal of help. I already have a housekeeper, Mrs Davies, but she has other occupations and cannot be expected to keep up a constant surveillance, so I am offering you that job, Leyla, at least during filming and afterwards if that doesn't conflict with your plans. All I am saying right now is that you should consider what I have said and let me know what you decide.' Clive smiled at the thoughtful look on Leyla's face. Rising, he picked up the riding crop. 'In the meantime, I still think that you need to be taught a lesson and then, perhaps, I shall fuck you. I have often found that this can be a tremendous aid in sublimating a strong will.'

Leyla's answer was an impassioned murmuring and frenzied struggling, which simply made Clive laugh. Bending lower, he whispered to the bound and helpless woman. 'After all, you are not in any position to argue, are you?'

In spite of herself, excited and intrigued, Leyla watched as Clive walked around the room, poking into drawers and cabinets inset into the wall of the small cell. Returning to the bed with the booty he had collected, Clive looked enquiringly at her.

'Leyla, I have a tremendous respect for you as a dominatrix. The only reason I have had to so treat you –' he gestured to her bound state '– is because, I think you will agree, you asked for it!'

Under such an intense gaze, Leyla could only nod.

'Now that you are somewhat calmer,' Clive continued, 'I propose removing your gag and untying you. I will only do this if I have your word that you will not repeat the vituperative abuse.'

Again, Leyla nodded and Clive set about undoing the ropes. When he had removed her gag, his gaze remained on her. 'Promise me that you will behave?'

Almost shyly, Leyla nodded. 'What do you intend to do with me?' she questioned.

'I am merely going to carry out my promises, my love. You still need to be taught a lesson and I would still like to fuck you. You will not be restrained during your punishment, because we are two dominant people who neither need or desire such treatment. Am I right?'

'Yes, Clive,' Leyla acquiesced. The excitement she felt was becoming an urgent arousal which the thought of punishment did nothing to deter. Clive had challenged her and she would endure her punishment – whatever it was – stoically and without complaint. Clive had reminded her of their joint status and she was a firm believer in being able to accept whatever punishments she dished out to other people. Now was her chance to prove to herself that she had the courage of her convictions. She also had to admit that if the reward for all that was to be sexual satisfaction at the hands of this mesmeric man, then it would indeed be worthwhile. She pushed the thought of how the battle for possession of Caroline might be resolved to the back of her mind. First things first!

'Would you like to come here, Leyla?' Clive invited, standing by the bed and flexing the handle of a vicious-looking whip. Inwardly, she shuddered, but the smile on her face remained in place as she rose and walked towards Clive.

'Would you prefer a blindfold?' Clive asked. She shook her head and allowed herself to be firmly pushed on to the bed. She clutched at the pillows, resisting the temptation to bury her face in them and, instead, looked towards Clive, her eyes signifying that she was ready.

Clive took a deep breath, unsure that what he was

doing was right but knowing that it had to be done. Leyla must learn who was boss and he could not afford to show weakness. Releasing his breath as the lash came down across Leyla's vulnerable buttocks, he began to whip her in a rhythmical way, placing the strokes across her bottom and the back of her thighs in a way that he knew would hurt but would not seriously mark. He knew that for a dominatrix such as Leyla to appear at an SM party with such markings could seriously undermine her credibility and he had too much respect for her to allow that. As the whipping continued, Clive marvelled at her self-control. He could see her muscles tensing and the hands that gripped the pillows turn white with the effort of enduring the punishment without audible complaint. As his admiration mounted, so did his desire. The body that trembled beneath his onslaught was superb in the shapeliness of its contours. The sleekness of the long black hair and the tanned firmness of the skin excited him, almost causing him to lose control and fall on her abused body. Instead, he completed his mental allocation of strokes and threw down the whip. For a moment, he simply looked at her, the marks on her bottom merely enhancing his desire. Silently, he removed his trousers and then his rollneck sweater. Turning a tear-streaked face to him, Leyla smiled. 'That was the punishment. Now, do I get the pleasure?'

Controlling himself with an effort, Clive picked up the roll of black latex material he had found in one of the cupboards. Bending, he gently rolled Leyla on to her back. Studying her for a moment, Clive admired the hard buds of her nipples and the pink lips between which her engorged clitoris was clearly visible.

'Now, my dear, you get the fuck of your life!'

Moving quickly, Clive unwrapped the latex and laid it across the bed. Gesturing to Leyla that she should lie on the material, Clive watched as she obeyed, her superb shape outstanding against the slippery material. Gently wrapping the thin rubber around her, he lay alongside and stroked the erectness of her nipples through the latex. Revelling in the feel and smell of the material, Leyla gasped, but that was only the beginning. For an almost agonising ten minutes, Clive stroked her body through the sensual material, gradually reaching her vagina, the wetness from which was already making the rubber achieve a quite unnatural additional slipperiness.

'Easy, darling,' Clive whispered, accurately judging her state of readiness to receive his cock. 'I want you to wait for me and I promise that it will be very special.

Bending his head, he parted her lips with his tongue and kissed her, probing her mouth and entwining his tongue with hers. Gently lowering himself on to her, Clive's cock at last slid home, her natural lubrication making for an easy journey as her vaginal walls contracted around his hardness. Soon they were both panting out their animal lust as he rode her to a mutually overpowering climax, the hastily pushed aside latex framing them both.

They had lain together for some time, enjoying the post-orgasmic feelings, warm and comfortable with each other. Leyla stirred slightly and Clive bent his head to gently kiss her.

'What now?' she asked softly.

'What now what?' Clive asked.

'What we were talking about . . .'

'Oh, you mean Caroline,' Clive said, again laying his head across her breasts. 'Is there still a problem?'

'I'm not sure. Is there?'

'My sweet, Caroline is mine. You are welcome to borrow her ... use her ... from time to time, but she will always be mine. Didn't I make that plain?' Clive asked, raising his head to look at her.

'I suppose you did. I just never expected to give in so easily.'

Clive chuckled softly. 'You certainly didn't give in, Leyla. My determination is just a bit stronger than yours.' Clive paused, running a finger around one of her areolae and smiling at the tremor that went through her body. Suddenly, Clive looked seriously at Leyla. 'Caroline has always been mine. It's just that there have been unavoidable ... interludes.'

'And is James another such interlude?' Leyla asked, wriggling her body on the sticky sheet and wishing that Clive would continue his stroking.

'Ah, James!' Clive sighed, lying back on his folded arms, then looking at Leyla through narrowed eyes. 'Are you threatening me, my dear?'

Puzzled, Leyla turned towards him. 'Threatening you? Why on earth should you think that?'

'Because of your bringing James into the equation.' Clive paused thoughtfully. 'If you were to tell him of my presence and of what has transpired between us, you could cause me a lot of trouble.'

Leyla laughed, winding her body around that of Clive. 'It sounds like you are the one doing the threatening.' Her expression serious, Leyla looked at him, eyes liquid with desire. 'Clive, I have no intention of telling James anything. If I did, I feel sure you would arrange it so that I didn't see Caroline ever again. In fact, James would probably spirit her away somewhere. I bow to your superiority. You have taught me something about myself and I am more than happy to share Caroline as you suggest. I would

128

quite like to make frequent trips to England, although I would never want to leave the States permanently.' She stroked her fingers across Clive's brow and then chuckled. 'I may even be able to make use of your Mrs Davies!' Her smile faded and she kissed him on the mouth. 'You have nothing to fear. Your secret is safe with me, provided . . .'

Clive frowned. 'Provided?'

Leyla smiled at him. 'It's only a very small piece of blackmail . . .'

'Blackmail! What do you mean?'

In a swift movement, Clive had rolled on top of her and pinned her wrists to the mattress, looking sternly at her although unable to hide the twinkle in his eyes.

'I won't tell James provided you fuck me again,' Leyla said. Running the tip of her tongue around the outline of her lips, she smiled impishly.

'I see. Insatiable as well as gorgeous,' Clive said, using his mesmeric eyes to cement even further the power he felt he had gained over this dominant woman. To Clive, power was the greatest aphrodisiac in the world. 'I accept your terms. Your place or mine?'

Laughing, Leyla burrowed into the warmth of his body, until Clive was also laughing helplessly. It was only the clearing of a throat that interrupted them. Raising his head, Clive stared straight into the triumphant eyes of Rudetska, who was holding firmly on to Caroline. Moving his gaze to the girl's stricken face, Clive knew he would have to tell Lee to move the schedule forward. He had to get Caroline back to England and safely imprisoned in his house; the place, he would ensure, from which she could never escape.

Twelve

Anxiously, Lee checked his watch. They were only just going to make the plane! Almost absent-mindedly, his hand clutched the knee of the girl sitting beside him. Caroline did not respond, staring blankly through the darkened windows of the stretch limousine in which they were travelling to the private airfield. Her thoughts were a mass of contradictions. She was longing to see England again, but at what price? She was under no illusion that she would ever be allowed to return to the States. Clive had made it quite clear that she was to stay at his house during filming and he had also made it very plain that she would not be allowed to leave. Thinking of Clive made her remember Leyla and the scene which Rudetska had taken great pleasure in ensuring that she witnessed. Neither Clive nor Leyla had volunteered any explanation. Rudetska had merely hustled her out of the room and locked her up in the cellar, obviously feeling that she had achieved her objective by inflicting a small measure of revenge on the man who had so humiliated her mistress.

Now, Caroline was unsure as to what she felt about either Clive or Leyla. Not for the first time, she felt betrayed by the men in her life and it seemed that, yet again, she was allowing events to sweep along her unresisting form. Lee had told her that the pre-production had been completed ahead of schedule and that she was therefore to be taken to England a week earlier than planned. She realised this would mean that she would not see James before she left and was almost relieved. What could she have said to him? What Lee had not told her was that Clive, worried by Caroline's taciturnity, had made him promise that the girl would be taken to England and delivered to his Hertfordshire home without being allowed the smallest degree of freedom. That was why she was wearing special white leather ankle boots which were linked together by a padlocked chain. Around her wrist was one half of a pair of white leather handcuffs, the other half being around Lee's own wrist. When Lee had demurred at such travel arrangements, Clive had smoothly parried such objections.

'I don't want her escaping, Lee. I have no idea what's in her mind, but I have no intention of losing her again. I can't return until later in the week, so I am relying on you. Leyla is due to host one of her SM parties tomorrow, so she also has to delay travelling. You need to be in England and I will feel much better with Caroline safely out of the States. You will be travelling by private jet and my staff are all extremely committed and very loyal. They will give you every assistance. I don't anticipate any trouble. At the moment she seems fairly docile and amenable, but you know what they say about "a woman scorned"!'

'You didn't exactly scorn her,' Lee had said, looking at Clive and thinking that perhaps he was starting to know how Caroline was feeling. Clive had not been near him since the night when Caroline had been his guest. Lee tried to keep his attitude sanguine. They were about to embark upon a twelve-week shoot. There would be plenty of time but, for all sorts of reasons, it would behove him not to upset his financial backer.

The chauffeur informed him that they were approaching the airfield. Lee felt in his pocket and removed the roll of adhesive tape which had been given to him by Clive. Turning to the already silent girl beside him, he tore off a strip of the tape.

'I'm sorry, Caroline. Boss' orders,' he said.

Caroline turned to him and, for the first time, smiled. Obligingly, she allowed Lee to seal the tape over her lips. 'When we're airborne, perhaps we might be able to remove this,' he said, pressing the tape firmly into place. There was a lot of money riding on keeping this girl safe and it would definitely not be in his own interests to allow her escape.

By the time that they arrived at the airfield, Caroline had almost become cheerful. Certainly, she felt more optimistic. As usual, she enjoyed her restrictions and felt the warm glow of sexual arousal. So what if Clive and Leyla had been enjoying each other's company. She would just write Clive's latest treatment of her down to further bitter experience. Yet again, he had managed to deceive her and, when she thought about James, she despaired of ever being able to maintain any kind of monogamous relationship. Perhaps she should come to terms with the fact that she thoroughly enjoyed sex with both men and women, and stop worrying about her lack of fidelity. She decided that she would no longer question her apparent lack of morals and just enjoy life. She was looking forward to going back to England and even to seeing Mrs Davies again. The filming could prove to be very exciting and she would just have to come to terms with living with Clive once more. Perhaps he really cared and perhaps he did not. Maybe she was just a challenge and she knew how Clive responded to those! Whatever it was, she decided to simply accept it. At least life was far from boring. She found herself idly speculating on what Lee might be like as a director and as a lover. As things stood, she would certainly find out about the former, and perhaps the latter would follow. As the limousine slowed and stopped, she realised that, in spite of Lee's earlier words, she was hopeful that the tape might remain in place. Now that she was relaxing, she found her very helplessness to be a distinct turn-on.

As the door of the limousine was opened, Lee turned to her and helped her from the car.

'I must say that it makes a pleasant change not having to wonder if my star is going to report to the set on time!' Lee smiled at her and was relieved to see that his smile was reciprocated. Feeling much happier, he turned to the steward and stewardess who stood at the bottom of the steps to the aircraft. Lee had to applaud Clive's choices: both were young and very attractive and wore identical uniforms of very soft black pigskin leather. He admired the way the steward's uniform fitted over a tightly muscled torso and how that of the stewardess held her body in a sensual embrace. The slashed neckline finished just above her navel. They both wore matching skin-tight trousers.

'Welcome,' said the blonde stewardess. 'My name is Kalia and this is Tony.' The equally blond-haired and blue-eyed steward bowed his head. 'We shall be looking after you during the flight to England. Our pre-take-off checks have been completed and if you would like to board, we can be airborne within minutes.'

She smiled devastatingly at Lee, who was in two minds as to which of the flight attendants he preferred. Remembering Caroline's bound state, he looked towards her and then, more hesitantly, at Kalia. The

133

stewardess merely smiled. The whole of the flight crew had been well briefed on their passengers and, besides, they were extremely well remunerated. As far as they were concerned, whatever their employer wanted was fine with them. They were also well used to Clive's little perversions.

Kalia held out her hand for the key to the handcuffs. 'If you would let me have the key, Mr Esslyn, I will ensure that you are both made perfectly comfortable. We have our instructions regarding Ms West.'

Lee opened his mouth to remind them that she was now Mrs Ogilby, but then remained silent. Clive probably did not want to be reminded of James' existence. Instead, he felt in his pocket and handed the key to Kalia, who accepted it with a smile of thanks that took his breath away.

'Thank you, Mr Esslyn.'

He watched the blonde head bow in concentration as she fitted the key in the lock of the handcuffs. As she opened and removed the cuffs, she looked at him again. Lee found himself mumbling as he told her that he would be very pleased if she would call him Lee.

'Certainly, Lee,' she said and gestured for them to precede her up the short flight of steps. 'Mr Craigen has told us that you are to be given everything that you desire.'

'During the trip?' Lee asked.

'During and after, if such is your wish,' Kalia said.

Putting his arm around Caroline, Lee ushered her up the steps and into the body of Clive's private Lear jet. On entering, they both looked around in amazement. It was just like stepping into the front room of a luxurious suite. At one end of the cabin, an inset walnut-panelled, well stocked bar gave on to a seating area furnished in cream leather with opaque glass coffee tables and in-flight seating for four passengers. In-built into each of the cream leather upholstered seats were cream telephone and fax consoles. The cabin had cream-painted walls, which directly matched the impossibly deep pile of the carpeting.

Smiling at their obvious amazement, Kalia gestured to the rear of the aeroplane. 'For your comfort, there is a double bedroom, an office and a well-equipped kitchen. If you need anything, please do not hesitate to ask.' With a sympathetic smile to Caroline, Kalia indicated one of the in-flight seats. 'There is a crew-call buzzer inset into each chair.' The inference was clear: in this instance, being deprived of the power of speech was not necessarily a disability.

Kalia moved to Caroline and laid a deceptively gentle arm on her back. 'Mr Craigen has asked us especially to look to your particular ... requirements.' The stewardess led an unresisting Caroline to one of the in-flight seats and watched as the girl seated herself. Moving swiftly, she arranged Caroline's arms along the arm-rests and buckled two leather straps around each of her wrists. Smiling apologetically, she fastened a similar strap around the girl's waist before kneeling down and securing her ankles to the base of the seat. Standing, she surveyed her work with satisfaction and gestured for Lee to take a seat next to Caroline. Lee did so and then looked appealingly at Kalia as he placed his arms along the arm-rests.

Smiling, she bent towards him and secured his seat belt. 'It is my understanding that you are only to be treated as an honoured guest!' Kalia finished securing the seat belt and, straightening, winked at Lee.

'Will there be any in-flight entertainment in this flying palace?' Lee asked.

135

'Your wish, sir, is my command,' Kalia assured her passenger.

The intercom activated with the captain's voice announcing the imminence of their departure. Kalia and Tony retired to the back of the plane to take their seats and Lee reached across to squeeze one of Caroline's hands.

'I'm sorry about all this, Caroline. As soon as we're airborne, I'll have you out of these.' Lee gestured to her restraints and was amazed when the captive girl shook her head. Curious, Lee leant towards her.

'Do you enjoy being like this?' he asked, his hand caressing one of her thighs, which was temptingly visible beneath the short white leather dress that barely covered her curves. Again she nodded, an invitation in her eyes. Lee's hand crept higher along the smoothness of her thigh, until it was cradled within the warmth of her labia. Touching her swollen bud, he smiled at this clear evidence of her arousal and stroked her clitoris until she was straining against the straps as her excitement mounted. With amusement, Lee looked down at the bulge within his beige trousers and chuckled softly. This time, filming might be more than usually draining!

After a very smooth take-off, Tony and Kalia re-appeared bearing trays of refreshments. Excusing himself, Lee left his seat and joined Kalia in the lounge area while Tony took his place at Caroline's side.

'Can I get you anything?' he asked the helpless girl.

Caroline shook her head, but her eyes invited him to stay. Placing his tray alongside their seats, Tony turned to Caroline. He was visibly excited as he looked at the beautiful, helplessly bound and gagged passenger. In common with all the staff, this was not the first visible evidence of Clive's preferences that he had ever seen, but there was certainly something different about this one. Almost involuntarily, his hand raised to gently travel along the curves of her breasts until it reached the front zip of her dress. Pausing, his turquoise gaze sought permission. Caroline smiled and blinked her eyes.

Tony was incredibly excited and extremely aroused. He was a very good-looking young man and had never suffered from a shortage of available girl-friends, but the situation in which he now found himself was very different to anything he had experienced before. He thought that his employer might object, but he didn't know that for sure. In any event, he felt he had witnessed enough peculiarities since joining Clive's staff to be fairly sure that he could not easily be dismissed. Staring again into those blue-grey eyes, he decided that the risk was worth it. Looking around, he saw that Lee was very busy with Kalia and, besides, the girl next to him, so appealingly restrained, seemed not to be at all averse to his attentions. Caroline's head rested on the cream leather cushioning of her seat. Her eyes were closed and her back arched as Tony's questing hand slipped inside the top of her dress. His hands closed around her breasts and he smiled as Caroline moaned her pleasure. He wondered if he should remove the tape from her mouth. He imagined the sensuality of those lips opening for his tongue and felt the tight pressure of his leather trousers against his straining cock. He wanted this girl and he would have her! Peeling down the zip of her dress, his mouth closed over each erect nipple, licking and sucking at each in turn. His eyes opened as he felt her buck beneath him. He had changed his mind about removing her gag. Not only might that really traverse his authority and jeopardise his job, but there was a definite added attraction to having this beautiful girl totally at his mercy. After all, what could she do? She was tightly strapped to her seat and he had no intention of releasing her. She was also unable to scream for help, even had she wanted to and, from the eagerness of her bodily response, Tony knew that, even if her mouth had been free, she would not try to summon assistance. Kneeling, Tony unstrapped her ankles and gently parted her legs. There was no attempt to close limbs now so invitingly spread apart. He moved his mouth in a trail of lingering kisses down the smoothness of her tanned skin. Now, Caroline was moaning in frustrated desperation, wanting him to go lower.

Smiling, Tony raised his head. 'Patience, my sweet,' he murmured. 'I'll get there, but you will have to wait until I am ready, otherwise I may have to make you wait even longer.'

Resuming his sensual trail, Tony gloried in the surge of power as she struggled against the straps that held her and twisted her head from side to side in a futile attempt to dislodge the tape. At the entrance to her vagina, Tony again paused, this time resuming his seat. Smiling, he leant across her and pressed his hand firmly over her mouth. She looked at him with eyes that sparked her frustration.

'Easy, my pet,' he said. 'I am only doing my job. One of our instructions for this flight was that you were not to be allowed to escape, so I'm just making sure that your gag does not become loose.' Again moving his hands to her breasts, Tony chuckled. 'Although, even if you should scream, at this altitude, no one would hear and we are all very loyal to Mr Craigen. So you struggle all you like, my pet, it will avail you nothing. You cannot escape and I don't think that you want to.'

Suddenly, he moved his body over hers, his knees on either side of her in the spacious seating. Caroline heard his zip as he released his straining cock and closed her eyes as she anticipated the feel of his hardness within her.

Suddenly, she felt a soft hand covering her eyes and tried to move her head to dislodge the obstacle to her sight. 'No, my pretty,' Kalia said as she replaced her hand with a securely tied black silk cloth. 'We don't want you telling tales on us, do we? Now, you won't be able to tell Mr Craigen who it was that did anything to you!'

Plunged into complete darkness, Caroline felt her whole body tingle with desire. What was going to happen? Now she had no way of knowing what was coming. And where was Lee? She could not know that the pair of firm hands so solidly placed on either side of her head, preventing movement, effectively blocking her hearing and contributing to her excitement, belonged to the director.

'Can she hear?' Tony asked.

'She will only be able to discern sounds without being able to identify voices or what is said,' Lee said. 'You were so right, Kalia. This in-flight entertainment is definitely first-rate!'

Lee watched as Caroline's frenzied struggles threatened to loosen her bindings. He thought he knew what she needed to increase her excitement. She needed to feel more and more helpless. 'Tighten those straps, Kalia. We wouldn't want any interference, now would we?' Lee smiled at the blonde stewardess. This was going to be a long flight and she had promised him that he would not be bored.

Obligingly, Kalia bent to her task, unbuckling each strap before pulling it cruelly tight and re-fastening the restraint. Forcing the girl's legs apart, she strapped them into a position that made her vagina very accessible.

Caroline felt Tony's cock pressing at her slit – or was it Tony? Had he moved from her lap or was he still there, and if it was not Tony, then who was it? As Lee had intended, Kalia's tightening of the restraints had fuelled Caroline's excitement and she was now desperate to feel someone's hardness inside her or someone's warm mouth on her clitoris. At such thoughts, her struggles increased and she felt the leather straps biting into her. She was totally unable to defend herself from these people. They could do anything to her and she could not resist. As her climax triggered around the thrusting organ that invaded her body, she bucked against her restraints. The obstruction to her hearing was removed and she felt Lee's warm breath against her ear as he whispered to her, 'Don't use it all up, Caroline. It's a long flight!'

Caroline lost all track of time, as she climaxed again and again. Hands and mouths were all over her body: strong male hands and softer feminine fingers stroked and felt her; mouths bit, caressed, sucked and grazed; hands covered her ears and were then removed. During a period of time that Caroline could not begin to estimate, she was penetrated on at least four occasions; once, she believed, by a softly buzzing vibrator. Just when she thought that she could not take any more, a soft tongue pushed into her labia and swirled around her clitoris which immediately pulsed with renewed demands. It had to be Kalia. Only a woman knew how to bring such intense pleasure to another. In the heat of her passion, Caroline could not have known that, as Kalia knelt before her and brought her such an immensity of pleasure, Tony was behind her, his rampant cock plunging into Kalia's bottom while Lee watched the two of them as they gave pleasure to each other and to Caroline, satisfied in his own knowledge of how firm Kalia's anus felt around a man's cock. Caroline thought that the young director seemed to want to explore all erotic avenues. It would certainly make for an eventful flight.

Gentle fingers peeling off the tape awoke Caroline. Her blindfold had been removed and she looked straight into Lee's eyes.

'Have to look after my star,' Lee said. 'We'll be landing in about half an hour and I need to get you fed and washed ready for landing, all right, my pet?'

Caroline smiled at him. She stretched languorously and then realised that the straps were still in place. Noticing her concern, Lee stroked her hair. 'I'm going to have to feed you, my love. I've spoken to Clive and he's most anxious that you should not be allowed too much in the way of freedom. Kalia will help you to shower. You will of course be handcuffed.' Caroline nodded and Lee felt that she would not have had it any other way. 'You know, Caroline, you amaze me. I've never seen a woman respond to bondage in the way that you so obviously do. You love it, don't you?'

Caroline blushed. 'Yes, I do. Ever since my first Master introduced me to bondage, I've loved it. That exciting feeling of helplessness.' She sighed. 'Of course, there has to be a great deal of trust involved. Clive . . .'

'Loves you very much,' Lee cut in, stroking her neck. 'I've never seen a man so obsessed before. If you leave him again, you'll destroy him.'

Caroline smiled a little sadly and shook her head. 'Clive is obsessed with the challenge. He doesn't want

141

me. He just wants to know that he owns me . . . body and soul.'

'You're wrong, Caroline. I know it may seem like that, but Clive is not very articulate –' seeing her look of disbelief, Lee hurried on '– when it comes to telling you how much he cares. That would make him lose his control over you. Don't you see, Caroline, that if Clive were to reveal how he really feels about you, he thinks it would make him lose face – that you would never respect him.'

Caroline sighed and turned her head to look out of the small window. 'Lee, I don't know. I was happy with James and then along comes Clive and suddenly I've been kidnapped . . .'

Lee laughed. 'You seem to me to be a very willing victim!'

'That may be so, but Clive doesn't know that.'

'Clive certainly does know that, Caroline. He's not a bad man and he wouldn't do anything which he felt was really against your will. He wants you to be happy and he believes that he is the person who can help you achieve that.'

'I was already happy with James . . .'

'Were you, Caroline? Were you really?'

'Yes, I was. Of course I was . . .' Caroline trailed off, realising how little conviction her voice contained. 'Oh, I don't know any more.'

Lee held her face in his hands.

'Caroline, we're nearly in England. Enjoy the experience. Enjoy being here. If, at the end of filming, you are still unsure, I promise that I will not let Clive keep you against your will. I'll take you back to the States myself, if that is what you want.'

'Clive wouldn't let you. You don't know him.'

'Oh, I think I do, Caroline. You're not unhappy now, are you?'

Caroline looked into his gentle, slate-coloured eyes and smiled.

'No, Lee, I'm not unhappy.'

Just then, Kalia arrived with a tray of food.

'Some sweet food for a very sweet lady,' Kalia said, winking at Caroline as she placed the tray on a table which folded down across the girl's bound wrists. Straightening, she licked her lips. 'And you are one very sweet lady!'

Caroline blushed her thanks and settled down to the novelty of being fed by her director. Lee watched patiently as she chewed and swallowed the delicious food before offering her another spoonful. Caroline did full justice to the meal, which was washed down with a glass of Dom Perignon.

When she had finished, Lee turned to her. 'Trust me, my dear. I think we are going to make a beautiful film together and you are going to really enjoy it. I promise that I won't let any harm come to you. Do you trust me?'

Caroline smiled and nodded. Lee bent forward and gently dabbed a napkin across her mouth.

'I'm sorry, boss' orders,' Lee said as he held up the roll of tape.

'Well, we can't disobey orders, can we?' Caroline said.

Thinking how adorable she really was, Lee tore off a wide strip of tape and pressed it down over her lips. As if on cue, Kalia appeared and began unstrapping the willing prisoner. With surprising strength, Kalia urged her to stand before forcing her arms behind her and snapping a pair of steel cuffs around her wrists.

'Bath time,' she almost sang as she propelled Caroline to the rear of the aircraft and opened the door to the bathroom. Caroline looked around her in wonderment. The marble floor was neatly bisected by a large sunken bath.

'Now, I'm going to remove your cuffs. Please don't give me any trouble. I am very strong and well able to control you,' Kalia said. 'I would also not recommend that you attempt to remove the tape. Do you understand?'

Caroline nodded and Kalia moved behind her to remove the cuffs. As soon as this was done, she unzipped the front of Caroline's dress to enable the girl to step out of it. The bath had already been filled with scented water and she gestured for Caroline to get into the steaming depths before starting to remove her clothes. Caroline did as instructed and revelled in the feel of the warm water as it closed about her limbs. Now disrobed, Kalia also slipped into the water and moved towards Caroline.

'This bathroom was designed with you in mind,' she said, urging Caroline to the side of the bath. Bringing the girl's arms out of the water, she stretched them along the sides until she was positioned to Kalia's satisfaction. Caroline had not noticed the gold cuffs attached to the two inset gold rails. Now she watched as Kalia snapped the cuffs around her wrists.

'Is this what they mean when they talk about a gilded prison?' Kalia asked, coming back to stand in front of her prisoner. 'My, but you look good. In fact, good enough to eat!'

With that, Kalia's head disappeared beneath the water and Caroline shivered with pleasure as she felt her captor's tongue sliding into her slit and swirling around her clitoris. Despite her arduous afternoon, she was again aroused, and twisted and turned in a futile effort to free her hands as the sexual tension mounted.

Coming up for air, Kalia smiled at her. 'I was told to get you clean, but no one said how that should be done.' She giggled mischievously as she again plunged beneath the water. Caroline felt her orgasm approach and strained to reach her nipples, but her imprisoned hands would not allow this and soon the water's warmth received an additional surge of moisture.

When Kalia re-surfaced, shaking the water from her hair, she answered Caroline's questioning gaze. 'Oh, don't worry about me,' she said. 'We still have another ten minutes in the air and Mr Esslyn has asked me to share touchdown with him! Although I suspect it might be closer to another lift-off!'

It was indeed a very flushed Lee Esslyn who joined Caroline for touchdown. Turning to his bound companion, he smiled. 'A very satisfactory flight, wouldn't you agree?' He was rewarded with a blushing smile from his new star and reached for her hand, gripping it with a reassuring pressure. 'Oh, I was told to tell you that everything has been prepared for our arrival,' he continued. 'Clive says he has had the house readied for us and, although he won't be arriving for a day or two, his housekeeper will look after us.'

Caroline stared unseeingly at the window. Mrs Davies was waiting for them. More particularly, Mrs Davies was waiting for her. Caroline's vision filled with images from her past; images of Mrs Davies whipping and caning her; Mrs Davies tying her so cruelly tight; Mrs Davies insisting that she go to bed wearing a nappy and then wrapping the soiled cloth over Caroline's face in order to teach her a lesson; Mrs Davies and her lessons, each more humiliating and painful than the last. Caroline closed her eyes as a shiver of fear thrilled through her. She could see the woman, see that iron grey hair and the cold eyes. Then why was it that, as well as the gnawing fear, she felt her clitoris pulse its need?

Thirteen

'Leyla! What the hell is going on?'

Startled, Leyla glanced round to confront an enraged James. As calmly as she could, she reached for the full-length black rubber macintosh she had previously selected and placed on her bed. Slipping the mac on, she turned to face him.

'My dear James. It's always lovely to see you, but some warning would have been preferable . . .'

'Cut the crap!' James shouted, moving to her and grabbing her arm. 'You know damn well what I mean. Where is Caroline?'

The picture of outraged innocence, Leyla shook off his arm. 'I presume she's at home. Where else would she be?'

As if explaining to a rather backward child, James' face took on a patient expression. 'She is not at home. I've just come from there. A lot of her clothes have gone and there was a rather curt note which she'd left for me, explaining that she had gone to England and she was sorry she couldn't wait until I returned. Well, Leyla, what is going on?'

James' voice had become almost icily polite, but Leyla was well aware of the violence that simmered just below the surface. 'James, I'm sorry, but I have no idea where Caroline has gone. Unless . . .'

'Unless?'

As if the thought had only just occurred to her,

Leyla turned away, her demeanour suggesting deep consideration of events. 'Lee Esslyn was talking about bringing forward the movie start date. Yes, I remember now. Something about pre-production being well ahead of schedule. He said it would enable him to bring the film in under budget and that would certainly please his financial backer. Why don't you speak to him?'

'I intend to, but even if what you say is true, why didn't you go with Caroline? I thought that was the plan.'

'I had to stay for the week in order to make arrangements for a long-planned party. Lee knew about that and presumably he planned to let me know of the change of plan.' Picking up her handbag, Leyla turned to the door. 'You can see yourself out, can't you James? I have to be somewhere.'

James' hands curled around her shoulders in a tight grip. 'You are a little underdressed, aren't you, my love?'

Looking down helplessly at her bare feet, Leyla smiled. 'I'm so excited about going to England for the movie! I guess I'm not thinking clearly.'

'I'd say you're not thinking at all. You are of course aware that you have nothing on beneath your coat?'

Angry at Caroline for the seeming thoughtlessness with which she had acted, James felt the need to assuage that anger in some way. He turned Leyla to face him; his burning eyes devoured her body, so excitingly clothed in nothing but the rubber mac. As he breathed in the sensual smell of the material, James' body language told Leyla all she needed to know. Smiling at him, she moved towards the bed.

'Never mind Caroline, James,' she said. 'She has been a very naughty girl and, when I reach England,

147

I will certainly punish her most severely.' Lying back on the bed, she patted the mattress invitingly. 'Perhaps you have some ideas as to how that punishment should be enacted?'

For a moment, James stood looking at Leyla. She had allowed the mac to fall open and he could clearly see her erect nipples. Running her tongue across her lips, she moved her hand down until her elegant fingers slid between the moist lips. 'Even better, perhaps you would like to show me?' she suggested.

James began to remove his clothes and Leyla smiled in gratification as she saw the bead of moisture at the tip of his straining penis. She and James had long been friends and, while she was a little sad about her deception, she was also very aroused. James needed some comfort after his new wife's seeming disloyalty and, after all, what were friends for?

'Lie on your stomach, Leyla. I think I would like to show you exactly how you should punish Caroline.'

Her excitement rising, Leyla did as she was told, the rubber mac rustling as she moved. 'Put your hands behind you,' James' voice, now rich with arousal, instructed. As she obeyed, Leyla felt her wetness increasing. She loved playing games and if, on occasion, the tables were turned, she was not averse to having a different type of fun. As she positioned herself and lay waiting, she wondered what was in store. Would James really hurt her or was this, for him, merely a game? Leyla squirmed at the thought. Submissives had often told her that the hint of the unknown – the need to trust someone, even though you could never be totally certain of them – was a distinct added turn-on and now she was feeling the truth of that. Would he really hurt her? She did not know. All she did know was that, right now, this was what he needed and, whatever happened, she was sure it would be very enjoyable for them both.

James seemed to have left the room, but the delay merely served to heighten Leyla's sexual tension. She wanted to bring her hands round and slide them beneath the rubber mac so that she could touch her nipples, but she knew that James would expect discipline, particularly from her. Against her body, the mac felt warm and slippery. She felt she could scream in frustration. Where was James?

'I'm sorry for the delay, my dear,' James' voice reassured her of his return. 'You will, however, appreciate my difficulties in finding suitable . . . equipment in a strange house.'

'Surely not that strange . . .'

'Silence! Your remarks are not required.'

At the sternness of the voice, Leyla felt a thrill of fear which quickly translated to an increase in her juices. This time she was really for it! She was conscious of James seating himself on the bed.

'Now, in this position, you will have Caroline at your mercy,' James said, stroking a gentle hand over her rubber-clad back. 'In fact, I think it would be a good idea if Caroline were to be similarly dressed. The rubber is very exciting.' His hand moved lower and she felt air on her bottom as the mac was raised above her thighs.

'You will tie her wrists together,' James continued, uncoiling a length of rope. Leyla shivered as she felt the cord sliding across her naked thighs. 'You will play with her, let her feel the rope caress her skin.' In her anticipation, Leyla wriggled, bringing the rebuke of a sharp stinging slap across her bottom. She felt her wrists being lifted and the rope sliding beneath.

'You will talk to her and tell her how she is to be punished. You will tell her that it will hurt and that, were she able, she would be begging you to stop.' As James spoke, he pulled the rope tightly around Leyla's wrists, tying the knots firmly, and making her gasp. 'You will take no account of her discomfort. You will ensure that she cannot escape and you will of course ensure that she cannot complain.'

Leyla felt her head being lifted; a wad of cloth was then pushed between her lips. 'Make sure that the cloth is tightly packed. She is not to be allowed to scream. To secure the cloth, tie a piece of rope in and over her mouth.' Sounding like an instruction manual, James carried out his own orders, knotting the rope securely behind Leyla's head. 'During the binding, you should occasionally give the slut a little pleasure; not too much, but enough to make her hope for ultimate satisfaction – which you may or may not supply.'

James turned Leyla on to her back and spread the mac to each side, allowing him access to her nipples. She groaned with pleasure as his teeth gently grazed her nipples and then with pain as the grazing became biting. Raising his head, James smiled as he looked into Leyla's eyes. 'The slut will love it, because she loves sex – especially when she is tied up. Tell her of the pleasure you are going to have as the whip comes down on her vulnerable skin. Tell her you are going to give her –' James broke off and looked consideringly at his captive '– forty, no, why be cautious, one hundred lashes.'

Leyla's eyes widened with fear. Surely James was not going to give her that sort of punishment? She mumbled her protests into her gag, shaking her head from side to side. Smiling, James slid his fingers between the wet lips and probed within her slit.

150

'Methinks the lady doth protest too much!' James said. 'You are soaking wet, my dear. I wonder why?'

Moving off and away from the bed, he returned with some more rope. 'I suggest that you tie her knees and ankles together, tightly mind, so that she can't wriggle around too much.' Almost in fascination, Leyla watched as he did just that. Her fear had dissipated. She knew that she wanted him and she knew that she was prepared first to suffer as James obviously intended. From past experience, Leyla knew that it would be worth it.

When James had finished tying her, he again sat on the bed, watching her. 'Once you have got the slut secured, play with her like this.' Leyla gasped into her gag as sensual fingers invaded her moistness, brushing lightly across her clitoris.

James bent his head and sampled her with his tongue. Leyla squirmed, fighting her bonds even though she knew it to be useless. His tongue played with her, while his fingers explored the swollen bud. James raised his head and looked at her, seeing the frustration in her maddened eyes. 'You will drive her wild in this way, until she wants nothing more than satisfaction, which you will of course withhold.'

Leyla grunted her fury into the gag. Smiling and staring intently at his prisoner, James arose slowly from the bed. 'You will take the whip and show it to her,' he said, picking up the black leather whip and holding it up for Leyla's inspection. 'You will tease her with the whip, stroking it across her breasts and thighs before pushing it into her vagina.' As the whip handle entered her, Leyla whimpered into her gag. 'If she becomes too noisy,' James continued, 'you will tie some more cloth over her mouth, making it difficult for her to utter a sound.' As he spoke, James roughly tied a thick piece of cloth over Leyla's already filled mouth, tying it so tightly that, with surprised recognition Leyla realised that James had forgotten who she was. To him, she was Caroline and she was going to get the punishment that James felt was well deserved.

James stood in the large window area of Leyla's luxurious house, gulping the whisky to which he had helped himself. He had nearly lost it. For a moment, he had forgotten that the woman lying bound and gagged and awaiting his just punishment was not Caroline. Finishing his drink, he tried to ignore his burgeoning erection. He should untie Leyla and just leave. He was not going to whip her, even though he suspected that she knew more about Caroline's precipitous departure for England than she was letting on. Glancing at his watch, he smiled. Ah well, she had been waiting for fifteen minutes, minutes that he hoped had been filled with at least a little apprehension. Absently, James stroked his cock. He was still naked and extremely excited by what he had so nearly accomplished. No, he was not going to whip her, but he sure as hell was going to fuck her. Setting his features into a grim mask, he returned to the bedroom. Hearing his soft footfalls, Leyla twisted her head and stared at him. Yes, the apprehension was there all right. Smiling, James approached the bed.

'That gag looks like it must be hurting your mouth,' he said gently, sitting beside her and stroking a finger over the wet cloth. Leyla nodded. The gag *was* hurting. The cloth inside her mouth had stretched it until her jaws ached, while the thick cloth over her mouth had been so tightly tied it would certainly leave a few temporary facial marks.

James leant over and kissed her forehead, before straightening and looking at her. 'Well, that's unfortunate, my dear. I haven't finished with you yet and I may leave you tied up for the rest of the day. However, first things first!'

James pushed her over on to her stomach and pulled the rubber mac above her buttocks. He smiled as he saw the faint red mark where he had slapped her earlier and decided that such a lovely bottom deserved to be spanked. Kneeling on the bed, he proceeded to slap Leyla's buttocks, reddening the whole area. She squirmed beneath the punishment, attempting to kick out with her bound legs. James stopped to slide a finger into her wetness, pleased at this clear evidence of her enjoyment. She was unable to make more than very muffled sounds beneath the tight gag.

'That gag is very efficient,' James commented. 'I must remember that.'

Feeling as if her arse was on fire, Leyla rode her punishment, glorying in the ecstasy of pain turning to pleasure. James' knowing fingers ensured that her enjoyment continued unabated and she forgot the discomfort of the tightly tied ropes and gag. James knew his job and, although the bindings were quite severe, she was in no danger of loss of circulation in any of her limbs.

She froze as James' punishing hand ceased. Surely he was not going to leave her like this? Leyla relaxed as she heard a buzzing sound and realised that this must indicate that at last he meant to give her pleasure. Her eyes were closed in anticipation, so she was totally unprepared for the dark cloth that covered her eyes before being tied behind her head.

Smiling to himself, James tied a thick rope around her waist, looping it down over her slit before again knotting it at her waist. She tried to whimper a protest. She knew what was coming. Sure enough, the buzzing vibrator was wedged beneath the rope and positioned just below her clitoris, ensuring the maximum amount of frustration. James smiled lazily at the furious muffled sounds, imagining what mental and bodily torment Leyla was enduring. He tapped her smartly on her already stinging buttocks.

'Must leave you now, my love. I hope you have a peaceful night.'

Laughing, James strolled to the door and watched his captive as she struggled futilely to dislodge the infuriating intruder. Settling himself in a chair by the door, he stroked his erection. He would let her wait. She deserved it. He would let her think that she would have to endure this punishment for the whole night. He would leave her for half an hour, and then he would release her.

James finished his musings and concentrated on his own pleasure, made easier by the sight of the lovely Leyla squirming helplessly beneath the ministrations of the strategically placed vibrator. As he massaged himself to orgasm, James' thoughts turned to Caroline and of what he would do to punish her. She had to learn that he was her Master and, as such, was not to be disobeyed or lightly treated. As his semen spurted over the soft brown matting of the hair on his chest, James smiled. Oh, she would learn all right, and he would be the one to teach her!

'This will be your room. It is to be kept clean and tidy. You will be punished if it is not.'

Nervously, the girl placed her battered suitcase on the floor and surveyed her new home. Kirsten Thomas ran a hand though her mousy chin-length hair and tentatively smiled at her new Mistress, who moved towards her and placed a reassuring hand on her shoulder.

'We will get on well, Kirsten, as long as you do as you are told and follow orders without question. Do you think that you can do that?'

The girl smiled at her Mistress and accepted without question the caressing hand that smoothed across her hair before slipping lower to her small breasts. 'Yes, Mistress. I think I shall be happy here.'

Kirsten meant what she said. She had been rescued from a dead-end job, waitressing in a run-down bar in the East End of London. This amazing woman – what was her name? Oh, yes, Mrs Davies – had come into the bar and Kirsten had served her. The woman had been kind and tipped generously. During the evening, Kirsten had become aware of the woman's eyes upon her and could not help responding to the attention she was receiving. Ever since she had turned sixteen, Kirsten had realised that her youthful dislike of boys was not just a teenage fad, nor were her schoolgirl crushes on other girls, and particularly her crushes on her female teachers. Every night, her masturbatory fantasies had become more extreme. They always concerned women and what those women did to her. She fantasised that she became a slave to a cruel Mistress, who treated her harshly, but also looked after her. Since leaving school, Kirsten had taken the job in the bar because she needed to earn money and, without substantial qualifications, she did not know where else to go. She learnt to parry the offers she received from the male customers without offending them. The women were another matter and she spent many enjoyable nights in the company of some of her female customers, but she knew that she wanted more. When this middle-aged, but still attractive, woman had shown an interest, Kirsten had responded quickly. This had led to a job offer for Kirsten; a live-in maid situation, which both women knew to mean that she would be little better than a slave. Accepting the job with alacrity, Kirsten now found herself taking stock of the sparsely furnished room. At least it was clean and the house itself was quite magnificent; a sprawling mansion with extensive grounds.

Kirsten felt her nipples harden at Mrs Davies' knowing touch. During that evening in the bar, she had allowed the grey-haired woman to touch and fondle her in such a way that they had both become excited. Kirsten had taken the woman home to her dingy flat and had started to apologise for it, when the woman had slapped her hard across her face. At first stunned, Kirsten had only been able to stare at her attacker. Suddenly, Mrs Davies had folded her arms around Kirsten and they had spent the night together.

'We are expecting a guest,' Mrs Davies now informed her. 'She should be arriving fairly shortly and it will be your job to assist me in looking after her.'

'Is she an invalid, Mistress?' Kirsten ventured.

Mrs Davies chuckled, kneading Kirsten's breasts with both of her capable hands.

'No, my dear. She is a young woman with whom I am well acquainted. She will be living here during the filming of her first movie.'

'How exciting,' Kirsten enthused. 'You can be assured that I will treat her with the utmost respect.'

Mrs Davies softly laughed as she began unbuttoning the girl's white cotton blouse. 'You will do nothing of the kind, my dear. She belongs to my Master, whom you will also shortly meet.'

Bending her head, Mrs Davies suckled the girl's teats.

'Belongs to your Master?' Kirsten asked.

Mrs Davies raised her head and smiled at the girl.

'Yes, my dear. She is nothing but a slave and it will be our job to look after her and treat her as befits her station.' Mrs Davies' eyes gleamed with excitement. 'She will not be allowed any freedom, other than that which my Master allows. We are to keep her very rigidly confined.'

'Suppose that she does not like this, Mistress?'

'Then she will be very severely punished, my dear. Very severely indeed!'

Fourteen

The limousine sped along lanes thick with summer foliage. Hertfordshire is a particularly beautiful part of England, never more so than in the height of summer. Caroline gloried in the unfolding beauties of the countryside, although her thoughts were elsewhere. She wondered about Clive's country home. Remembering his love of sparseness and unencumbered surroundings, she tried to imagine the sort of home in which she was soon to reside. Would it be a real home for her? Would she want to stay and, if she did not, would she ever be allowed to leave? She tried not to think about James. They had once been so happy together and she had felt her future to be secure, but now she wondered if she would ever again set eyes on him.

'Clive certainly lives in a beautiful part of the world,' Lee commented, breaking into her thoughts.

Caroline turned her head and looked at the American sitting beside her. She murmured in agreement and Lee smiled. 'I think we can dispense with this,' he said as he gently peeled off the tape from her mouth. He looked down at the handcuffs on both their wrists. 'I don't think you'll be going anywhere!'

Seeing her look of disappointment, Lee looked inquiringly at his new star. 'You really don't mind this, do you?' he asked.

Caroline looked out of her window. How much

could she tell him? Even after all that she had been through, she was still reluctant to discuss feelings so deeply held, feelings that even she could not always explain. Deciding to trust him, she turned her face to his. 'I can't really explain it,' she began. 'I like being in bondage, and having very little say in what happens to me. Being tied makes me feel so ...' She broke off.

'Helpless?' Lee offered.

'Yes. It means I don't have to make any decisions. They're all made for me. I can relax and just go along with events.' She laughed. 'When I'm tied up, that's all I can do.'

'What about trust?' Lee asked. 'Surely you have to be sure about the person who has control.'

'Yes, of course, but there's always that element of not being quite sure; that niggling little doubt that adds to the excitement.'

Swiftly checking that the panel between the driver and passengers was firmly in place, Lee turned to her, roughly pushing her back against the soft leather cushioning of the car's luxurious seating. Fuelled by the excitement that had been rising since he had snapped the handcuffs into place, Lee pinned her back against the seat and put his hand over her mouth.

'Like this? Does this excite you, Caroline? No one can see us. You can't scream or run away. You are totally at my mercy. How does that feel?'

The sexual excitement that he saw in her eyes gave him his answer. Now sure of his ground, Lee released her mouth and felt in his pocket for the key to the handcuffs. Her eyes huge in her oval face, Caroline watched him. She made no effort to struggle or scream. She was excited and curious. What would he do? Would he risk Clive's wrath by taking his most prized possession? Even as Lee released the cuff that was around his wrist and forced Caroline's arms behind her, she didn't think so. Lee smiled as he locked both cuffs around her wrists. 'Now, my darling, you are truly helpless. If you so much as attempt to scream, the gag goes back on. Perhaps I will try you for myself – see what all the fuss is about.'

In spite of his words, Lee remained staring at her, making no move to carry out his implied threat. Caroline's nipples were erect and she felt the wetness beginning between her legs. She had long ago ceased to question her own motives and actions. If Lee wanted her, she was not about to raise any objections.

For a long moment, they remained in their respective positions. Caroline's eyes were telling Lee that he could take what he wanted and she would not tell Clive. Lee was full of indecision. He could have this beautiful girl and she would not resist. In truth, she could not, even if she wanted to, but Lee did not think that was likely to happen. He felt he was reading her correctly, but he kept seeing Clive's face and finally knew that, if he gave in, the truth might one day come out, and then what? Clive would withdraw his financial support, the film could not be made and that could just about finish Lee in Hollywood. Regrettably, it was just not worth the risk.

Caroline felt the tautness leave her companion's body. Brushing his lips lightly across hers, Lee sighed and resumed his seat. The remainder of the journey took place in silence, both passengers occupied with their own thoughts and silent frustrations.

'Miss Caroline! Welcome home!'
Lee helped Caroline to alight from the limousine and face the woman she had never expected to see

again. Carol Davies folded her arms around the helpless girl, the hug seemingly more an affirmation of relative positions than a mere greeting. Standing back, she eyed Caroline from head to toe as the two women each took the measure of the other. Lee stood awkwardly beside his new star. Mrs Davies turned to him and, in greeting, extended her hand.

'Mr Esslyn?'

Somewhat overwhelmed by the effusiveness of the woman, Lee nodded. 'Yes, and you must be Mrs Davies? Clive has told me all about you.'

Almost girlishly, Mrs Davies chuckled. 'Only the good things I hope. Master Clive telephoned yesterday to tell me to get the house ready for our ... guests.' As she spoke, the housekeeper's eyes travelled to Caroline. 'I was told to ensure that you were comfortable,' she said, her eyes full of menace and the sexual desire that this girl always roused. 'Kirsten will see you to your room, Mr Esslyn. I am to take sole charge of Miss Caroline.'

Now suitably adorned in a pert maid's outfit, Kirsten moved forward and gestured for Lee to follow her inside the imposing Georgian mansion. As he walked into the house, Lee had already forgotten Caroline. His mind was full of the house's filmic possibilities and also the more immediate prospect of getting the quietly pretty Kirsten into his bed.

With her hands still secured behind her back, Caroline remained staring at Mrs Davies, her mind full of recollections from the past. This was the woman who had kept her as a sexual prisoner at the behest of Liam, whom she had once loved, and then Clive whom she ... whom she what? Caroline still did not know. If a total fascination with someone was love then perhaps that was what she felt, but she had more immediate concerns. The woman into whose care Clive had now committed her had formed a large part of her life. This woman had tied and beaten her, dressed her as a schoolgirl and a baby. She had arranged for her to have a labial piercing. This was the woman who had tied her to a tree and whipped her breasts with stinging nettles; who had made her wear a nappy and then had tied that sodden nappy over her face as punishment when Caroline had been unable to last the whole night without wetting it; the woman who had pissed over her; the woman whose face was now devoid of the kindness she had previously shown to Caroline in contacting James and bringing him to her rescue. As Caroline looked into the woman's eyes, she felt the conflicting emotions that this woman always provoked: fear and resultant sexual excitement.

'Well, Caroline,' Mrs Davies said. 'Do you have nothing to say to me?'

Caroline hesitated, turning her head to look back down the driveway to the house. Hundreds of thoughts seemed to be fighting for space in her mind. Her feet were unbound. She could turn and run, screaming for help. Perhaps she should try an emotional appeal to the implacable woman, begging for help, or alternatively she should appear pleased to see Mrs Davies and pretend that she had missed the housekeeper. She could assume an imperiousness she was far from feeling; after all, she was Clive's guest. As the contradictory thoughts flooded her mind, Caroline became aware of a firm hand on her arm and the fact that the housekeeper's face was close to her own.

'Forget all thoughts of escape, my dear. I have strict orders from Master Clive and I will do what I have to in order to carry them out,' Mrs Davies said, her voice soft and low but leaving no room for doubting her intentions. 'As for running away, how far do you think you would get?' Startled, Caroline looked at the housekeeper. 'Oh, yes, my dear. I know exactly what you were thinking. You are forgetting how well I know you.' She stepped back and gestured towards the house. 'As for screaming, this house is miles from anywhere and anyway we will soon have you inside and properly . . . restrained. Besides, is that really what you want? Do you really want to get away from me . . . us?'

Caroline felt a weakness in her knees. How well this woman knew her. She could see right through any façade that Caroline might try to erect. She could see the hard little nipples pushing against the leather confines of her dress and could probably smell her excitement.

'Shall we go inside, my dear?' Mrs Davies asked, moving her hand to Caroline's elbow in an unmistakeably firm grip. 'Master Clive expects to be here early tomorrow and has given me firm instructions as to exactly how you are to be presented.'

With an almost despairing backward glance at the sunlit grounds, Caroline walked into the house. She wondered how long it would be before she would again see the outside world.

'Strip please.'

Lee stood rooted to the spot, shocked because of the commanding tone in which the order was given as much as for its content.

'I beg your pardon?'

'I said remove your clothes please, Mr Esslyn.'

Kirsten was standing in the middle of the high-ceilinged room into which Lee had been shown. To Lee, she suddenly seemed to be much taller as she waited for his compliance, her manner one of polite tolerance.

163

'I'm sorry. I don't understand.'

With a small sigh of impatience, Kirsten advanced towards him and started to remove his jacket. 'Master Clive has given us a complete dossier on the guests to which we have been assigned.'

'By we, I presume you are including Mrs Davies?' Lee asked, more to gain thinking time than from a genuine desire to have his question answered.

'Of course,' Kirsten said, folding his jacket before beginning to unbutton his leather trousers. 'Master Clive gave orders regarding Miss Caroline and informed me as to your likes and dislikes.' Kirsten watched as Lee continued the removal of his trousers and then gestured to the bed, on which was displayed a formidable array of correction equipment. 'You will observe that I have catered to your every need.'

Lee shook his head in bewilderment. 'But how did . . .?'

'Master Clive makes it his business to find out everything about his intended guests. He likes to make them feel at home. He prides himself on his ability to discern their every need.'

Still mystified, Lee stood helplessly as the once timid Kirsten unbuttoned his shirt. Thanks to Mrs Davies, she had discovered a previously hidden dominance in her personality, which the housekeeper had brought out and improved upon. Mrs Davies, having spoken to Clive about her protegée, had received permission to train Kirsten in any way that she saw fit to make her an ideal assistant. Lee did not know any of this, nor did he know of how Clive had accurately guessed at Lee's heretofore hidden submissiveness. As Kirsten approached, carrying a stout pair of leather cuffs, Lee gave a mental shrug and placed his hands behind him. As he did so, Kirsten hid a small, triumphant smile. As she looked appreciatively at Lee's burgeoning cock, she knew that accepting this job had been the best thing she had ever done.

'This will be your room,' said Mrs Davies, pushing Caroline through the open doorway to a large, darkened room. The housekeeper flicked a switch by the door and the room was flooded with light, revealing that it was in fact little more than a well appointed cell. There was no bed. Instead, a black leather bench seemed to be the only available resting place. The bench was well padded and raised at the head. Ominous-looking black leather cuffs dangled at various points along the bench. A series of leather straps ran from the head of the bench to the bottom and Caroline gave a small shiver of sexual excitement, threaded through with just enough fear to heighten her arousal. Other than the bench, the room was sparsely furnished with a sturdy wooden chair and a central wooden post to which further hand and ankle cuffs were appended. There was a door at the farthest end of the room which was firmly closed. Caroline's eyes went to the window and saw that the reason for the room's darkness was the heavy wooden shutters which obscured all outside light.

'Mrs Davies, I . . . I thought I was to be a guest,' Caroline faltered.

'Oh, but you are, my dear. A very honoured guest, and we shall do our best to ensure that your stay with us is a long one! In fact, Master Clive has informed me that this room is to be regarded as your new home . . . Your very permanent new home.'

Caroline looked at the housekeeper. 'You know that I am only staying here for the duration of the filming?' she asked, trying to keep the fear from her voice. 'I haven't agreed to anything else.'

Mrs Davies smiled as if with a secret knowledge. 'I know all about the filming. You are to be allowed to partake in that as per your contract. You will of course be supervised at all times. Mistress Leyla will accompany you to the set and I will be here waiting for you upon your return. Mistress Leyla will give me a full report on your behaviour during each day and I will personally administer any punishments you incur. While you are in this house, you will be subject to my orders and you will obey me without question. Master Clive has given me total control.'

Caroline sat on the chair and regarded Mrs Davies, feeling the old combination of fear and excitement. 'I haven't yet thanked you for sending James . . .'

'Forget James Ogilby!' Mrs Davies thundered. 'As far as you are concerned, he no longer exists! You belong to Master Clive and I intend to see that you never again forget it. I would prefer to gloss over the shameful part I played in allowing you to escape from Master Clive. He himself is prepared to forgive and forget and I am determined to make up to him for my betrayal. Now, enough of this.' She forced Caroline to her feet. 'We must get you ready for the Master. He will want to see you the minute he arrives.'

In the darkened room, Caroline lay on the surprisingly comfortable bench and strained her ears for any evidence of an arrival. She did not know how long it had been since Mrs Davies had replaced the handcuffs with some securely tied strong rope before dressing her in a floor-length diaphanous plastic cape, very similar to the one she had worn when Clive had first set eyes on her.

How well she remembered that day. Master Liam had bid for her in an auction where she was the only prize. That was when she had been living with Lynne and Francis and Liam had refused to return her after the agreed one night. She had first met Clive on that evening. She remembered how fearful she had been at the initial sight of the man who was now responsible for bringing her to his home. Then, Clive had seemed so darkly sinister – so menacing. In spite of that, she had been fascinated by him; fascinated by his economy of speech and movement and by his dark mesmeric eyes.

She moved restlessly as she thought of him. Even though only one of the thick leather straps had been used to secure her to the bench, she was unable to do more than turn slightly. With her body heat, the thin plastic of the cape adhered to her body, making it impossible to struggle usefully with her wrist bonds. The material prevented the use of her fingers to search for the knots which might be untied. Thinking this, Caroline almost smiled. Mrs Davies did not tie loose ropes, and although only her wrists and ankles were bound, she knew that she would be unable to free herself. She sighed into the gag that the housekeeper had so gleefully tied into her mouth. Even though Caroline's screams would go unheeded in this lonely area, Mrs Davies had assured her that they were not taking any chances and, besides, Master Clive had given strict instructions. Caroline shivered, aware that the plastic was sticking to her very erect nipples. She knew she was wet with her anticipation of Clive's arrival. Would he pleasure her when he arrived or would he make her wait? As she tried to rub herself against the plastic material which enfolded her, the room was again flooded with light. She blinked as she tried to accustom her eyes and endeavoured to make sense of the dark shape that she could see.

'Well, Caroline, this is just like old times, isn't it?'

The strong voice with just a hint of his Scottish ancestry made her strain against her bonds. As her vision adjusted, she heard a low chuckle. She could see Clive as he stood there watching her. As usual, he was dressed in black and, as usual, it suited his dark features. Clive moved to the bench and sat on the edge. 'Patience, my love. It's going to be a long night and we have much to discuss . . . or at least, I will talk and you will listen. However, first things first. I have been hearing all about your flight over. I have been reliably informed that you were a most enthusiastic participant in all that occurred.' Bending towards her, Clive stroked one of her nipples, which strained against the plastic. 'You should remember that I demand obedience and I do not recall giving you permission to have such fun.'

Caroline moaned into her gag as Clive's touch ignited the smouldering flames of arousal within her. There was a knock on the door and Clive raised his head. 'Come in,' he called. The door opened and Caroline's eyes widened as Mrs Davies, clad only in a black leather corset and matching boots, entered the room, closely followed by a similarly attired Kirsten. Smiling, Clive got to his feet and gestured to the two women.

'Caroline, may I present Kirsten, whom I don't believe you have met. She is going to assist Mrs Davies in ensuring that you are suitably rewarded for such disobedience.' Caroline struggled futilely with her restraints. Clive walked to the door, then turned and smiled at her. 'Learn your lesson well, my pet. If it has to be repeated, it will be even more painful!'

Fifteen

Clive strolled into his lounge, contemplating with satisfaction the scene that was taking place in Caroline's room. Sighing with pleasure, he opened the drinks cabinet and considered the selection.

'How did you know?'

Surprised, Clive turned and looked at a bathrobe-clad Lee Esslyn who had entered noiselessly.

'Not that I'm complaining,' Lee said. 'Just curious.'

Waving the brandy bottle in Lee's direction and receiving an affirmatory nod, Clive poured the rich amber liquid into two glasses, then walked across the room to proffer one to his companion. 'I make it my business to study people,' Clive said. 'I like to know their weaknesses and strengths. You, my friend, were quite obviously barking up the wrong tree so I took the liberty of demonstrating what it was that you really needed.' Clive paused as he sipped his drink. 'I trust that all was satisfactory?'

'Eminently,' Lee said, seating himself on one of the comfortably padded cream leather chairs. 'You have my thanks.'

'As you have my money,' Clive said, his eyes growing suddenly colder.

'Which is much appreciated.'

'I require a little more than that, my friend. Now that your star is in residence, I would like to ensure that she remains exactly that.'

169

'I'm not sure I follow,' Lee said, placing his empty glass on a marble coffee table. 'Caroline is certainly here, but she will have to report to the studios for filming. Surely you knew that? After all, it's your studios we are using.'

Clive took his time in selecting a long, slim cigarette from his monogrammed case. Apparently deep in thought, he applied a similarly monogrammed lighter before inhaling and then exhaling the smoke in a leisurely fashion. 'I'm afraid there has been a change of plan.'

Alarmed, Lee sat up straight. 'What change?'

'The filming will not take place at Cliveden Studios.'

Lee's jaw dropped. 'Clive, we are due to commence filming the day after tomorrow. We came to England on the promise that we could use your studios . . .'

'Which don't exist.' Clive smiled at the blank astonishment on Lee's features. 'Oh, don't look so worried. Filming will begin as planned . . . in the new location.'

'What location? Clive, this is impossible. Locations have to be scouted and inspected. We just haven't the time . . .'

'The new location will be right here.'

Lee sat back, digesting this new information. 'But the equipment . . .'

'Is already installed and ready for use. I have taken the best possible advice and I think you will find everything that you need. Whatever is missing will be procured immediately.'

Some of the tension had left Lee's face. 'Why the change?'

'Because things have occurred which would have made filming off site rather . . . difficult.'

Lee looked inquiringly at Clive, a look which invited him to continue.

'When I first heard of this project, I was keen to be

170

included. I lost Caroline once and I have since been watching and waiting for a way to get her back. Now that she is here, I do not want her to leave. Leyla, who was to have accompanied Caroline and kept an eye on her, is unable to join us.'

'Is she all right?' Lee asked, alarmed at the information.

'She is fine. In fact, more than fine. She has been discovering a few things about herself that have surprised her. She will be staying in Los Angeles in order to keep someone company.'

'And that someone . . . Do I know them?'

'Yes, I believe you do. Caroline's husband, James. He is rather anxious to join his wife and I am just as anxious that he shouldn't. I need time with Caroline. I need to convince her that her place is with me. That can best be accomplished without unnecessary interruptions. Leyla will keep James occupied for a while at least and then, when he begins his search for his wife seriously, he will have no way of locating her. That is why the filming will take place in this house. From you, my dear friend, I require an assurance of secrecy. I want you to ensure that not one of your team will divulge the unit's location.'

Slowly, Lee nodded. If Clive was right and all requirements had been taken care of, there was no reason why it was not possible. 'It could work . . .'

'No, my friend. It will work. I am counting on you to ensure that it does.' Clive's tone brooked no arguments. Lee looked at him and saw the implied threat. If he did not play ball, Clive's financial arrangement would come to an end. Lee rose and walked over to Clive. Extending his hand, he smiled.

'In all the circumstances, you have a deal,' Lee said. 'James will not discover his wife's whereabouts from this film crew. You have my word on that.'

* * *

Fearfully, Caroline watched as Mrs Davies unbuckled the strap which held her to the bench. Caroline's eyes flicked to Kirsten who stood watching, flexing a harsh-looking whip in her hands. The younger girl's mousy brown hair had been scraped back off her face and secured in a high ponytail. Although she wore the same outfit as her mentor, the black leather corset containing the lithe slimness of her young body was very much more alluring than that which clung to the housekeeper's thickset figure. In just a short period of time, Kirsten had changed from the timid young girl who had once served Mrs Davies. Now, she continued to serve her Mistress, albeit in a greater capacity. Her expression as she surveyed the helplessly bound and gagged captive was one of extreme pleasure. There was no hint of sympathy.

'Does the gag stay on, Mistress?' Kirsten asked Mrs Davies.

The housekeeper ran a finger across Caroline's mouth. 'Yes, I think so. No one will hear her screams, but *I* would find them very distressing.' The inquisitive finger slipped lower and Caroline felt herself tensing with sexual anticipation. 'Kirsten, bring me the gloves,' Mrs Davies ordered.

'At once, Madam,' Kirsten said and hurried to the housekeeper's side. Caroline's eyes widened as she watched the housekeeper accept the proffered gloves. Smiling at Caroline, she proceeded to work the short black rubber gloves over her fingers. Once they were in position, she pushed the plastic cape off Caroline's shoulders and then stroked her rubber-clad fingers over the girl's body. Caroline felt the excitingly gloved hands exploring her soft skin, and struggled as arousal consumed her. Mrs Davies chuckled lightly and pushed three fingers inside the wet lips of her captive's sex.

172

'Such a beautiful body,' Mrs Davies crooned. 'Such a pity to have to punish it so cruelly.' As she spoke, the housekeeper's fingers grazed across Caroline's clitoris, sending a pre-orgasmic shudder through the girl. Kirsten stroked the whip handle along Caroline's legs.

'Untie her ankles and secure them in the cuffs, Kirsten. That will allow easy access for your whip. Ensure that the cuffs are very tightly strapped,' Mrs Davies ordered, still smiling at Caroline. 'We don't want any slip-ups, now do we?'

Kirsten hurried to obey, untying the ropes and forcing Caroline's legs apart. She laughed at the audible gasp which escaped from Caroline as the straps were tightly secured around each of her ankles. Mrs Davies observed and approved.

'You are doing very well, Kirsten. Your Mistress is very pleased with you. Now, fuck the girl with your whip!'

Without hesitation, Kirsten slid the whip handle inside Caroline, smiling at the girl's futile struggles. 'I don't think that she likes that too much, Madam,' Kirsten said.

'It doesn't matter what she likes. She is here to serve us and she has no choice in the matter! I want you to fuck her hard!'

Had Kirsten been a little more experienced, she would have realised that Caroline's struggles were not entirely those of resistance. When the whip had entered her, she had been surprised by the power of the thrust. Now that she was attuning her body to the rhythm of the movements inside her, she was far from unhappy, especially as Mrs Davies was stroking and sometimes sucking her nipples. Caroline knew that she was riding the crest of an orgasmic wave and turned her head from side to side, moaning into her gag.

'Stop!' Mrs Davies commanded. 'Let the little slut wait!'

Kirsten stopped her thrusts and looked at Mrs Davies. Totally frustrated, Caroline's eyes pleaded with the housekeeper. 'The first scene that they are shooting requires the heroine to have been whipped by her lover. As the actual whipping cannot be shown, she must simply be seen to bear the marks. Master Clive has given me strict instructions as to where each stroke of the whip is to be laid. We had better turn her over and secure her, then she can be given the forty strokes required.'

As Caroline listened to these words, she shivered in anticipation. She knew that forty strokes would be hard to bear, but she also knew that the pain would turn to pleasure. To her surprise, Mrs Davies pulled the gag from her mouth.

'Be patient, my dear,' the housekeeper said. 'We have to prepare you. Master Clive says that sensory deprivation can make the body much more sensitive to pain and it is pain that he wants you to feel. Don't be deceived into thinking that two women cannot inflict such pain as perhaps a man would. When you left Master Clive, you also left me, and I need to punish you for that. Kirsten is now my assistant and she understands what I and the Master require. She does not want to lose her job, so you can be assured that your punishment will indeed be most severe!'

In total darkness and silence, Caroline lay on her stomach waiting for her punishment to begin. She had been divested of the cape and her wrists and ankles had been released. Her arms had then been forced into the wrist cuffs attached to the bench and the waist strap had been reinstated. A soft black leather hood had been placed over her face and then laced into position. As each of the laces was pulled tight at the back of her head, she had become aware of the extra soft padding placed strategically at various points in the hood. Once in position, Caroline became fully aware of the hood's restrictive capabilities. There were soft pads over her eyes, ears and across her mouth; pads which efficiently shut out all light and the ability to hear and speak. As she lay there, her whole body quivering with arousal and anticipation, Caroline could only guess at the activity going on around her. She certainly could not know that the two women, incredibly excited by their prisoner's helplessness as she struggled against the tightly strapped cuffs, were locked in each other's arms. Kirsten was twisting Mrs Davies' nipples and Mrs Davies had inserted her fingers inside Kirsten's anus while she probed the younger girl's mouth with her tongue. Caroline also did not know that Clive and Lee were two very attentive members of a voyeuristic audience, which included a third man who watched with a high degree of excitement. After all, the girl about to be punished was his co-star and Clive had promised the young actor plenty of off-screen activity.

Stewart Osman could not believe his luck. Here he was about to witness a genuine punishment scene and one in which he might be able to partake. The six foot, dark-haired actor could not take his eyes off the scene in front of him. He could not see Caroline's face, but he had seen the catalogue layout and knew that she was gorgeous and certainly had a very tempting body. Stewart found himself rubbing the stiffness of his erection as he thought of the whip so soon to inflict punishment on that very tempting arse. After two years of porno movies, this was finally the real thing. He remembered the only bondage movie he had made and, as there seemed to be a lull in activities, his mind went back to that film and to the two lovely girls he had worked with and the things he had had to do. Had to do! That was a joke. He had loved every minute. He had played a dominant character whose predilection for tying up the girls with whom he had sex meant that his working days had consisted of arriving on set, stripping off his clothes and then putting two beautiful girls in bondage. He well remembered the excitement of tying and gagging his co-stars and then fucking them while they lay helpless. Apparently, it was that film, seen by Lee Esslyn, which had resulted in his being awarded the male lead in this new film.

As the whip was raised over Kirsten's head, preparatory to the first stroke, Stewart felt his cock throb with pleasure. Soon he would be paid for simulating sex with his lovely co-star, who would of course be an enthusiastic participant in his bondage games. His hand rode up and down his cock furiously as he visualised it. He could not wait!

The silent darkness of Caroline's world exploded into pain as the whip connected with her bottom. Crying silently, she bucked uselessly against the tightly strapped restraints. Within the confines of the hood, her cries sounded alarmingly loud, but she knew that, outside the hood, they could hardly be heard. She flared her nostrils to suck in much-needed air as the pain coursed through her, but she was allowed no respite. The blows rained down upon her in quick succession and there was nowhere she could go to escape them. Clive had subjected her to this. It did not matter that he was not the actual perpetrator. He had given the orders for her punishment and he was

176

the one who wanted her to feel such pain. Confusedly, she thought of Mrs Davies. The woman had said that the punishment was as much for her as it was for Clive, but Caroline knew that, on her own, Mrs Davies would never have been given such permission. In the darkness of her silent prison, Caroline could not even hear the swish of the whip or the crack as it landed on her buttocks. Each blow brought an explosion of colours into her darkness. She tried to ride the pain and then, amazingly, became aware of an exquisite tingling in her clitoris. Gently insistent fingers aided the feeling as each blow became interspersed with delicate strokings across her bud. Gradually her struggles became sensual, until she was writhing with excitement as her approaching orgasm wiped away all the pain. Who was it? Which woman was her benefactress? Caroline was sure that it must be one of the women. Who else could touch and stroke that way? Who but a woman would know exactly what to do and when to do it?

As he used the expertise gained during his work on so many sex movies, Stewart's semen sprayed across the abused buttocks of the woman who writhed beneath him. Of course, she would not feel such an invasion on skin that was red and well marked from the whip, which had been expertly wielded by Mrs Davies and a little less so by Kirsten. At Clive's urging, Stewart had joined the two women and massaged his co-star to the orgasm she craved.

Sixteen

'I was passing, so . . .'

Smiling at James, Leyla held open the door. 'Come in. I didn't expect to see you this morning.'

Walking into Leyla's palatial lounge, James waved a dismissive hand. 'Well, as I say, I was passing and saw your car.' Turning to her, he took a moment to survey his desirable companion. Leyla was dressed in a skin-tight silver rubber catsuit, cinched at the waist with a black corset belt. She was not wearing shoes. Tearing his eyes away from her breasts, James tried to look fierce. 'I thought you were flying to London in order to join my wife,' he said. Deliberately, James' eyes travelled to her bare feet. 'You don't exactly look ready for travel.'

Gesturing to the tray of coffee set on a long marble coffee table and receiving an affirmatory nod, Leyla rang for her maid. There was an uncomfortable silence as they waited for the maid to appear and receive her mistress' request for an extra cup. When the door shut behind the girl, Leyla sat in one of the deep leather armchairs, indicating that James should join her. 'I'm not going,' Leyla finally announced. Startled, James looked at her.

'Can you tell me why not.'

Taking a deep breath, Leyla looked directly at James. 'I don't know where they are.'

Swiftly moving to her, James grasped her wrists,

unaware of the immediate effect this had on Leyla. 'What are you talking about? They are filming at Cliveden Studios and Caroline and Lee are staying at the home of Lee's financial backer.'

Leyla looked challengingly into his eyes. 'Do you know where that is?'

'No, I thought that you . . .'

Leyla shook her head. It was true that she had no knowledge of the actual whereabouts of Clive's property other than that it was in Hertfordshire, and Hertfordshire is a big county. When the two had spoken on the phone, Leyla had informed Clive that she would be quite happy to stay in Los Angeles and entertain James. Clive had volunteered the information that filming would in fact take place at a secret location, but he had not told her where that was. When asked how Leyla could get in touch, Clive had answered that he could see no reason for her to need to contact him and that he would be in touch when it suited him. Reading between the lines, Leyla had imagined Clive's determination to keep Caroline and not allow her return to the States. That was just fine with her. Ever since James had been so dominant, releasing her only after she had been well and truly fucked, Leyla had looked at him with anything but the eyes of a mere friend. She had had a taste of something quite foreign to her and she wanted the chance to explore these new feelings further. For almost the first time in her life, she felt a strong attraction to a man. Strangely, that man had been a long-time friend. Now she wanted something more.

'I spoke to Lee Esslyn this morning,' she told him. 'Caroline is perfectly safe. They have moved to a secret location in order to avoid excessive media interest. The subject matter of the film is the sort of thing that makes the English tabloids sit up and take

179

notice. That is why they will not be using the studios and I'm afraid I do not know where they are. Lee felt that the fewer people who knew, the better. He assures me that Caroline will be well looked after, but apologises to you because, for security reasons, she will not be able to make contact with you. If there is any problem, Lee assures me he will let us know immediately.'

James stared at his lovely companion and the thought crossed his mind that she might not be telling the truth, but for what reason? What could she hope to gain by concealing information from him? James felt his cock stiffen with arousal as his eyes scanned Leyla's rubber-clad breasts. Her nipples seemed un-usually well defined. Raising his eyes, he wondered if her obvious sexual excitement had anything to do with him. James was an extremely sexual man and, with Caroline away, he needed some female compan-ionship. Keeping his eyes on hers, he ran a gentle hand over her breasts and enjoyed the immediate stiffening of her already erect nipples.

'Well, Leyla, I have the feeling that you may be hiding something. Perhaps I had better stay awhile and see if I can persuade you to be totally truthful and, just in case, I think a little punishment might be in order, don't you?'

For answer Leyla opened her arms to him, her willing mouth opening for his kiss.

'Quiet on the set!' Lee shouted, joining his camera-man to assess the suitability of the proposed shot. It was the first day of filming and the air was tingling with an electrical charge of excitement. He nodded to his cameraman and walked over to Caroline. 'It's all set, Caroline. Are you ready?' he asked.

The girl nodded, unable to speak because of the

gag tied over her mouth. Lee looked behind her and checked that her wrists were tightly bound. 'Now, you know what I want from this scene. Your boyfriend Carl has become obsessively jealous to the extent that he has decided to make his sexual games a reality. He is keeping you in his charming little dungeon and has returned from work very sexually aroused because all day he has been thinking of you helplessly awaiting him. This scene is a very erotic one. You have only been kept prisoner for a day and you are still highly sexually excited. You believe that this is merely an extension of his games and you are more than willing to go along with it. Is that clear?'

Caroline nodded. She was partially clothed in a torn lycra dress, which fully exposed one breast. Signalling to Stewart Osman, Lee rose to his feet. Stewart positioned himself on his designated mark close to Caroline and stood looking down at his co-star. He was wearing a dark business suit and was grateful for it. Hopefully, no one had noticed that his cock was fully erect. He knew that Caroline was tied for realism's sake and that the ropes and gag were indeed as securely tied as they appeared. How he would enjoy fucking her while she was so helpless. Firmly reminding himself that he was acting, Stewart forced himself to concentrate and assume the character of Carl. They were both unaware of a shadowy figure watching from the background.

'You look so nice like that,' Carl/Stewart said. 'Before I met you, I used to fantasise about having a woman who would let me play these sort of games.' Carl/Stewart sucked on the visible nipple, sending shivers of arousal through Karen/Caroline's body. Caroline was gagged, and therefore had no lines. Her clitoris was pulsing its need and moisture was seeping into her white cotton briefs. She twisted her wrists, struggling against the tightly tied ropes that bound her.

Dropping his voice to a mere whisper, Stewart turned his attentions to her swollen clitoris. 'You are really turning me on, girl. I could fuck you right here and now.' The cameras were still filming as Caroline arched her back with desire. There was no need for acting. The wanton lust in her eyes was all too real.

The watching shadow tightened his clasped hands. Once before, Caroline had introduced Clive to these unfamiliar feelings of jealousy, but he had put that down to the fact that, at the time, he was competing with James to win Caroline. Now, in reality, she was again his sexual slave. This time, there was no competition. He himself had okayed Stewart Osman's casting in the rôle of Carl. The guy was just acting. But even as he told himself this, Clive watched Caroline as she writhed beneath Stewart's expert caresses. There was also no denying the naked lust on Carl's face. Clive knew he had been right to attend the filming. If things continued in this manner, Osman could be replaced and as for Caroline, she would be well and truly punished for this latest transgression.

'No, don't do that!' Clive's imperious tone stopped the wardrobe assistant from untying Caroline. Surprised, she looked at Clive.

'I'm sorry, sir. Now that filming has finished for the day, I was merely making Caroline more comfortable.'

Clive flashed his mesmeric gaze in her direction, making the middle-aged woman go weak at the knees. 'I'll attend to that. I'm sure you have other things to do.'

182

Hurriedly, the woman rose. 'Well, yes, I could check tomorrow's wardrobe.'

'Why don't you do that?' Clive asked pleasantly, smiling hypnotically at the assistant. 'I will see to Miss Caroline.'

Clive watched the woman retreating and then turned back to Caroline. Kneeling beside her, he gently brushed his lips across her gagged mouth. 'I will ensure that Miss Caroline is comfortable,' Clive whispered and leant over to Caroline's bound wrists.

Expecting him to remove the cords, Caroline waited patiently. She was rewarded with a sharp tug on the ropes securing her wrists as Clive tightened the knots even further. 'How's that? Is that more comfortable, my dear?' Caroline whimpered into her gag as the ropes chafed her wrists, but Clive was far from finished. Because of the nature of the film, there was plenty of rope around the set and it didn't take him long to retrieve a sizeable handful.

Lee came across to them as Clive bound a length of rope across Caroline's partly exposed breasts, tying each knot cruelly tight. Caroline did not need to ask why she was receiving this treatment. During the day, she had become increasingly aware of the feeling of being watched. As she was being securely bound, she knew that she had been right and that it must have been Clive who had been watching. She blushed as she realised what it was he must have seen.

'Caroline, is everything all right?' Lee asked.

Clive pulled hard on the ropes he was binding around her elbows. 'She's perfectly fine, thank you, Lee. Aren't you, my darling?' Clive grabbed her hair and pulled her head back, forcing her to look at the director. Slowly and painfully, she nodded her agreement. 'You see,' Clive continued. 'Your star is perfectly fine and has no complaints, so we needn't bother you again for the rest of the night.'

Lee hesitated, even though the inference was clear. Clive was making it plain that he should leave them alone.

'Well, if you're sure,' Lee said, turning to leave.

'We are. We'll see you tomorrow, my friend.' Clive watched Lee return to a discussion he had been having with his lighting cameraman. 'Although your star may find it rather difficult to sit down,' he muttered.

On returning to the bedroom, Clive called for Mrs Davies.

'Carol, I think we have been a little too generous with our guest. Her quarters are far too luxurious and today I have had plenty of evidence that she is forgetting her place. I think it is time for a removal to slightly more appropriate surroundings, don't you?' As he spoke, Clive tugged on the rope he had bound around Caroline's long hair, causing her to whimper into her gag.

'I agree, Master Clive. I was rather surprised that you chose to place the slut in here. I will prepare another cell for her immediately.'

'Make sure this one looks like a real prison cell. In the meantime, I will take the opportunity to administer some discipline.'

Smirking, Mrs Davies left the room. Using the improvised ponytail, Clive dragged Caroline to the wooden post in the centre of the room. Without a word, he lashed the trailing end of the rope around the top of the post, forcing Caroline's head back. Swiftly, he tied rope around her arms and waist, imprisoning her to the post. Not yet satisfied, he roughly bound a cloth over the girl's eyes. Caroline could not struggle. She had been too well tied for that.

'Now, my little slut. Let's see. You were enjoying yourself rather too much with Mr Osman. A little more than just acting, wouldn't you say?'

Caroline had never heard such icy coldness in Clive's voice. She wished that she could use her eyes to beseech him not to hurt her, but the thick cloth prevented that. Suddenly, she felt a sharp pain in her left breast and she screamed into her gag. The right one was soon similarly treated and she knew that Clive had applied some vicious nipple clamps to her breasts. 'Hurts, does it?' the taunting voice asked. 'Let's see what you think of these.' Suddenly her labia were stinging as Clive applied clamps to her tender lips. She was grateful for the ropes that held her. Without them, she would have tried to run away. Gradually, numbness replaced the pain, but she wondered what was to come. She was not long in doubt as the cracking of a whip across the floorboards foretold the extent of her punishment. 'Are you sorry?' the icy voice hissed in her ear. 'Would you like to beg for forgiveness, or maybe you haven't yet had enough.'

Caroline whimpered into her now sodden gag. Clive's response was to twist one of the nipple clamps, causing fresh waves of pain to enfold her. The first stroke of the whip across her thighs was almost welcome, as it obliterated all other sensation.

'This is what you get for being a naughty girl. This is what disobedience brings.' The coldness of the voice surrounded her, mingling with the pain. Though her eyes were blindfold, she could see those mesmeric eyes blazing into her own. She could feel their power and suddenly, she could feel something else. The whip again sliced through the air and caught her across her thighs. Her legs were unbound and she tried to kick out, but this only resulted in blows raining down upon her defenceless thighs. However, the feeling she had previously experienced returned and she knew it for what it was. She was sexually aroused and the pain was slowly turning to pleasure. She felt something solid being strapped around her neck and heard the snap of a closing padlock. 'From now on, you will wear this collar at all times. It will have to be written into the script, because you are not taking it off. Perhaps it will serve as a reminder as to who and what you are and to whom you belong!'

Clive's words added to her excitement. Despite her discomfort, she yearned for sexual release. Her clitoris was throbbing with desire and, at last, she felt a finger stroke frustratingly around it. 'Will you promise to be a good girl from now on?' Clive asked. 'You only need to nod your head and I will give you the relief you need. Otherwise, well . . . it could be a long night.' In spite of the pain such movements caused, Caroline nodded her head frantically. 'That's my girl,' the voice said, now liquid with promissory warmth. 'Not too difficult now, was it?' The finger moved to the centre of her swollen bud and her orgasm erupted and flowed over her, leaving her spent and shaking.

'Here we are, my dear. Your new quarters.'

Mrs Davies shoved Caroline through the stout wooden door and pushed her on to the rough woollen blanket that covered the narrow bed. Caroline looked around her. She had been forced downstairs into the cellar, which had been partly converted into a dungeon, complete with barred cells and stone walls and floors. Her bonds had been removed and, although her thighs still felt hot and painful, the dull throbbing caused by the removal of the clamps had subsided. When she was able, she reached upwards with her hands and felt the leather-covered iron of her collar.

She sat in her new cell and shivered. It was cold and every vestige of clothing had been removed from her. Mrs Davies gazed approvingly at the red rope burns across her wrists, breasts and arms.

'It's a pity that, while you are down here, you are to be chained. You look so good with those marks on your tits. Still, we have to make the best of it,' Mrs Davies said, closing and locking the door. 'Before I settle you for the night, I think that you can give me a little pleasure.' She moved to the bed and grabbed the rope that was still tied around Caroline's hair. Bringing the girl's face close to her own, she smiled warningly. 'You had better make a good job of it, little slut, or I will complain to the Master.'

On her knees before the housekeeper, Caroline sucked enthusiastically at Mrs Davies' labia. Her arms were manacled behind her back. Chains ran from her heavy iron collar to her wrist cuffs and then to an iron waist belt. Chains ran from there to the metal cuffs that encircled her slender ankles. The weight of the chains alone would stop any escape attempt. One of the chains ran from her waist belt down between her legs before joining its companions in the heavy padlock that rested between the cheeks of her arse. This particular chain was very tightly cinched and would have pressed on her clitoris had not this position been supplanted by the thick dildo that buzzed angrily beneath its confinement. In a constant state of arousal, Caroline was very happy to pleasure the housekeeper whilst writhing in her exquisite torment. She was constantly on the verge of an orgasm as her tongue plundered the wetness before her, spurred on by the constant tugging on the thick chain attached to her collar, the other end of which was firmly grasped in the housekeeper's hand, as she moaned her own sensual pleasure. Any slacking in Caroline's tongue movements resulted in a sharp tug on the tautly held chain which caused the otherwise comfortable iron collar to chafe against her neck. As Caroline twisted in her chains, she welcomed her approaching orgasm and redoubled her efforts to bring the housekeeper similar pleasure. Her shivering had now been replaced by delicious shudders of ecstasy. She forgot the pain in her thighs and the discomfort of her chains. All Caroline knew was pleasure and, as a particularly sharp tug on her collar triggered her orgasm, she revelled in the release. Mrs Davies chose that moment to buck furiously as her own orgasm lifted and shook her.

Eventually sated, the two women lay exhausted. The dildo still buzzed against Caroline's clitoris, giving her little shocks of pleasure. She felt a gentle hand in her hair and raised her head. Mrs Davies was smiling at her. 'Thank you, my little girl. As good as ever!' Sighing, she sat up. 'Now, I had better settle you down for the night.' She rose and helped Caroline to stand, before gently pushing her on to the bed, to which she was chained. Holding up a ball gag, the housekeeper frowned in mock severity. 'You know the form. Open wide.'

'But, Mistress, please . . .'

Raising her eyebrows and looking quizzically at the prisoner, Mrs Davies paused.

'The vibrator, Mistress. Please . . .'

'Oh, I'm sorry, my dear. You gave me such pleasure that I completely forgot.' Bending down, she pushed the switch on the vibrator to full strength, smiling at the increased level of buzzing.

'No, Mistress, please! I thought you would remove it!'

Mrs Davies reached down and closed off Caroline's

nostrils by squeezing them with her thumb and finger. When Caroline was forced to open her mouth in order to breathe, she pushed the large rubber ball between the girl's lips, buckling the strap tightly in place. Moving to the door, she rested her hand on the light switch before turning and smiling. 'Good night, my dear. I hope that your little friend will aid pleasant dreams!' With that, the housekeeper snapped off the light and left the cell, locking the door behind her.

Seventeen

James leaned back against the silken padded head-board of Leyla's vast circular bed. His brown eyes were clouded and confused. Just a short while ago, he had been one of the happiest of bridegrooms, but now he did not know the whereabouts of his bride and he was not sure if that was a situation he cared to change. Impatient with himself, James sighed. He was usually so sure of himself, certain of his goals and the means of achieving them. Right now, he was not at all sure what it was that he did want. He and Leyla were friends of fairly long standing. Why was it that now she had become so much more? Thoughts of Leyla encouraged his cock to stiffen. She had slid from between the black silk sheets saying that she had a surprise for him, and Leyla never exaggerated. His thoughts turned to Caroline, the girl he once thought of as the answer to his every sexual desire: submissive, lovely and very willing. Was it just the abruptness of her departure that so worried him? Lee Esslyn was a man of his word and his assurance that Caroline was safe would not have been given lightly. With that assurance, James had become much less concerned and had been able to concentrate on more immediate matters. One of those matters now stood in front of him. The sight of her made him catch his breath.

Leyla was dressed in a black rubber catsuit, which was covered by a transparent latex cape, the glossiness of her hair seemed to merge into the shining material. Submissive dark eyes regarded him, awaiting his pleasure.

'Why, Leyla?'

Startled, she frowned slightly. 'Why what?'

'Why this incredible change? For all the years that I've known you, you've been a confirmed dominatrix. You had your own stable of submissives and I've seen the way that you treat them. This ... this complete turnabout has me more than a little confused.'

The material of her cape rustling deliciously, Leyla moved to the bed and sat next to him. 'I'm not sure that I really understand it myself. Something happened to me that night you were so angry and so dominant. Nobody had ever done that to me before. At first, I hated you, but then, lying there unable to move just waiting to see what you would do next and feeling totally helpless, I realised that I actually liked it. Your threat of a beating excited me and I wanted you to do it and do it hard.' Smiling, she looked down. 'I was rather disappointed when you didn't.'

James put his fingers beneath her chin, raising it so that she was forced to look directly at him. When she did so, James ran his fingers through the silkiness of her hair which covered the firmness of her breasts. As his fingers brushed against her nipples, Leyla arched her back, desire coursing through her. 'I see your cape has a hood,' James said, gesturing to the loose latex folds which covered her shoulders. 'I think we should get you properly dressed, don't you?' She nodded and surrendered to the pleasure of his hands smoothing the warm rubber which pressed so excitingly over her breasts.

'Yes, I think we should,' she whispered and gasped in surprise as James tangled a hand in her hair and pulled her face to his.

191

'I think you have omitted something, slut!'

'Master!' Leyla gasped, experiencing the thrill of pain at the hands of her dominant lover.

'That's better. Don't ever forget it! If we are to have any kind of relationship you must be totally subservient to me. I will accept nothing less!'

James released her hair and resumed stroking her breasts.

'What about Caroline?' Leyla whispered the question which she had previously forbidden herself. 'You love her.'

'I did and maybe still do. You are . . . a revelation. A friend whom I had only ever looked on as just that has suddenly become very important to me. Don't yet ask me about Caroline. I am confused by lust for your gorgeous body and cannot truthfully answer your question. We will have to wait and see.'

'If I told you where she was . . .'

James grabbed her hair, his other hand finding her neck. Exerting an erotically gentle pressure, he stared at her. 'You do know where she is.'

Sexually aroused by the power of this man, Leyla returned his stare. 'I know roughly where she is, but I don't have an address.'

'You will tell me, you slut, or I will beat it out of you.' James' voice was silky but no less dangerous for that. 'Or perhaps you'd like that?'

Filled with sexual daring, Leyla twisted out of his grasp and ran for the door. As she grasped the handle, a strong arm wrapped around her upper body, while a firm hand clamped over her mouth. 'Oh, no you don't! We have something to discuss!'

Entering into the spirit of the game, James' tone had become sensually threatening. Leyla shook her head furiously and managed to bite down on the hand that covered her mouth. Now thoroughly aroused, James' fingers, strong as steel, pressed down on her lips, sealing them shut. Allowing Leyla to struggle wildly, he managed to untie the belt of the black satin robe which he wore and, removing his hand, quickly tied the smooth material over her mouth, winding the satin of the long belt again and again around her head until her attempted screams became no more than heavily muffled mumblings. Dragging her back to the bed and throwing her roughly on to the satin-covered quilt, he grabbed her wrists and used the belt from his discarded jeans to wrap tightly around her slender arms, buckling it into place with a harshness which made her moan and continue to struggle wildly.

'You've had things your own way for too long, Leyla. Now I'm going to make you do what *I* want.' Threading a piece of silken rope through the leather that now bound her wrists, James none too gently forced her hands above her head, knotting the rope around the headboard mercilessly tight. Having restrained her flailing hands, James turned his attention to her legs, forcing them apart roughly and using her own discarded silk stockings to tie her ankles to the metal rings which protruded from the bed at convenient points. Making a tutting noise, James shook his head. 'Very useful, my dear. Perhaps you should have remembered that you too could be restrained in this way, but I suppose you dominatrixes don't usually have to worry about that!'

Sitting on the bed beside his captive, he looked at the bound woman. 'You have to learn that I am not a man to be trifled with,' James said and then looked around. 'I seem to remember seeing you in that suit some time ago and I also recall that you told me of various extras, which you of course didn't wear.'

Rising from the bed, James went to one of Leyla's

walk-in wardrobes and looked inside. 'Aha! I thought so!' he exclaimed. For a moment, James disappeared and then emerged, bearing a few items. Leyla's eyes widened in alarm as she recognised the black latex hood. Desperately, she shook her head from side to side on the pillow, straining to make her protests heard through her satin gag. James resumed his seat beside her. Her struggles became wilder as he held up the hood for her inspection. Suddenly, he threw down the items, roughly pulled down the soft gag and forced his tongue into her mouth.

Raising his head, he pulled the gag back over her mouth and glared at her. 'Isn't this what you want, slut? Isn't that why you tried to run away?' As she was still struggling futilely, James gripped her chin, forcing her to remain still. 'Listen to me, you little idiot! If we are to have a chance together, you'll have to get used to this! This is the way I like to have sex! I don't intend to go back to apologising to a woman if I handle her a little roughly. Listen to me, Leyla, and listen good. I've had all of that. For years I felt I had to apologise for my sexuality and behave as others expected it. I've had it with trying to fit in. I thought I'd found the answer with Caroline and perhaps I was wrong about that – not about what I did but about who it was done with. I thought you and I understood each other. Tell me if I'm wrong, Leyla, and I'll stop immediately. I'll untie you and we can hopefully still be friends. If I'm wrong about this, now is the time to tell me. Do you understand? I am not going to change and you have to accept me as I am or not at all! There is no middle ground.'

Leyla was making such pleading noises that James pulled down her gag again. There were tears in her eyes as she looked at him, and it was some moments before she could control her voice enough to speak.

'I'm sorry, James. I was so afraid . . .'

'Afraid of what? We're not kids, Leyla. I wouldn't have attempted to force you unless I genuinely believed that that is what you wanted.'

'It *is* what I want, James, but I'm afraid . . .'

'At the risk of becoming repetitious, Leyla, afraid of what?'

'At having my face totally covered. I've never . . .'

James laughed softly as he bent to kiss her. 'You silly little girl. Is that all?' With a sweetness Leyla had never seen from him before, James covered her face and neck with warm little kisses. When he raised his head, he looked into her eyes. 'Leyla, I'm sorry,' he said. 'What I want to do to you is just part of me being a dominant and treating my submissive as I see fit. That's how it is and while I would never seriously hurt you, there are things I command to be done and, if we are to become a partnership, you will be expected to obey unhesitatingly.' Gently, he stroked the glossy hair splayed out on the pillow. 'I want you to enjoy our sexuality and the only way that you can be sure whether it is going to work for you is to go along with what I want. If, having tried it, you don't like it, then perhaps you are not the convert that you seem. If that is the case, well, we'll have done our best and we'll be better off calling it a day.'

James' stroking fingers caressed her rubber-clad breasts. 'Do you know, you seem so different now, much softer and infinitely more desirable,' he said soothingly. ' You excite me, Leyla. We know a lot about each other and we could have one hell of a good relationship, but it has to be on my terms. Shall I put the hood on you and we'll take it from there, or shall we simply forget it?'

Leyla lay still, considering all that she had heard. In spite of James' words, she had no doubt that this

195

was truly what she wanted and, that being the case, she had no choice but to accept James' terms. Smiling at him, she ran her tongue over her lips. 'Perhaps my Master would be so kind as to kiss me before he conceals my face?' she suggested.

Returning her smile, James bent forward to part her lips with his tongue. As they kissed, the sexual energy crackling between them, both knew that together they were embarking upon a new and exciting journey.

Rendered totally immobile, Leyla lay inert, unable to see, speak or hear, awaiting whatever her Master might decree. James had slipped the rubber hood over her face, strapping it tightly behind her head. Whilst doing this and before she became unable to hear, he had kept up a running commentary. He told Leyla exactly what he was doing and of his future intentions. Initially, she felt swamped by feelings of panic as the hood began to close over her face, but James' reassuring voice kept her calmer than might otherwise have been the case. When he buckled the final strap, James spent a few moments admiring the picture that Leyla presented. The hood clung to her face and so did nothing to conceal the beauty of the wearer's classical features. Her hair had been carefully scooped up into a high ponytail and pushed through the opening designed in the hood for just such a purpose.

James' arousal grew at the sight of his shapely captive and he spent several delicious moments stroking Leyla's rubber-clad breasts and allowing his fingers to slip through the zipped crotch of the suit and delve into the wetness beyond. Muffled moans escaping from the hood demonstrated that his feelings were reciprocated. James could feel Leyla gradually relaxing as she became sexually excited. Gently rolling her on to her stomach, James tied silk rope around her upper arms, elbows and wrists, before proceeding to tie her thighs, knees and ankles tightly, but not uncomfortably so. When he was finished, he knew that she would find it hard even to struggle.

Collecting an ebony-handled whip from the drawer where he knew it to be kept, James stood admiringly, selecting the areas that were most deserving of a whipping. He knew that a good deal of Leyla's fear had evaporated and that she was highly aroused. Once before, he had promised her a good whipping and subsequently had changed his mind. Deciding that this time Leyla would come to appreciate exactly what he wanted from his partner, James decided to test her, to see where her limits might be. They had agreed on a signal to be used by Leyla if things became too much. She was to splay her fingers in a certain pattern which would be a clear sign to James that he should stop. Hoping that sign would not soon be forthcoming, James brought down the whip across her rubber-clad buttocks. As much as she was able to, she jumped, as much in surprise as in pain. James was under no illusion as to the amount of protection the tight rubber might afford his slave. The sting would be slightly lessened, but with the amount of strokes he intended to administer, it would not really matter. James whipped Leyla until his arm ached, always looking for any tell-tale sign that she wanted him to stop. He was not really surprised when Leyla's hands remained clasped together. Her wrists were tightly bound, but she could still splay her fingers if she so required; she obviously did not. As the beating continued, James felt a surge of pride and pleasure. Leyla was a dominatrix, but she obviously intended to show him that she could take as well as give punishment.

197

From the way her body squirmed, James knew that her pleasure was growing in intensity. After thirty hard strokes, James threw down the whip, needing rest but also sexual release. Kneeling on the bed, he parted Leyla's arse cheeks, feeling her tense as she realised his intention. He smiled as he felt her bear down to accommodate his cock, now pushing urgently at her anus. As he slipped inside, James squeezed the firm breasts so excitingly clad in rubber, feeling Leyla's answering movements as her muscles tightened around his cock. Mindful of her undoubtedly sore buttocks, James tried to moderate his thrusts, but heard the unmistakeable sounds emitting from the hooded woman. She was urging him on, telling him to ignore her bruised bottom and take his satisfaction. Only too gladly, James' thrustings into Leyla's anus became harder and faster. He felt her shiver in his arms as her orgasm approached and James' mind flooded with pride in his slave, even as his orgasm flooded her rectum. He had cause to be grateful for Leyla's inability to hear as his orgasm peaked and he shouted out the name of the woman who was most in his thoughts.

'Caroline!'

Eighteen

'His name's David Parnall,' Lee said, consulting a notepad. Looking up at Clive, he smiled. 'We have to pacify him.'

Clive frowned. 'Why? What's the problem?'

'There isn't really a problem. We are making a film, the content of which is – to say the least – contentious. Obviously, the media are interested. We're lucky. Parnall works for one of the more erudite journals. Besides, the film needs publicity.'

'Good or bad. Isn't that the accepted logic?'

'Well, yes, but what we've got so far is dynamite and I think the film deserves a damn good audience.'

'Even if you do say so yourself?' Clive's tone was only mildly sarcastic.

'Clive, you've seen the rushes. You know it's good!'

Clive smiled at Lee's indignance. 'Calm down. Of course it's good,' he said as he selected a cigarette from the carved wooden box on his desk. They were both seated in comfortable wing chairs set before an elaborately carved coffee table in Clive's luxurious office. Thoughtfully, he lit his cigarette and smiled as he exhaled a perfectly proportioned smoke ring. 'I want you to see this gentleman of the press. Invite him for dinner here at the house.'

'What are you planning, Clive?' Lee asked.

'I just want to give our Mr Parnall a little exhibition and then warn him off!'

'Thanks.' David Parnall accepted an after-dinner glass of port before settling back into the inviting depths of the soft black leather sofa. The perfectly groomed butler bowed slightly and departed, leaving David to assess the other guests. Running a hand through his thick black hair, he resumed his fascinated study of his host. As usual, Clive was perfectly dressed in a slim-fitting black suit with a white silk shirt and patterned silk tie. Aware that his being here was something of an honour, David watched Clive's perfectly precise movements as he sipped his port, at the same time languidly running a hand across his blonde partner's thigh in a fluently sensuous movement. Sexually aroused as he had been at the sight of Caroline's blonde beauty draped in a low-cut, figure-hugging black satin dress, with its waist-high slit clearly advertising the wearer's lack of underwear, it was Clive that held his attention. Refusing to acknowledge his latent homosexual tendencies, David had continued to resist the advances of some of his male colleagues and instead engaged in several unsatisfactory heterosexual couplings. Now, however, he was confronted with this sensuous animal whose effortlessly sexual mannerisms took David's breath away. Well aware of the effect his presence was creating on the hapless journalist, Clive settled back to enjoy himself.

'Have you prepared your questions, Mr Parnall?'

'Sorry?'

'Your questions,' Clive patiently repeated. 'Have you come prepared? I don't see any microphones or note pads.'

'Oh, there aren't any. I don't work like that.'

Empathising with the young journalist's difficulties, Lee smiled. 'And how do you work, Mr Parnall?'

Wishing that he had a cold cloth to press against his burning face, David managed a small laugh. 'Oh, please call me David. I have very good recall.'

'Well, David,' Clive said, his voice silkily sensuous. 'Perhaps you would like a demonstration.'

'Demonstration?'

'Of the film's content. You are of course already conversant with that?' Clive asked, keeping his intense gaze focused on the young journalist's face.

'Yes, of course. I mean, I know the bare outline, but . . .'

'Then a demonstration is a must,' Clive said pleasantly. Turning to Caroline, he kissed her upturned face before again looking at his guest. 'Unfortunately, Caroline's co-star was not able to join us tonight and so I will have to be the somewhat insufficient substitute.' Clive's confident smile showed that he thought he was anything but insufficient. His next words were uttered whilst he still held David's eyes.

'Play with yourself, my darling.'

Without hesitation, Caroline slipped a hand beneath the black satin of her dress. Although obscured by the material, there could be no doubting the activities in which that hand was engaged. Almost unwillingly, David dragged his eyes away from Clive and fixed on Caroline's lower body. As he watched the slow and sensuous movements, his eyes moved upwards to where Clive was stroking the erect nipples that were clearly outlined against the black satin. Moving further up to Caroline's face, David saw that her eyes were half closed as her breathing quickened.

'On your knees, my love.' Clive's command was unexpected. Even so, Caroline immediately slipped to the floor and knelt in front of Clive. 'Pleasure your Master, my love.'

David realised that he was holding his breath as he watched Caroline free Clive's penis and bend her head. He felt an unmistakeable stab of jealousy as he watched the blonde head bobbing up and down. His eyes moved to Clive's face, only to be disconcerted by the directness of the gaze that met his own. Clive's eyes were expressionless; displaying neither pleasure nor any involvement whatsoever.

'Do you wish that you were in her place, David?' Clive asked.

David did not respond. He knew that his face was suffused with the crimson glow not only of the heat of embarrassment, but also his own desire. His eyes returned to Caroline's head and the increasing fervour of her movements. Suddenly, Clive wound a hand through her hair and forced her to stop. 'That's enough, my love.' Obediently, Caroline remained in position, awaiting the next command. 'You see, David, the essence of the film concerns the obsessive love that Caroline's Master feels for his slave,' Clive continued. 'They both indulge in and enjoy a variety of sexual games, which are enough for the Master, until he feels that he wants more.'

Looking down at Caroline's bent head, he relaxed the firmness of his grasp. 'Go and get your lead, my dear.' Immediately, Caroline started to rise. 'On your knees, my dear.'

David watched as, on hands and knees, Caroline crawled to an oak cupboard. Opening this, she removed a silver length of chain before crawling back to Clive and presenting it to him. Clive patted her on the head, then bent and fastened the chain to the black leather-covered iron collar already fitted around her slim neck.

Twisting the chain around his fist, Clive brought Caroline's face close to his own. 'You know what you are to do, don't you, my dear?' he murmured. Awkwardly, because of the shortness of the chain, Caroline climbed on to Clive's lap. Releasing the chain, Clive pulled up the black satin material which covered her bottom. Running his hand appreciatively across the rounded globes, he looked up at David. 'You see the perfect whiteness of her arse, David. Wouldn't you like to own this lovely girl? If she was yours, wouldn't you like to make sure that she always stayed with you?'

Unable to speak, David nodded mutely.

'Of course you would and that is what her Master wants. You see, David, in the film Caroline is caught playing around with another man. Of course, her Master cannot accept this and decides to keep her a prisoner in his house, away from all temptations. Once he has made that decision, naturally he feels that she deserves to be punished for her misconduct.' As he bent closer to Caroline, Clive's voice became a whisper. 'She has to learn to whom it is that she truly belongs, doesn't she?'

Caroline nodded and David looked in confusion from the pair to Lee. Was Clive talking about fictional characters or was he talking about himself and Caroline? Guessing the line that David's thoughts had taken, Lee merely shrugged.

'David, perhaps you would care to participate?'

David's head snapped back at Clive's words. 'Me? I don't know what . . .'

'I am about to administer punishment, David. Do you not think that the slave needs to be restrained?'

His face burning, David shook his head. 'I . . . I don't know. I'm . . . I'm sorry, but . . .'

'David! You'll find the handcuffs in that cupboard!'

David felt as if all the breath had been knocked from his body. Impossibly embarrassed and yet also aroused, he knew that he was out of his depth. Feeling like a small mouse looking into the hooded eyes of its hawk-like predator, he stood up and almost staggered across to the cupboard from which, only moments earlier, Caroline had extracted her lead. Opening the door, he saw the steel handcuffs and picked them up, but remained standing irresolutely by the cupboard.

'Bring them here.' It was a command and David found himself obeying. Returning and proffering them to Clive, he waited silently. 'Put them on her,' Clive ordered.

'I . . . I can't. I've never done this sort of . . .'

'Are you disobeying me, David?'

In the ensuing silence, Lee held his breath. Had Clive gone too far?

'No . . .'

'No, what?'

'No . . . sir.'

Lee released his breath and settled back in his chair.

'That's better,' Clive said in a soothing voice. 'Now put them on her.'

David bent down and fastened the cuffs on to Caroline's wrists. He was horribly aware that he had just conceded something to this intractable yet fascinating man, but wasn't there just a hint of enjoyment in the way he checked that the cuffs were properly fastened? As he finished, he looked directly at Clive and was rewarded with an appreciative, almost conspiratorial smile. 'Thank you, David. Now, there is one more thing you can do for me.'

Now thoroughly involved in the game, although still in doubt as to whether it was only a game, David waited. He realised that he would do anything to please this man and he also realised that the girl did indeed deserve to be punished. She was where David realised that he would like to be: the focal point of Clive's attention.

'Take the handkerchief from my top pocket.'

This time, his hesitation was merely fractional. David leant forward and extracted the white silk square from Clive's pocket. As he did so, he was acutely aware of the scent of arousal, although whether it was his, Caroline's or Clive's was too difficult to distinguish.

'Gag her,' came the quiet command and again David hesitated. 'You do want the slave to be punished, don't you?' Clive asked.

'It's just that I've . . .'

'You've never done this sort of thing before.' A little impatiently, Clive sighed. 'I thought you were an investigative journalist, David. Used to exploring new things and relishing new experiences.' There was another embarrassed pause. 'Well?'

David gazed at Caroline, remembering his previous jealousy at their respective positions: she the captive and he merely the voyeuristic observer. Experiencing a resurgence of those earlier feelings, David bent forward and thrust the silken square between Caroline's lips, thrusting with such force that she whimpered a small protest. Clive watched approvingly as David paused momentarily whilst searching mentally for a securing implement. Smiling as an idea came to him, David removed the leather belt from his waistband and used it to tie over the protruding handkerchief, buckling it almost unnecessarily tightly behind the girl's head. After he had completed his task, David stood back, breathing heavily. Clive smiled at this palpable example of the young man's excitement.

'Well done, David. Innovative as well as clever.'

David blushed at the compliment. Lee watched in admiration as Clive so easily manipulated the young journalist.

'Perhaps you'd like to administer the first few spanks?' Clive asked.

David stared at Clive. The idea excited but also frightened him. Seeing Clive's encouraging nod, he smoothed his palm across Caroline's buttocks, which still bore faint traces of her earlier ordeal at Mrs Davies' hands. David realised that he wanted to do this; because he was excited, but most of all because he wanted to see the light of approval in his host's black eyes. Deciding that Caroline probably deserved all she got, David brought down his hand and administered a stinging slap which made the girl moan into her tightly strapped gag. This only caused David to make the next slap even harder. Raising his head, he received a further encouraging nod from Clive and proceeded to administer five further slaps, enjoying the sight of Caroline's reddening buttocks and the fact that Clive had to hold her more firmly on his lap as she struggled beneath her punishment.

Pinned on Clive's lap, Caroline was indeed struggling as her orgasm continued to mount. She had become very aroused as she had carried out Clive's orders under the embarrassed gaze of their guest. Fervently she hoped that Clive would allow the young man to continue long enough for her to climax. She had been very excited by her Master's total control of the room and everyone in it. Beneath her, she could feel the hardness of his erection and admired his total bodily control. She knew that he had allowed her to suck him almost to the point of orgasm, only stopping her before that had occurred. She felt an increase in her sexual juices as she thought about the coming night.

Clive had been watching her closely and knew that she was on the verge of an orgasm. Bending his head and whispering so that no-one else could hear, he let her know his intentions.

'Not yet, slut. I don't recall giving you permission!'

Raising his head, Clive smiled at David.

'I think that you can stop now, David,' he said.

Immediately, David stood back, his chest heaving.

'Perhaps you had better retrieve your belt,' Clive suggested.

Confused, David bent forward and retrieved the belt, threading it through the loops on his trousers. His face was red from exertion and excitement.

'David you have performed well,' Clive said before turning to Lee. 'Did we get it all?'

'Every single slap,' Lee answered.

'David, we have very much enjoyed having you as our guest. You have proved most ... entertaining. Please go away and write your article on the film and its content.' Clive leant back, his voice hardening. 'I would of course appreciate sight of the article before publication.' Uncertainly, David looked at Clive. 'The butler will see you out,' Clive said, indicating the tall figure standing by the door. David started to move towards it. 'Oh, and David ...'

The journalist paused and turned towards Clive.

'I don't expect the article to contain anything but praise and enthusiasm for the film. If there is anything in it of which I don't approve, or if I discover that you have – shall we say – been telling tales after school, I will ensure that your editor receives a copy of the video which has been recording your every movement since you arrived. I think, once the results are made public, you would not find it easy to gain journalistic or, in fact, any other sort of work anywhere in the world. Do I make myself clear?'

David had listened in horrified fascination to Clive's litany. Now he opened his mouth to speak, but thought better of it, merely averting his eyes and nodding his acceptance.

The water was soothing on her smarting backside, as Caroline twisted around to maximise the beneficial effect of the warm spray. Her hands were still cuffed behind her back. Clive had removed the cuffs as well as her dress, before re-locking the cuffs around her wrists. The silk square remained stuffed into her mouth, but a strip of tape had replaced David's belt. Even under the warmth of the water, Caroline shivered with excitement. Her bondage indicated that Clive had not yet finished with her. As she was thinking this, Clive appeared beside her in the shower cubicle. He was naked and caught her to him, pressing her against his bare chest so that she could feel the strength of his erection.

'I am pleased with you, my love,' Clive told her, as his hands smoothed shower gel over her back. 'You behaved well and obeyed my commands. I am sorry that you were not allowed to complete your orgasm. Perhaps we can rectify that.'

Suddenly she felt herself turned around until her cheek was pressed against the cubicle wall. Clive pushed against her from behind, his hands kneading her breasts as he soaped her body roughly.

'You are mine, Caroline. I always knew it, just as I knew that some day we would always be together. Have you forgotten that husband of yours yet?'

Caroline shook her head. She still wasn't sure enough of her feelings. Then she realised, judging by the violence of Clive's reaction, that at this moment, that was exactly what he wanted from her. His hands crushed her nipples as his cock probed for entry to her anus. Screaming with desire into her gag, Caroline met the force of his thrusts as she bore down and opened her sphincter to accommodate him.

'That's my little slut,' Clive almost snarled into her ear. 'You are a real anal slut, aren't you?'

His words caused an answering tide of excitement in Caroline's clitoris, to which she knew Clive would respond. He released his hold on one of her nipples, bringing his free hand down between her legs. She screamed with a new sort of pain, as the exquisite flood of her orgasm tore through her. She could feel Clive's thrusts increasing in ferocity and then his hand clamping over her already gagged mouth as he shouted out his own release. She felt the heat of his sperm invading her rectum and the vision of James' face, which had been invoked by Clive's words, faded into the blackness of her pleasure-dulled mind.

Nineteen

The first-class cabin steward regarded his beautiful passenger appreciatively. Showing the dark-haired, leather-clad figure to her seat, he asked if there was anything he could do for her.

'I will take care of the lady's needs,' James said, smiling as he slid into his seat. 'Thank you for your assistance. If we need anything, we will let you know.'

'Certainly sir,' the steward almost bowed in his obsequiousness. 'I hope that you both have a good flight.'

As the steward departed, James turned to his companion, his eyes taking in every inch of the form-fitting soft black leather of her catsuit and coming to rest on the newly acquired black leather collar. Running his finger along its rim, he smiled at Leyla.

'Does it feel comfortable, my dear?'

Leyla returned his smile. 'It feels like a badge of ownership.'

'Which is of course precisely what it is.' James transferred his finger to her lips, watching as she opened her mouth and gently bit down on the intruder. 'Any regrets or second thoughts?'

'Regrets none, second thoughts . . . not exactly.'

'Not exactly?'

'A little concerned, perhaps.'

'About what?'

'About going to England and seeing Caroline.'

'You have nothing to fear. I'll be with you.'

Leyla stared into James' eyes. 'That's what bothers me. How will you feel when you see her?'

James looked away. He had thought of little else since he had ordered the air tickets. Turning back to Leyla, he cupped her face in his hands.

'Leyla, what we've had these past weeks has been ...' James broke off, bending to kiss her lips before resuming. 'It's been fantastic, unexpected, breathtaking, but I need to see Caroline and tell her of what's happened between us. I need to discover my own feelings when I talk to her. Leyla, I've made mistakes before. I want to get this right and, to do that, I need to close one chapter before I begin another. I need to be sure.'

Leyla nodded. 'James, I understand. This is all new to me as well. I know that you've turned my life upside down. You've made me question many things that I thought were firm and solid. What we have is new and exciting and I don't want it to end, but you're right. Whatever the outcome, you need to see Caroline and talk to her. I just hope that I'll like the outcome.'

James bent his head and kissed her with a rising passion which Leyla answered fervently, opening her lips and thrusting her tongue into his mouth. His hands slipped to her breasts, warmly encased in the soft leather. The smell of it further excited him and he was aware of his erection pressing against his own neatly tailored beige trousers.

'Champagne?'

Laughing, they broke apart and gazed at the attractive stewardess. Winking at her, James smiled. 'Champagne would seem to be appropriate.'

As the stewardess filled two crystal flutes, Leyla

hoped that their return trip would indeed be a cause for celebration.

'The flight is on time,' Francis informed Lynne. 'They should be here in about ten minutes.'

Lynne was dressed as startlingly as ever in a red PVC mini dress with matching thigh-length boots. She frowned.

'Oh, Francis. What do you think has happened?'

'James said he would tell us everything when we meet. He said that Caroline is fine . . .'

'Then why aren't they together and who is this Leyla that James is bringing?'

Francis smiled at his wife. 'Darling, we'll soon find out everything. There's no point in worrying.'

'But, Francis. The wedding was such a short time ago and they seemed so happy.'

'Lynne, we know from experience that life doesn't always go as planned. James and Leyla are staying with us for three days. Time enough for a full interrogation!'

Nothing was said concerning James' wife until the maid had brought them after-dinner coffee. Francis had spent the meal studying James and Leyla. Having met James' companion, Francis had been more concerned about the fate of his and Caroline's relationship. There was no doubt that Leyla was absolutely gorgeous and there was certainly no doubt that they were more than mere friends. They had chatted about inconsequential things, always steering clear of the name that was uppermost in all their minds. Now, sipping his coffee, Francis decided that they had waited long enough.

'And how is Caroline?' Francis asked innocently.

There was an embarrassed silence, eventually broken by James. 'She's well . . . I believe.'

'Don't you know?'

'Well, she's been over here for a number of weeks and, as you know, she's been busy. I'm told that she is well . . .'

'You're told!' Lynne broke in. 'James, don't you know? What's been going on between the two of you and why aren't you with her?'

'It's a long story, Lynne,' James began. He looked at Francis who caught the desperation in his eyes and stood up.

Placing his coffee cup on the table, Francis smiled at Lynne. 'Why don't you show Leyla around the house. I know how you girls are about that sort of thing. James and I can have a stroll in the gardens.'

Immediately catching on, Lynne rose from her seat and held out her hand. 'Come on, Leyla. Let's leave them to it,' she said.

Uncertainly, Leyla looked at James who nodded encouragingly. Standing, she smiled at her hostess. 'Good idea, Lynne. The house is lovely and I've been hoping for the guided tour.'

After the door had closed behind the two women, Francis turned to James.

'Now what's all this about?' he asked. 'It had better be good, James. Caroline is a very special girl and I'm warning you that if you've hurt her in any way you'll pay for it!'

'OK, Leyla, what's all this about?'

'Sorry?'

Lynne placed her black leather-clad body squarely in front of the startled Leyla. They had reached the main bedroom and Lynne had closed and locked the door. Sometimes submissive but at the moment very dominant, Lynne had decided to find out the truth. Like Francis, she was concerned about Caroline and anxious for the girl's well-being.

213

'Shouldn't we join the others?' Leyla queried, trying to edge past her interlocutor. 'They'll be wondering where we are.'

'You, miss, are going nowhere, at least until we've had a little talk!' Lynne said, glowering at Leyla. For her dinner outfit, Lynne had chosen to wear a skintight Mistress dress which reached to her knees and covered the tops of her black leather boots. She made an imposing figure.

A little out of her depth, Leyla tried to push past her and reach the door. Lynne reached out and gripped Leyla's PVC-covered upper arm. 'Oh, no you don't. I said we were going to have a talk and I meant exactly that.'

Trying unsuccessfully to free her arm, Leyla attempted to swing at Lynne. Very quickly, Lynne wrestled James' companion to the floor, where she pinioned her captive's arms behind her back and lashed her wrists together with leather thongs which she had retrieved from a bowl of water usually kept on the dressing-table and which, on entering the room, she had quietly placed on the floor. Wrapping a long length of Leyla's luxuriant black hair around her fist, Lynne pulled the other woman's head off the floor and held it at what she knew to be an uncomfortable angle.

'Right, you slut! Answer my question!'

'You're hurting me,' Leyla wailed.

'Damn right I am, and it's only the beginning unless you tell me what I want to know! Where is Caroline?'

'I . . . I don't exactly know.' Leyla screamed as Lynne pulled her head back even further. 'Please . . . I really don't know. We know she's here filming, but we don't know exactly where.'

Very slightly, Lynne relaxed her grip. She was

panting, not just with her exertions, but also with arousal. Her eyes flicked lasciviously over Leyla's helplessly pinioned body. Lynne admired the sleek lines clearly visible beneath the form-fitting black PVC of Leyla's suit. Although genuinely concerned about Caroline, the situation had caused her body to ignite with excited longing and she knew that her sexual arousal would have to be sated.

'Leyla, you should know that I have bound your wrists with strips of wet hide. Do you know what that means?'

'No.'

'The Indians first used this method to extract confessions from their captives. Rather appropriate, don't you think? As the hide dries, the leather tightens. If you don't tell me the truth, darling, you will become rather uncomfortable and I would so prefer it if we could become friends.' As she tightened her grasp on Leyla's hair again, Lynne's voice hardened. 'Come on, slut! What's it to be? The truth from you means I will cut you free. Otherwise, I shall simply gag you so that your screams go unheard.'

'All right, I'll tell you. Only first, please release me. The cords feel as if they are cutting into my skin!'

Smiling, Lynne fetched a sharp knife, knowing full well that her words had instilled such fear into Leyla that the woman was actually suffering imagined physical discomfort. Lynne was well aware that, although she had spoken the truth, the hide had not even begun to dry.

'I'm going to release the leather from your wrists,' Lynne said warningly, 'but I am going to tie you with ordinary rope. Then we can have our chat.'

Feeling incredibly excited, Lynne sliced through Leyla's bonds, only allowing the other woman to rub her wrists momentarily before forcing them behind her back once more and re-tying them with silken cord. As Leyla lay helpless on the floor, Lynne peeled off her captive's tight PVC leggings and tied her ankles together. Satisfied, she leant back. Resisting the urge to fondle her own nipples, Lynne tried to appear stern. 'Now, Leyla. I believe that you have something to tell me?' she prompted.

Haltingly at first, Leyla told her captor everything; from her instigating the meeting between Lee and his financial backer, through her unexpectedly sexual encounter with James, to the growing knowledge of her own submissive tendencies and how she now felt about James.

'How does James feel about you?'

'I think ... I think he cares, but he's still confused as to his feelings for Caroline. We agreed that he needs to see her and get things properly sorted out. Then we'll see.'

'And you genuinely don't know where Caroline is?'

'Not exactly. I know which county and I know that she's all right. James thinks that Francis will be able to help in locating Caroline.'

There was a pause as Lynne digested all this new information. Leyla watched her and realised how very much she wanted this woman to believe her and also how strongly sexually attracted she felt. Tentatively shifting her position, Leyla ventured, 'Lynne, will you please untie me?'

Apparently deep in thought, Lynne rose to her feet. Striding to the window, she stood with her hands on her hips and her legs apart.

'How did you feel when you realised that you had these submissive feelings?' Lynne asked. 'Surprised? Disappointed? Secretly glad?'

Leyla wriggled herself into a more comfortable position. Studying the beauty of Lynne's leather-clad form, she felt excitement stirring as she pondered her answer.

'Surprised certainly. Not disappointed, though. Excited and perhaps a little nervous.'

'Nervous?' Lynne asked, unfolding her arms and strolling over to stand in front of Leyla.

'Yes, a little. I'd always been in control and now I was handing over that control to someone else and I wasn't sure that that was what I truly wanted.'

'And now?' Lynne asked, squatting down beside Leyla.

Leyla looked into an unfathomable gaze. 'Now, I'm still not sure . . .'

As Leyla trailed off, Lynne smiled. 'Shall we find out?' she asked pleasantly.

'What do you mean?' Leyla's voice was no more than an excited whisper.

In answer, Lynne leant forward and probed with her tongue between Leyla's lips. The answering pressure as their tongues intertwined sent thrills coursing through both women. Sighing as if disappointed about what she now had to do, Lynne broke the embrace and studied her captive.

'If we're going to do this, Leyla, it has to be done properly,' she said. Leyla watched in fascination as Lynne removed the belt from her slim waist. 'I am going to treat you as my slave, Leyla, and I don't want to be disturbed by your screams.' As she spoke, Lynne covered Leyla's mouth with the thick belt, buckling it tightly behind her head. Leyla felt a huge surge of excitement as she made a futile effort to free her wrists. Lynne watched her with the intent of a scientist scrutinising an experiment. 'How do you handle pain, Leyla? Do you think you'll like it?' Leyla shook her head. 'Ah, but slaves are not given choices. As you are my slave, Leyla, you are at my mercy and

217

I shall do whatever I choose. You, of course, are not in a position to make choices.'

Feeling an undeniable thrill searing through her clitoris, Leyla could only watch helplessly as Lynne stripped off her clothes. Standing naked before her captive, Lynne picked up a leather whip, idly tapping it against her bare thigh. 'I think you should be whipped, and whipped thoroughly. Just in case you are not being entirely truthful.'

Smiling as Leyla shook her head furiously, Lynne positioned herself so that she was standing astride the helpless woman. Leyla found herself staring at Lynne's slit, which was clearly wet. She found herself longing to push her tongue between the inviting pinkness of the proffered labia. Lynne was relentless. Well aware that her desire for Leyla's body was mutual, she decided that their ultimate coupling would be much enhanced by a good whipping. She felt her fingers itching to administer the lash to Leyla's beautifully smooth thighs, but everything had to be perfect. Kneeling and swiftly untying the rope from Leyla's ankles, she pushed a leg spreader between the other woman's legs and strapped her ankles securely to either end. Remaining in position, she inserted the handle of the whip into Leyla's vagina, until the woman was writhing and whimpering with excitement.

Unexpectedly, Lynne removed the whip handle and got to her feet. Swinging the instrument in a practised gesture, Lynne struck her captive across both thighs, leaving a weal in its wake. Giving Leyla little time to recover, she proceeded to whip the other woman steadily and with increasing ferocity. She could tell from the moans and struggles that the pain was becoming pleasure and on seeing this her own excitement became orgasmic. After she had laid a wide network of red weals across her captive's thighs, she threw down the whip and knelt with her knees on either side of the woman's head. Reaching down, she unstrapped the makeshift gag.

'Now, slave. You will pleasure me. Do it properly or it will be the worse for you!'

Eagerly, Leyla watched as Lynne moved slightly, positioning herself over her captive's face before lowering herself so that Leyla could easily reach up with her tongue. Leyla slipped an eager tongue into Lynne's slit, finding the engorged clitoris and swirling her tongue around the hard bud. Feeling her orgasm approaching, Lynne stroked and squeezed her own nipples until Leyla's questing tongue had done enough work to trigger her climax.

Sated with lust, Lynne found that it was not easy to move. She just wanted to remain drifting languorously in reverberations of pleasure. Only groans and desperate struggles aroused her. Smiling, she looked at her frustrated captive.

'Want some pleasure, do we?' she asked.

'Yes, please, Mistress.'

Pleased at the form of address, Lynne untied the ropes from Leyla's wrists and released her from the leg spreader.

'Now, what does the slave require?' she asked, unable to conceal a superior smile.

Suddenly, Leyla demonstrated her own strength as she swiftly reversed their positions, holding Lynne pressed to the floor, her hand firmly clamped over the other's mouth. 'Your slave requires some vengeance, Mistress,' Leyla said, moving to sit on Lynne as she looked around. Spotting a robe lying on the bed, she grabbed it with her free hand and managed to remove the belt. Smiling at Lynne, she removed her hand and tied the belt across the woman's mouth, ignoring her mumbled protests.

'I understand that you also have some submissive tendencies,' she purred. 'Shall we find out how deep they run?'

With amazing strength, she flipped Lynne on to her back. Grabbing the flailing wrists, she used the discarded rope with which she herself had been tied to subdue her would-be Mistress. Tying the rope tightly around Lynne's wrists and ankles, she stood up and looked at her opponent.

'Now, how many strokes of the whip did you consider to be a fair punishment?' she mused, running the whip through excited hands. 'I think I counted twelve. Is that right?'

Lynne uttered a protest into her gag and Leyla nodded approvingly. 'Yes, I think that was right.' Stroking the whip along Lynne's bottom, she selected the angle of her aim. She would make the whipping hard enough to exact punishment but also hard enough to fuel her own already high level of excitement. 'Are you ready, my love?'

Lynne gave a muffled moan in answer to the rhetorical question and Leyla decided that enough time had been wasted. Bringing down the whip in a stinging arc, she watched with approval as the network of weals grew and spread. Carefully counting out the twelve strokes, she seemed to hesitate on the last. 'Now, was that twelve or have I lost count?' she muttered. Ignoring Lynne's muted cries, Leyla resumed the whipping. 'I think I probably made a mistake,' she continued, as though to herself. 'I got so carried away ... I remember eight, but not any more. I think I'd better start again, just in case.'

As the whip cracked again and again across Lynne's defenceless buttocks, both women became intensely aroused. Throwing down the whip, Leyla abruptly turned Lynne on to her back, removed the gag and then spreadeagled herself on the other woman, so that she was lying over Lynne with her mouth on her labia and her own legs widely spread on either side of Lynne's head. With enthusiasm, each woman licked at the other, moaning as their orgasms reached a peak and wriggling fervently as they were both simultaneously swept up in an excitingly intense stream. Afterwards, there was the smell of sex and the laboured sound of breathing as both women recovered. At last, Leyla moved and sat up. She untied Lynne and helped her into a sitting position. Both women smiled at each other and then Leyla opened her arms and cradled Lynne.

'That was very nice, but what did it prove?' she asked.

Lynne sighed as she snuggled happily into the warmth of her companion's body.

'It proved that we are both very happy submissives,' Lynne said and then added an afterthought, 'who occasionally like to play around!'

As they dressed, Lynne thought back on their earlier conversation.

'You said that you were the one who introduced Lee to his financial backer. It might help if we knew the identity of this person,' she said. 'Is it a big secret?'

'He did say that he didn't want his identity to be generally known, but things are different now,' Leyla said. 'It's important that we find Caroline and that she and James have a chance to talk.'

Zipping up the long front zip of her leather dress, Lynne turned to Leyla.

'Agreed. So who is this paragon?'

'He's British, actually. His name's Clive Craigen.'

Twenty

'Cut . . . and print!'

Lee walked across the set to the ornate double bed and smiled at his newest star.

'Perfect, Caroline. You are turning out to be one hell of an actress!' he exclaimed.

'Who's acting?' Clive asked as he strolled up to join them. 'I would think that they're both enjoying every minute!' Anyone less acquainted with Clive than was Caroline would have accepted the lightness of his tone and facial expression at face value. Caroline, however, being more cognisant of his moods, immediately latched on to the heavy sarcasm as Clive took in the scene before him. Caroline and Stewart were lying between baby pink latex sheets. Both were naked and Caroline was positioned on her back with her arms raised above her head, both of her wrists being firmly manacled to the metal scroll-worked headboard. Clive thought that she had never looked lovelier. Glimmering with lust and suppressed anger, his gaze swept over the shapely contours of her body, clearly visible beneath the clinging latex. He frowned as he looked at her face. Above the white silk gag which covered her mouth, her cheeks were suspiciously pink and her eyes alight with arousal. She and Stewart were enacting a scene in which her co-star had just declared his intention to keep her permanently as his slave and had demonstrated the sort of sexual treatment which she could anticipate.

'Acting or not, Clive, we are getting some great action!' Lee said before turning away to discuss the next day's scenes with his cameraman.

'I believe that you have finished for the day,' Clive said coldly, indicating to Stewart that he should leave the set.

'Yes, of course. I was just going to release Caroline,' Stewart replied.

'I'll do that,' Clive returned in a voice which did not invite arguments. Without another word, Stewart scrambled off the bed. Stopping only to retrieve his clothes, he hurried from the set.

'I do like obedience,' Clive murmured as he turned to Caroline and sat beside her on the bed. Looking around to ensure that the set was now clear, he resumed his contemplation of the helpless girl. 'Are you obedient to me, my dear?' he asked, running a finger along her breast bone and being rewarded with the immediate reaction of her hardening nipples. Mutely, she nodded. 'I wonder if you are obedient with Stewart,' Clive continued, circling her nipples with a gentle finger. 'I wonder if you are really acting with him or just following your normal inclinations.'

Suddenly, the gently sensual movement on her breasts became pain as Clive twisted both of her nipples. Staring intently at her, Clive lowered his face until it was close to her own. 'You are mine, slut, and you'd better never forget it! Act your little heart out with Stewart, but remember who is the real controller.' Clive's voice had become little more than a whisper, but the underlying steel in his tone left no doubt as to the seriousness of his words. Caroline whimpered into her gag, not with fright, but excited arousal. Like no other, Clive had the ability to do this to her no matter how threatening his manner might become. As Caroline twisted her body in growing anticipation, she found herself wanting Clive's touch on her nipples to become a caress, and yet she was mentally urging him to exert even more pressure on them. As always, any pain she experienced at Clive's hands quickly became pleasure. She yearned for him to tell her of all the things he intended to do to her and of how much pain this would entail.

As though reading her thoughts, Clive released his hold on her nipples and leant back. He laughed softly. 'Caroline, you are such a slut. You look so innocent, but your thoughts are pure filth!' He rose to his feet and looked down at her captive form. 'I was going to release you, but I think you should stay as you are for a while. Perhaps you need time to reflect on your behaviour with Stewart and consider what amends you can make. Oh, I know you, Caroline. I know that your performance derives from your genuine desires and not your so-called acting abilities.' Again, he laughed. 'Oh, don't worry. I don't really mind. You are what you are and it's because of how you are that I want you so much. I think that you are amoral, little Caroline, not immoral. You really don't see anything wrong in your behaviour or if you do, you manage to make excuses for yourself.' Bending down to brush his lips gently across her gagged mouth, Clive chuckled softly. 'Don't worry, my sweet. You are the perfect mate for me. We both know what we are, but we can live with that. You are my sex slave, Caroline, and I will teach you to use that wonderful body to satisfy my every need and desire. Don't worry about measuring up, my darling. What I can't teach you can always be beaten into you!'

Leaving just a small area of the set illuminated, Clive walked off the sound stage. Straining her ears, Caroline heard the main door close before there was the unmistakeable sound of bolts being shot into position. As far as she was able, Caroline raised her head and looked around. Apart from her small circle of light, the rest of the sound stage was in total darkness. Still gagged and therefore unable to scream for help, Caroline considered her situation. Bathed as it was in the after-glow of warmth from the strong lights, the stage was not cold and would not become so for some time. Surely Clive did not intend to leave her there all night? Caroline realised that he was battling with the still unfamiliar feelings of jealousy he had experienced only since meeting her. It was true that she had not been acting with Stewart. She was very much enjoying this new experience of filming, particularly since the rôle she was being called upon to play was so close to her heart, but she knew that there was no need for Clive's jealousy. Stewart meant nothing to her other than a participant in the film, although he had also become a friend.

She had forced herself not to think about James. It was still too recent and too painful. She knew that Clive intended to keep her and she was still unsure as to her feelings about that or about him. As he always had done, Clive fascinated her. She was also strongly attracted to him, but so much had happened since she had married James. Did she love them both? Could she love two men at the same time? Impatiently, Caroline decided to give up that line of thought, at least for the time being. She decided to concentrate on her current predicament. Moving restlessly on the latex sheets, she became aware that the excitement generated by Clive's words had not abated. As she moved, she noticed that the latex had become adhered to her body and she felt enveloped in the rubber. She looked up at her chained hands and realised that there was no hope in that direction. Not only were her slim wrists handcuffed, but a length of heavy-link chain had been wrapped around her wrists, firmly securing them to the headboard. She was able to move her fingers but her wrists were anchored into position. The gag which covered her mouth, although made of soft white silk, had been very tightly tied and all her attempts to dislodge it by even a small amount had proved to be futile. She faced the prospect of a frustrating night, her sexual arousal unable to be satisfied.

Smiling mischievously, Caroline wondered if there might be a cleaner interested in some extra-curricular activity. Just as she was thinking about the possibility of getting satisfaction from some such quarter, a shadow fell across her and her eyes widened in alarm. She strained to make out the figure standing just outside the circle of light. She had not heard footsteps. Moaning softly into her gag, she waited for the silent figure to identify itself. Her apprehension mounted as the silence seemed only to deepen. Becoming aware of her extreme vulnerability, Caroline twisted her chained hands feebly.

'My poor Caroline. Helpless and at the mercy of anybody who might want to take advantage of her situation,' her husband reflected. 'This is obviously a case of typecasting, wouldn't you say?' James asked rhetorically as he moved into the pool of light around the bed. Caroline could only stare at him. Laughing softly, James sat on the side of the bed. Running his hand appreciatively over the dusky pink latex sheets, he studied Caroline.

'You're looking very well, my sweet, particularly for such a lying little slut.'

Caroline shook her head, moaning with frustration. Using her eyes, she pleaded with James to remove her gag. Understanding completely but unwilling to co-operate, James continued looking at her.

'No, Caroline. I will not remove your gag. I rather like the fact that you are unable to speak or move. You will therefore have no choice but to listen to me. I must say, though, you look absolutely gorgeous.'

Caroline moaned a half-hearted protest into her gag as James gently stroked her breasts. Instantly erect, her nipples almost begged him to touch them, but James simply continued his smooth stroking motions, well aware of the sexual arousal he was responsible for instigating. When he bent his head to suck in turn at both of her nipples, Caroline almost screamed with wanting. Her husband was back and it seemed that she wanted him as much as ever. She wrestled with her chained wrists until a sharp pain warned her against such futility. She desperately wanted to be free to hold James and tell him how much she loved him. Irritatingly, he merely raised his head and stroked a gentle finger along the outline of the white silk, delineating her helplessness in a way that made her juices flow on to the rubber sheets.

'My poor little Caroline. Still don't know who it is that you want, do you? I'd prefer to think of you as a very mixed-up girl rather than the slut that you undoubtedly are.' James' finger stroked lower, circling her breasts before beginning its painstakingly sensual journey down her body. 'I cared for you, Caroline, and I thought that the feeling was mutual. But it's always been Clive hasn't it? He's always been the one to whom you turned. I'm not really surprised to find you living in his house. You probably deserve each other.'

As he spoke, James started to undress in a languorous fashion, stopping every now and then to slip his fingers inside her slit and afterwards taste her juices on his fingers.

'I've been busy as well, Caroline. You remember

227

Leyla who was a guest at our wedding? Well, little Leyla has sprung a real surprise. She's really quite the submissive and I've been discovering how much that pleases me.'

Suddenly, James' hand went around her throat, squeezing slightly. He knew that this would only excite the helpless girl.

'She's different from you, Caroline. She's honest and she doesn't have old boyfriends hiding in the closet. She says she loves me and I believe her. I once believed you, too, didn't I? I know better now. I think that Leyla and I could be good together, Caroline. What do you think?'

If she could have shaken her head, Caroline would have done so but, although not threatening, James' grip allowed for no movement. Desperately, Caroline moaned into the white silk, but James merely smiled. Releasing her neck, he looked around the set.

'I must come and see this film, my darling. I expect that you will be rather good. Art reflecting life, wouldn't you say?'

The gag was now soaked with saliva as Caroline made desperate attempts to speak. If only she could talk to James, explain.

'It's no good you struggling, Caroline,' James told her. 'I have no intention of releasing you. I like you just the way you are. I think, however, I would like to have a little trip down memory lane, just for old times' sake.'

James climbed on to the bed and positioned himself so that his knees were on either side of her shoulders.

'Now, Caroline, I am going to pull down your gag just enough to get my cock into your mouth. I think you owe me a good blow job, don't you?'

As James slipped a finger inside her gag, Caroline took her chance and tried to call out.

'Ja . . .'

Effectively gagged by the throbbing penis that was stuffed into her mouth, Caroline could only stare at her husband. Automatically closing her lips around the shaft, she began licking and sucking in the way that she knew he liked. Kneading her breasts with urgent fingers, James pushed roughly into her mouth, knowing that Caroline was revelling in his treatment. Caroline was conscious of her approaching orgasm, fuelled by James' pinching fingers at her nipples and his unrelenting thrusts into her mouth. She forgot everything; where they were and James' hard words. The world had narrowed down to their joint needs and desires. Both knew what they wanted and were determined on mutual satisfaction. Surprised at how much the familiar intensity of Caroline's response meant to him, James rode to his climax thinking of nothing but the blonde girl writhing beneath him in her excitement and ultimate satisfaction on the pink rubber sheets.

Almost regretfully, James pulled up the white silk until it again covered Caroline's mouth. Shaking his head at her whimpered protests, James sat up and began dressing.

'I'm sorry, Caroline. I don't want to talk to you – at least not right now. I need time to think and I need to talk to Clive . . .'

Caroline struggled desperately with her chained hands, until James held her arms and looked at her, gently shaking his head. 'No, Caroline. You'll only hurt yourself and I truly don't want that. Just now . . . well, I had feelings that I thought I had managed to get under control. I want to get this right, Caroline. I feel things for you, but I also have feelings for Leyla. I don't know what's going on here, Caroline, and I'm not sure that I want to. Now that I know

229

that you're safe, I can concentrate on what's right for me.' James smiled at her. 'Yes, that's right, Caroline. I said for me. For too long I've been living my life in a way that I thought would suit other people. I thought I'd found what I was looking for with you, but now I'm not so sure. I want to decide on the right thing to do so that I can get on with my life in the way that's right for me. If that turns out to be not so good for you, I can only apologise. I need to talk to Clive and get his side of the story and then, when I'm in possession of all the facts, perhaps I will know what to do.'

Caroline again twisted in her bonds, moaning into her gag. Softly, James laid a finger across her gagged mouth. 'No, Caroline. I don't want to discuss it with you. I'm glad you're safe and perhaps you'll be happy with Clive – if he is what you want. I have to sort out my own life and I'm going to be totally selfish about it . . .'

'Well! A man after my own heart.'

James turned around and looked at the voice's owner.

'Clive. Just the man for whom I was about to go and search,' James said, his tone equally sarcastic. Retrieving his trousers, he slipped them on unhurriedly. 'May I congratulate you on your superb house and your superb slave.'

In the sparsely furnished lounge, Clive and James sat across from one another. Taking a sip from his glass of brandy, James studied his companion. Something in him had always responded to Clive. Perhaps it was his seemingly effortless control over people or the economy of speech and movement that dictated the way in which the other man lived.

'You won't believe this, Clive, but I have always

230

had a sneaking admiration for you and the way you live,' he said. 'You use people with an almost callous indifference to their feelings and yet afterwards they can't seem to forget you.'

'You're thinking of Caroline?'

James shrugged and replaced his glass on the coffee table. 'Caroline, yes of course, but she's not the only one, is she? If you want something, you will use your ability to manipulate anyone ... man or woman. I admire that.'

'James, this is all very flattering, but let's get down to cases. You didn't come here to admire me or even just to fuck my slave ...'

'Then she is your slave?'

Clive settled back in his chair. He found himself responding to James in an unexpected way. 'I like to think so.'

'But do you know so?'

'I know that I am not willing to let her return to the States. I know that, if I have to, I will fight you for Caroline.'

'Fight me?'

'Yes, by fair means or foul,' Clive said, leaning forward and fixing James with a piercing gaze. 'Caroline and I belong together. I've known that since I first met her. I want to control her, body and soul.'

'But do you love her?' James asked.

Puzzled, Clive sat back. 'Love her? I don't know. I find her exciting. When I'm with her, I never want her to leave. When she's not with me, all I can do is plan on how to get her back. I have even tried to forget her, but I find that to be impossible. Is that love? I don't know. I've never experienced it.' James shook his head. 'We are both experiencing doubts. I have come here to find out what are my true feelings for Caroline and so far all I have done is succeeded in furthering my confusion. Clive, if I felt that you truly loved Caroline and that she felt the same way, I would be on the first flight back to LA, but I'm not at all sure about this . . .'

'I think I might have the answer,' Clive said. 'Tomorrow we are shooting the penultimate scene of the movie. There is to be an Egyptian-style slave auction, during which the heroine is to be sold off to the highest bidder. I think we might waste a day's filming. After all, I'm paying for it!'

James frowned. 'Clive, I would like to say that I understood, but . . .'

Smiling, Clive leant forward, pouring more brandy into both glasses.

'Oh, you will, my friend. You will.'

On the now darkened set, Caroline lay frustrated and helpless. Filled with concern about what the two men might be doing to each other and still aroused after her unexpected encounter with her estranged husband, she could only try uselessly to struggle within the confines of the sheets which Clive had tightly tucked beneath the mattress, effectively rendering her immobile inside her rubber cocoon. The gag had been tightly re-tied and, although her hands had been unchained, they were now pinned firmly to her sides as the increasingly warm rubber moulded to her naked body. Clive had informed her that, as a punishment, she would remain in that position until he came at daybreak to release her. She couldn't help smiling as she thought of her 'punishment'. As Clive and James well knew, being kept prisoner in such a manner could certainly not be regarded by her as anything other than a pleasure – albeit a very frustrating one!

Twenty-one

A hand gently playing with a strand of her hair woke Caroline from the shallow sleep into which she had finally fallen. Opening her eyes, she looked straight into Clive's unfathomable eyes. Murmuring into her gag in the hope that she was about to be released, she was rewarded with a simple shake of her captor's head.

'Not yet, my darling. I just want to look at you.'

Clive unpeeled the rubber sheets from their adherence to her body and then just sat on the bed gazing at her nakedness. Wanting to speak to him, Caroline raised her hands to her face, but before she could pull down the gag, Clive had gathered her wrists together. Puzzled, she watched him as he remained motionless, his grip on her wrists firm enough to maintain control, but gentle enough not to cause her discomfort. They remained like that for several minutes. Clive seemed to be trying to imprint her body on his memory so that, when desired, he would always have total recall. Finding herself blushing under such close scrutiny, Caroline tried to free her hands from his grasp. Tutting as if at a naughty child, Clive reached into his pocket and extracted a length of white silk rope. Wordlessly, he tied her wrists together and then ran the cord down to her knees, winding it around them before tying the knot tightly. The exercise had rendered Caroline unable to move her tied wrists even as far as her waist. Completing his task, Clive extracted a further length of rope and tied her ankles together. With the gag still in place, Caroline was unable to move or talk and could only watch helplessly as he resumed his quiet study. It was several minutes before he spoke.

'I like to see you this way, Caroline. I don't want to frighten you. I just want to remember you like this.'

In spite of his words, Caroline felt an unreasoning fear. What did Clive mean? Why was he so intent upon remembering her? Was she not his slave? The answer, when it came, was very unexpected.

'I've always wanted you, Caroline, ever since I first met you. Do you remember how that was? Liam introduced us and you looked so scared and vulnerable. I remember so well how you looked. That wonderful plastic cape you wore that hid nothing except the fact that your hands were tied behind you and that you were gagged. I resolved from that moment that you would be mine. I lost a good friend in Liam when I took you away from him and I've never regretted it. When I lost you again, I was determined more than ever that I would get you back and that this time you would never leave. I wanted to control your mind as I knew that I controlled your body, but you always eluded me, Caroline. You always managed to keep that stubborn little mind of yours well away from my grasp. Once or twice, I thought I had overcome your resistance, but I knew that it was not quite right. Then I realised what was wrong. I wanted you to surrender to me voluntarily. I needed you to give yourself to me without holding back any little part.'

Now more than ever frightened by his words, Caroline struggled with the ropes and the gag. She needed to talk to him and tell him that he was wrong and that she had almost come to the conclusion that she really did want to stay with Clive.

'Hush, my little darling,' Clive said, laying a finger across her gagged mouth. 'Now do you see why I didn't want to remove your gag? I just wanted a chance to tell you how I feel, without interruption. I saw you with James and I know that you still have a great depth of feeling for him. In your own way, my sweet, I think you would like to be loyal.' Clive smiled as he removed his finger from her mouth and trailed it softly down her breast bone. Caroline stopped struggling as sexual arousal took the place of fear. As Clive's finger progressed lower, she resumed her struggles. This time they were an indicator of her excitement.

Clive rested his finger on the smooth skin over her pubic bone. Caroline still shaved her pubic area each day and she saw Clive's eyes glisten with appreciation as he looked at her slit and the wetness oozing from its depths. She moaned into her gag, willing him to enter her. Clive raised his head and looked with deep intensity into her eyes.

'No, Caroline, I'm not going to give you what you want, although that's not easy for me,' he said. 'I would like nothing better than to ram my cock into your sweet little pussy, but the time is not right.'

Smiling at her frustrated bewilderment, Clive bent towards her and chastely kissed her forehead. 'Not yet, my love. The others will soon be arriving and then we can begin the penultimate day's shooting. There has been a slight script change, my darling.' Caroline's eyes widened with alarm and Clive shook his head laughingly. 'Nothing for you to worry about, my love. You will, after all, be chained and gagged throughout the scene and you will be taken to the right place on the set.'

Almost reluctantly, Clive rose from the bed and stood looking down at her. 'I am taking the place of your co-star and will perform the slave auction. You may well recognise some familiar faces amongst the bidders. Just react normally, my love. For today, forget the script. Just follow your inclinations. At some stage, your gag will be removed and you will have the opportunity to choose.' As he turned to leave, Clive's voice became harsh. Studying the floor, he paused before continuing. 'I know you don't understand, Caroline, but you will. For today, you have total control over your own destiny and no-one will argue with your decision.' So softly that she could hardly hear him, he said, 'Choose wisely, my darling.'

James smiled as he glanced at the DO NOT DISTURB sign still dangling on the door of his suite. Fitting his key into the lock, he felt a stirring of excited anticipation. He had had a surprisingly good meeting with Clive and now wanted to spend the balance of the night with his new slave. Satisfied to leave the final outcome of the situation until the following day, he decided that he would set aside his confused thoughts. Opening the door, he slipped quickly inside and closed it again. As he snapped on the light, he gazed with admiration at the picture that Leyla presented. Before leaving to confront Clive, James had ensured that his new slave would wait with – albeit enforced – patience for his return.

Leyla was firmly secured to a chair and James regarded her with complete satisfaction. Her dark hair was held in an upswept style by the thick rope wound around her pony tail and secured to the back of her thick leather collar. Further rope led from the collar to the chair back, ensuring that her posture

remained nicely erect. Rope bound the top of her
arms to the chair back, behind which her tightly tied
wrists were effectively restrained. She was further
bound by thick coils of rope around her waist, thighs,
knees and ankles; all firmly secured to the chair
making any movement impossible. As the chair was
of a heavy wooden type, he had no fears of any
escape attempts causing it to topple over and thus
alert any of the hotel staff to her imprisoned status.
Any efforts that she might have made at speech were
effectively thwarted by the rope coiled around her
head and forced between her lips.

Satisfied at his captive's helpless status, James drew
up another chair and sat in front of her. 'You are a
lovely vision to return to, my love,' James said,
slipping his fingers beneath the constricting ropes that
were looped over and around her naked breasts. As
he squeezed one of the invitingly presented nipples,
James slid his other hand between her bound thighs.
Smiling at her frenzied moans of protest, James
slipped a finger into her wetness and played with her
clitoris. 'You might be interested to know that I have
had a most illuminating chat with Clive. You know,
I think I actually like the guy.'

Smiling again at her futile attempts to free herself,
James shook his head. 'No, my love, I think not. I
will take a leaf out of Clive's book and keep you quiet
while I talk to you. Clive is keeping Caroline tied up
and gagged until morning and, although she is somewhat more comfortable than you, I think that is an
excellent idea. You see, my love, if you are to be my
slave, you will have to learn that discomfort has to be
borne, if such is my decree.' Seeing the questioning
look, he took pity on her and relented. 'I'm sorry,
Leyla. I will know the answer to your question
tomorrow. All I can say is that I promise that

237

tomorrow the matter will be resolved one way or the other. Tonight, however, I don't want to think about it. I just want to enjoy the delights of my slave . . . if that's all right?'

To his enquiring gaze, Leyla nodded. James smiled as he contemplated the best way to spend the intervening hours between then and the execution of the agreement that he had reached with Clive.

People were moving quietly around the set, holding whispered conferences, moving parts of the set and substituting others. No one seemed to take any notice of Caroline despite her muffled pleas for help and renewed struggles to free herself. As the morning wore on, spent with seemingly pointless exhaustion, Caroline stopped struggling and lay still. In spite of herself, she realised that she was fascinated by the scene unfolding before her eyes. What had once been the refurbished cellar room in which she had supposedly been kept by her obsessive lover was now a mock-up of an Egyptian slave auction site, complete with a solid wooden post which had been draped in ominously exciting loops of thick chain. Realising that they would need to turn their attention to the undoubted obstacle in this authentic scene, Caroline was content to patiently wait until they got around to her. She was so engrossed that she failed to notice the stout woman who had appeared by the bed, until a voice broke into her thoughts.

'Well, Miss Caroline. It seems I have to get you ready.'

Caroline turned her head, surprised to hear Mrs Davies' voice. Since filming had begun, she had hardly seen the housekeeper. Mrs Davies sat on the bed and untied the ropes around Caroline's knees. The housekeeper smiled at her and gently stroked her hair. 'Just like old times, isn't it?' she said. 'I am to get you ready for the slave auction. I have very clear instructions. Master Clive does not want you to be told anything and he does not want you to be able to ask any questions. I am to get you shaved and showered and then make you ready for the auction.' Mrs Davies untied the ropes from her ankles and then attached a longer rope to Caroline's tightly bound wrists and pulled the girl up into a sitting position. 'We'd better go. They need to clear away the bed. Please don't give me any trouble. Everyone here has instructions to ignore you and, as you are due to get a whipping during the scene, I have been instructed not to mark you.'

Tugging at the lead rope, Mrs Davies hauled the girl to her feet. 'In any event, Master Clive says that, all being well, I will have plenty of future opportunities to administer punishment.' As the rope was pulled taut, Caroline had no choice but to follow the housekeeper. She was excited and aroused at the mention of a promised whipping but also puzzled at Mrs Davies' reference to Clive saying that all being well there would be opportunities for future whippings, which indicated some uncertainty on Clive's part and only added to her confusion. Clive was never uncertain. He was always in control, sure of himself and of the people he sought to control.

Caroline was given no further time for reflection as Mrs Davies took her into one of the studio bathrooms, closing and locking the door behind them. Gesturing to Caroline that she should enter the shower cubicle, Mrs Davies started to remove her own clothes. As Caroline had paused in front of the cubicle, Mrs Davies pushed her inside, looping the lead rope over the shower head and tying it firmly in place. Swiftly removing the white silk gag,

239

the housekeeper gave her no chance to speak, and sealed a strip of adhesive tape over her mouth. To Caroline's muffled protest, Mrs Davies merely shook her head.

Removing her dress and revealing that she wore nothing underneath, the housekeeper joined Caroline in the shower and turned on the water. 'Before filming begins, you will be allowed to eat and drink under supervision,' she explained. 'Today, you are to be treated exactly as a slave who is truly to be auctioned. That is why, before the auction commences, you will be whipped. Now hold still!' Mrs Davies had a razor in her hand and was soaping Caroline's pubic area. Massaging the soap into a lather, she constantly slipped her fingers into the girl's slit, stroking her hard little bud. As Caroline writhed with sexual excitement, Mrs Davies pretended to be displeased. 'Stay still, girl, or I will have to disobey Master Clive and whip you myself!'

Knowing that her words would only inflame her captive, Mrs Davies continued her sensual probing, watching appreciatively the way the girl's erect nipples caused the water to bounce off their tips. Bending her head, she caught one of them between her teeth, biting gently. Caroline was moaning into her gag, desperate for some relief. Mrs Davies pretended to pause and consider the situation. 'Well, we have time and I don't suppose Master Clive would object too much. Of course, if he does, I shall have to punish you severely. Do you understand?' Shivering with anticipation, Caroline nodded eagerly. Laughing softly, the housekeeper increased her thrusts into the willing girl's vagina, feeling her own orgasm begin to climb. 'Before we are finished, you are going to have to pleasure me, my girl.' Wrapped in extremes of pleasure, Caroline did not hear and would not have cared if she had. Getting immediate satisfaction was what counted. As her orgasm overwhelmed her, Caroline's knees buckled, the tightly tied rope being the only thing that stopped her from falling.

Both replete with satisfaction, Mrs Davies and Caroline stood in the wardrobe department as Caroline was fitted with her slave outfit. After bringing the girl to orgasm, Mrs Davies had shaved her pubic area before untying the lead rope and forcing the girl to her knees. Placing Caroline's tightly bound wrists on to her bush, Mrs Davies had leant against the wall of the shower cubicle as she had swiftly and expertly brought her to orgasm. Afterwards, the housekeeper had thoroughly soaped and cleaned her captive and had allowed Caroline to reciprocate. Now she stood silently watchful as Caroline was prepared for the day's filming. Under strict instructions not to utter a sound, the tape had been removed from Caroline's lips and she had also been untied. Caroline's slave costume consisted of a dark brown leather corset belt which was tightly strapped. A thick leather and metal chastity belt was buckled into position. Over this, a pair of diaphanous soft plastic harem pants were fitted. The pants left her buttocks bare and Caroline shivered with excitement as she recalled Mrs Davies' promise of a whipping. Next, dark brown leather wrist and ankle cuffs were buckled into place, thick chains connecting all four. The chains were only just long enough for her to walk and Caroline could only hope that she would not be expected to move too fast.

When the wardrobe mistress and Mrs Davies were satisfied, Caroline found herself plunged into darkness as a thick leather strap covered her eyes and was securely fastened. Before she could protest, a smooth wooden object was forced between her lips. The thick leather strip to which it was connected was tightly fastened behind her head and Caroline realised that she was incapable of making more than the most muffled of sounds. The wood was not uncomfortable but filled her mouth and made speech totally impossible. At last Mrs Davies and the wardrobe mistress were finished, and Caroline stood before them, the very image of a truly helpless slave. Fettered with thick, dark brown leather and heavy chains, Caroline was unable to see or speak. The dark brown leather gag and blindfold saw to that.

Totally disoriented, Caroline was led on to the sound stage. She was guided up a short flight of wooden steps and forced to stand against the wooden post, the positioning of which she had observed earlier. The chains which had been looped over the post were now wound around her helpless body. Firm hands held her in position as the chains were draped and tightened over her body. When they had finished, Caroline was held totally immobile, all too aware that the post neatly dissected her exposed buttocks. She felt a thrill of excitement as she realised how very helpless she truly was and also how accessible her naked buttocks were for the promised whipping. For several minutes, nothing seemed to be happening. Then a loud voice rang out.

'Take your places, please! The auction will begin shortly! You have ten minutes to inspect the property and see if she meets your requirements! You may examine the slave in any way that you choose before the public flogging!'

Supremely sensitive to touch in her world of darkness, Caroline felt a thousand tiny jolts of shock as hands, both male and female, explored her chained body. A warm hand caressed her face and slid down to her naked breasts, squeezing the hard nipples before a wet tongue replaced the fingers. Caroline moaned with pleasure as her nipples were expertly teased and sucked. An unknown male voice commented on the pleasures offered by the slave's body and of how his bidding would reflect his anticipation. Caroline shivered as she felt a long nail slithering down her back. Her buttocks were softly kneaded by softly feminine hands before something hard and slippery was inserted into her anus. Caroline struggled desperately with the tightly secured chains as the vibrator buzzed into life. The owner of the teasing implement touched her lips to Caroline's cheek, allowing the girl to inhale her expensive perfume.

'I have long desired to have my own slave,' a soft voice purred into the girl's ear. 'I hope that we are to be offered the opportunity of flogging those beautiful cheeks because if you are to be my slave, your punishments will be many and very, very severe.' With a soft, light laugh the perfume and the vibrator were withdrawn.

Caroline sucked at the hard wood lodged inside her mouth, feeling the intense feelings of frustration beginning to rise. The unknown woman's words had excited her as much as the buzzing vibrator. She wondered if this was indeed a change to the scheduled filming or whether it was real. So many strange things had been said to her and there had been no explanation for the unplanned scene that was currently being enacted. Whether it was for the cameras or not seemed to be very debatable. Caroline gasped into her gag as something soft slithered across her bottom. Instantly, she knew it to be a whip. She was aware that previously during filming the whip had been no more than a prop, visually very convincing but not at all effective when wielded by her co-star. This time, however, Caroline knew that this was no prop. She felt the leather strands of the whip as they came into contact with her skin, and a corresponding increase in her juices as she realised that she was indeed about to be whipped. For a further few moments, the exploring hands roamed across her body. Several fingers investigated her anus while others pinched and squeezed her nipples. Sometimes the pinching was so hard that Caroline groaned into her gag, which only seemed to encourage the perpetrator to further severity. Caroline was aware that her clitoris had become hard and swollen and she could feel her own wetness against the insides of her thighs.

Suddenly, all the hands were withdrawn and Caroline heard the rustling of clothing and the gradual subduing of voices as the bidders settled to watch the promised whipping. Caroline tensed as she recognised the voice that announced her punishment. As always, full of control, Clive's words informed the assembled gathering that the slave had been found guilty of several misdemeanours and subsequently would need to be reprimanded. As of old, her reprimand would take the form of a beating. Holding her breath, Caroline tensed as the fronds of the whip slithered across her legs, tickling the backs of her thighs and knees. There was not a sound as the gathering watched in silent fascination as the slave master prepared his captive. Behind the blindfold, Caroline was lost in a confusing series of images and feelings. She could smell her own arousal and twisted within her chain bondage as the silence continued.

Seeing her desperate movement, Clive raised his whip. 'The punishment will be twenty hard strokes! This will enable all the bidders to see how well the slave responds to punishment, how she craves and adores the pain that it brings.'

Caroline barely heard the swish as the whip descended through the air. She had been trying to prepare herself for the first wave of pain. It was always the hardest to bear before it started to become pleasurable. Her teeth clamped around the hard wood in her mouth. Caroline felt the increased tension in the chains as she pulled against them. The pain was working its way across her buttocks and there was no escape. Locked in her darkness, she could only fight to ride the waves of intense sensation, as brilliant colours seemed to pulsate before her eyes. Desperately, she fought to remember the waves of pleasure occasioned by the probing fingers and the vibrator inserted into her anus. There was no pause between the first and second stroke, but this time Caroline succeeded in her battle to ride the pain and felt the first thrill of pleasure in her clitoris as the chains firmly resisted her struggles and held her body rigidly in place, delineating her total helplessness.

The watching crowd murmured its approval as they noted that the slave's struggles were becoming much more sensuous, and they yearned to slip their fingers between her labia and dive into the sweet wetness they knew that they would find. Now, Caroline's smell of sexual arousal became substantially augmented as the watching crowd added its own aura. As the whipping progressed, Caroline lost count of the number of strokes, the pain becoming completely submerged in her sexual excitement. When Clive at last threw down the whip, she was trembling with desire.

Thoroughly exhausted by his endeavours, Clive strolled across the stage, his leather waistcoat straining as he sucked in deep breaths. He made a magnificent sight as he walked around, his dark brown slave master uniform soaked in sweat. He had shared the pain with Caroline and also the excitement. He turned to look at the girl and acknowledged to himself that all he really wanted was to thrust his swollen penis into her backside. Taking a deep, shuddering breath, Clive turned to the edge of the stage and summoned the woman who had been standing there, watching and waiting.

'Carol Davies, remove the slave's gag and blindfold.'

Dressed only in a thick leather corset and knee-high boots, Mrs Davies walked over to the trembling girl. Unstrapping the gag and blindfold, she stood back and waited as Caroline blinked in the unaccustomed brightness of the sound stage lighting. Her buttocks felt as though they were on fire and her desire was at fever pitch. Looking around, she saw Clive and opened her mouth to call to him, but he only shook his head and moved to the front of the wooden stage. Puzzled, Caroline looked at the watching faces in the crowd and caught her breath as she recognised Lynne and Francis, Liam and James. Soundlessly, her lips moved in shock. Gathered in front of her, mingled amongst the other anonymous faces, were all of the people to whom she owed such a great debt: Francis and Lynne who had first made her their slave; Liam who had stolen her from Francis in order to keep her for his own, and James – James her husband for whom she still felt such love and affection. Then, another face joined them as Clive walked from the stage to stand with the others. Clive, for whom she felt – what? Looking at all their familiar faces, Caroline felt her confusion rising in a crescendo. What were they all doing there and what did they all want from her? Clive moved to the foot of the stage.

'Caroline, there is not going to be an auction other perhaps than an auction of your feelings. You mean a great deal to all of us: myself, James, Liam, Francis and Lynne. All of us would like you to choose – and it is a free choice – whom it is that you would most like to be with. We will abide by your decision. All of us have, at one time or another, forced you to obey our dictates. Now the choice is yours. I feel that James and I have perhaps the most recent claims upon you. Both of us would like to have you as his partner, slave and lover. Perhaps I, more than any of the others, have tried to control you. Now I want you to choose freely and, even though I might not like the result, if it is your choice, Caroline, I will let you go. More than anything, I want you to be happy and in order truly to become a slave, you have to make that choice yourself. Life with James will be great fun. You will have everything that you need and James loves you . . . very much.' Glancing at his rival, Clive smiled. 'With me, you will have everything that I can supply, but you will live as my slave subject to my demands. Sometimes, those demands will seem cruel and unreasonable, but I will expect your total obedience. Mrs Davies will help me to look after you and you will also be expected to obey her commands.' Clive paused and fixed her with his mesmeric gaze. 'I still want to control you, Caroline, and that will not change. What I offer you is a life of servitude and something more. I offer you my total love and devotion and my promise that, if you choose me, I will never, never again let you get away from me.'

Twenty-two

Love's Obsession *has squeezed past the censors by the skin of its teeth and has been granted an 18 certificate. Controversial film director Lee Esslyn has not disappointed with this one. In a sensual tale of an obsessive love which, for once, has a satisfactory outcome, he manages to handle the sensitive material with courage and wisdom, securing top-notch performances from his two stars who are both newcomers to the mainstream. Stewart Osman, usually only seen in pornographic features, acquits himself well in the rôle of the man obsessed with his girlfriend to the point that he keeps her under lock and key. The real surprise is Caroline West. Sensually beautiful, she is more than convincing in her characterisation of the girlfriend, who happily plays along with her boyfriend's sex games until things take a more serious turn. Having seen a sneak preview, I am a definite fan. Without giving too much away, the ending leaves one literally panting for more. The film premieres tonight and I would strongly recommend it with one proviso. Do not watch it alone. Take your partner and be prepared for a very long night!*

Mrs Davies entered the bedroom and stood looking down at Caroline. Gagged and strapped firmly to the mattress, a buzzing vibrator inserted into her vagina and secured with a rope belt, Caroline was not aware that she was being watched. Mrs Davies smiled as she reached down and switched off the vibrator, causing Caroline's eyes to open. Unable to keep the dismay from her eyes, she could only stare helplessly at the housekeeper, with an expression that a child wears when its toy has been forcibly removed.

'Master Clive says that you will by now have had enough to put you very firmly in the mood.' Mrs Davies studied the girl's eyes critically. 'I think he's right. You have the look of a slut who adores sex.'

Unstrapping Caroline from the bed, Mrs Davies also removed the gag and helped her into a sitting position.

'Just a few more minutes, Mrs Davies. Please.'

Ignoring Caroline's imploring look, Mrs Davies washed the vibrator in the vanity unit of the small dressing room which opened off the bedroom.

'Master Clive does not want you to orgasm until after the premiere,' Mrs Davies called out from the dressing room. 'He wants every man and woman present to respond to your obvious sexuality and to desire you for themselves. I am to stay with you until he comes to collect you . . .'

Breaking off as she returned to the bedroom, Mrs Davies stopped as she saw that Caroline's fingers were busily massaging her clitoris. The girl's eyes were closed in approaching ecstasy. Suddenly, the pleasant interlude was shattered as Mrs Davies marched over to her and grabbed her wrists.

'Master Clive will not be pleased with you, my girl. Later, you will have to be punished. Right now, though, I will make sure that you behave!'

Caroline gasped as her arms were forced behind her and thick rope was tightly tied around her wrists. As always, the bondage only increased her sexual excitement and, in this instance, her frustration. 'Please, Mrs Davies. Please bring me off. I won't tell Clive and . . .'

'But I would, my girl. You have only served to complicate matters. You have forced me to tie you up, which means that I will have to wash you myself.'

Although her tone was a stern one, Mrs Davies felt her nipples harden as she contemplated the pleasing prospect. Returning to the dressing room and selecting some stout handcuffs, she stood in the doorway, dangling the cuffs and unable to conceal her pleasure.

'You are fortunate that we have plenty of time. Get on your feet and we will take a shower together.'

Watching with delight at the difficulties Caroline experienced in trying to stand without being able to use her hands, made more difficult by the fact that she was sitting in the middle of a very large bed, Mrs Davies fondled her nipples. Perhaps there was even time for a little taste of the promised punishment. Going back into the dressing room, Mrs Davies stroked the handle of a black leather whip. Yes of course there was time.

'A little taste of pain before you shower, my dear?' Mrs Davies said as she walked towards her tethered charge.

Caroline said nothing but attempted to back away. She knew that calling for Clive would be pointless. He had clearly informed her that Mrs Davies would have a free hand and he would not interfere, besides which the prospect of a whipping only increased her arousal.

'We ... we had better not be late,' she managed, backing into a wall and unable to do anything other than watch her tormentress approach.

'Oh, we won't be late, my dear. Now, I want you to be a good girl and go and bend over that chair.'

Caroline looked at the softly padded chair to which Mrs Davies had indicated. 'But ... but, Mrs Davies. I can't. My hands are tied.'

'Then I suggest you think of a way to obey me, my dear. Otherwise we may indeed be late.'

Staring at the housekeeper's implacable face, Caroline felt mounting excitement. She was able to walk over to the chair, but was unwilling to let herself fall forward into the required position. She was conscious of Mrs Davies' eyes watching every movement. Suddenly, she felt a small push at her back and overbalanced. She hit the chair with a small thud which slightly winded her but otherwise did not cause her any injury. Feeling terribly vulnerable with her bottom so presented, Caroline could only wait for the first stroke of the whip. Instead, she felt a soft hand travelling across her buttocks, coming to rest just over her anus.

'You will learn obedience, my dear, and Mrs Davies will ensure that your lessons are deliciously painful.' Caroline quivered as she heard the voice of her Master. 'Unfortunately, there is no time for anything other than a shower before we get you dressed. When we return, well, that is another matter. Every bit of disobedience that has been observed will have to be paid for and you will pay, my darling, you will pay.'

As Caroline opened her mouth to speak, Clive slipped the whip handle between her teeth. 'No talking, my dear. Mrs Davies will get you showered and then we will both get you dressed.' Straightening, he faced the housekeeper. 'Carol, see that the slave maintains that whip between her teeth. If she does not, I want to hear about it.'

'Yes, Master Clive. You can rely on me.'

As Mrs Davies helped Caroline to stand, Clive reached the door and turned.

'Be a good girl, Caroline,' he said. 'You have already incurred several punishment debits. For your own sake, I would suggest that you do not incur any more.'

'This place looks more like a fetish club than a film premiere!'

Laughing delightedly, Leyla looked around at the crowded lobby. The Odeon in Leicester Square had probably never seen anything like it. Men and women milled around, all dressed in rubber and leather outfits. Squeezing her arm, James smiled at his partner. She was dazzlingly dressed in a moulded black latex dress which clung to her body as far as the hips and then draped in shining folds to the floor. Her recently acquired black rubber collar encircled her slender neck. The shining dark fall of her hair concealing the glistening gold padlock which secured it in place. The draped folds of the lower part of her dress effectively concealed the black rubber dance pants. Only she and James knew of her discomfort as she moved. Every step seemed to push the thick rubber penis further inside her vagina.

James' well-cut beige leather suit just about concealed his erection and only the two of them knew of the pleasures they intended to enjoy on their return to their hosts' home. Thinking of Francis and Lynne caused James to look around for the couple who had become firm friends. They had all arrived together, but Francis and Lynne had been swamped with greetings from old friends. Clive had personally vetted the guest list, consulting with James and Francis as to the eligibility of the invitees. Spotting Lynne's elegantly rubber-clad figure, James waved and they were soon joined by the sensually garbed pair. Lynne was wearing an electric blue skin-tight mini dress while Francis had contented himself with a black leather suit. Cameramen were going frantic. Used to celebrities at such events, these assignments normally followed a pattern. Now, they vied with each other for the closest shot of each of the sexily dressed men and, more particularly, the women.

Rumours were buzzing about Caroline and who would escort her. It was generally accepted that, at these functions, the stars would arrive together, but it had been made plain that Caroline would be the last to arrive and that she would be accompanied by her Master. Leyla and Lynne were not immune to the excited speculation as to Caroline's outfit. After the auction, these two had become the best of friends and Lynne felt that James and Caroline had both made the wisest of choices. Over the past few weeks, she had seen another side to Clive and was now certain that the man she had once despised had redeemed himself by his undoubted devotion to Caroline. They had all been moved by Clive's little speech and none was therefore surprised when Caroline chose her mate.

'You know, I think they're going to be very happy,' Lynne said to Leyla. 'Clive really loves her and I think that James feels the same way about you.'

Smiling her gratitude, Leyla surprised James by giving him an enthusiastic kiss, to which he responded with equal fervour.

'Hey, break it up, you two,' Francis said. 'I think our lovely Caroline is about to make her entrance.'

The black limousine that drove up to the entrance had darkened windows. No one was to be allowed a glimpse of Caroline until her Master decreed it. With pre-planned aplomb, Stewart Osman leapt forward to open the door. The television lights were reflected in the shining PVC suit that he wore as the cameras jostled for shots of him and of the girl they had all come to see.

Clive stepped out first, turning to offer his hand to his slave. Himself looking debonair in a well-cut black leather tuxedo, he found himself shivering with excitement as he waited to present the girl he loved to the watching world. There was a slight pause before Caroline finally emerged. There was a moment's stunned silence and then a blinding barrage of flash-bulbs as cameras from all the newspapers and journals in the world went off together. Caroline was dressed in a tight white rubber catsuit with matching white high-heeled boots and elbow-length rubber gauntlets, but it was the cape that caused the most comment. Fitting tightly over her skull, it clung to her face, leaving only her eyes and nose visible. The hood blended into a tight neck collar before flowing across her shoulders and down to the ground. As she moved, the cape fell open, revealing shapely rubber-clad curves. As Caroline moved away from the car, further interest was caused by a black rubber-clad figure alighting next. Swathed in clinging latex which concealed her less than perfect figure, Mrs Davies took her place behind Caroline and Clive, a position she was happy to adopt, since from there she could keep an eye on her charge and watch and report any misdemeanours. As the party moved into the elegant foyer, Clive bent his head and whispered softly to his slave, 'I am very pleased with you, my dear. You are a complete success. This will not of course affect the just administration of your punishment.'

As he held her arm, Clive could feel Caroline's shiver of excitement. Could anyone have seen beneath the leather of his suit, his own pleasure would be plain to see. Caroline did not reply. Beneath the white rubber of the hood which covered her mouth, the thin, firmly sealed adhesive tape ensured her silence.

* * *

'Well, I think that was a success, don't you?'

Caroline could only look at Clive, her eyes conveying her affirmation.

'I think the papers will be full of your appearance, undoubtedly hailing the mystery masked woman who didn't say a word. Little did they know that you were unable to speak because you were gagged, but it's just as well. We don't want to risk the censors withdrawing the film's certificate, do we?'

Caroline and Mrs Davies listened to Clive's rhetorical questions, one in enforced silence, the other maintaining her muteness as a mark of respect. Looking towards Mrs Davies, Clive inclined his head in an imperceptible nod. Without hesitation, the housekeeper turned towards Caroline.

'Hands, please,' she ordered.

Obeying the instruction, Caroline held out both her wrists to enable Mrs Davies to snap metal handcuffs over the gauntlet gloves. Nodding his approval, Clive returned to his reverie concerning the delights of the evening.

'The gentlemen of the press were falling over themselves to know why the star remained silent,' Clive said, chuckling as he ran a playful hand across his slave's breasts. 'If they had only known the truth,' he sighed. 'But they will never come close, my dear. People believe what they want to believe. They don't want to be too shocked. The idea that you truly are my slave and that you willingly allowed yourself to be taken to the premiere gagged and with your prison wardress in attendance would not have been acceptable.' Looking at Caroline with his intense dark eyes, he smiled. 'And you are my slave, aren't you, my darling?'

Almost shyly, Caroline nodded her head. She had been unbelievably excited by the events of the night.

Even more than Clive, she had enjoyed her captive state and the fact that, other than Mrs Davies, no one had guessed at the real reason for her silence. She knew that she would be labelled enigmatic and that Clive was assumed to be her manager. Of course he was, but he was the manager of her whole life. He decided when she got up and what she wore. Most excitingly, he decided whether or not she would spend the day in restraints. He decreed when she was to be punished and by whom. Sometimes he attended to it himself and at other times he watched while Mrs Davies administered the punishment. In all other ways, he was concerned for her well being and ensured that she was happy and that she had everything she needed. All he demanded in return was her complete obedience and unswerving acceptance of him as her Master. She acknowledged that he had at last achieved his aim. She was truly his and she allowed him to control her completely, happy in the sure knowledge that now she really had exactly who and what she wanted. She also knew that in the event of any real problem, she could turn to him and share it. She knew that he would never hurt her, except by her consent, and she was completely happy as she acknowledged the fact that she could relax and enjoy the fetish dressing, the restraints and all the sex games. It was her fantasy become totally beautiful reality.

'You look so far away, my love,' Clive whispered. 'Are you all right?'

Eyes brimming with happiness, Caroline nodded.

'James told me that you looked wonderful and that he was very jealous of me. I thanked him, but pointed out that a woman like Leyla was not exactly a consolation prize!' Stroking her breast with increasing excitement, Clive told her about a message he had received from Liam. 'He says that he was sorry to miss the premiere, but was having a pirated copy of the film despatched to his new home. I said there was no need for that and I would talk to the distributors and get him a copy. He and Selina send their love and best wishes to both of us.' Beneath her gag, Caroline smiled. Dear Liam, he was so kind. She was very pleased that he was making a new life for himself with Selina, a woman to whom James had introduced him. Suddenly aware of a strong pressure on her upper arm, she looked up at Clive. 'Well, my dear. What form will your punishment take? I think that I will allow Mrs Davies to take you downstairs while I have a nightcap and consider your chastisement. Carol?'

'Certainly, Master Clive. I will make sure that the slave is suitably prepared.'

'Excellent. The dungeon cell, I think.'

The dungeons in Clive's house were just that, albeit that the originals had been refurbished to offer a little comfort. As Mrs Davies led a naked Caroline down the carpeted steps, warmth from the central heating engulfed them. The only reason for Caroline's shivering was the sheer excitement which permeated her whole being. The premiere had been gloriously exciting and the evening was now about to culminate in the promised punishment administered by the man for whom she now had no doubts as to her feelings. He did control her totally and she surrendered with complete happiness. Mrs Davies had not removed the tape from her mouth and had in fact added another strip to ensure her silence under whatever punishment lay in store. The housekeeper's harsh grip on her arm offered no escape and only added to Caroline's excitement.

Pulling her roughly towards the metal barred cell

in one corner of the dungeon, Mrs Davies forced her to stand facing the bars with her arms raised. Caroline felt a renewed thrill of excitement as thick rope was wrapped around her slim wrists and coiled around the bars of the cell. Caroline grunted as Mrs Davies tied the knots firmly. When she had secured the girl's wrists, she fed rope through the bars and tied it securely around her waist. Forcing Caroline's legs apart, the housekeeper roped her ankles to the metal bars, leaving the girl immobile and with her bottom appealingly presented. Smoothing her hands across the white skin, Mrs Davies chuckled. 'What a nice little chicken! All plucked and nicely trussed!'

Turning her head as far as she could, Caroline was able to watch as the housekeeper left the dungeon, leaving her charge to await her punishment. Experimentally, Caroline pulled at her bonds. Mrs Davies did not disappoint. As always, her ropes were securely tied. The extra layer of tape on her mouth ensured that Caroline could not dislodge it. Truly a prisoner, she could only wait. Her excitement had almost become unbearable when warm hands caressed her bottom and an exploratory finger slipped inside her anus.

'A very pretty parcel, my dear,' Clive said and then moved inside the cell and sat on the low bed. Smiling up at his captive, he squeezed the nipples on the tips of breasts that Mrs Davies had forced between the bars. 'What shall I do with you, I wonder? Shall I whip you as you undoubtedly deserve, my darling? Shall I do that and then shall I push my cock into that delicious little anus?'

Beneath the tape, Caroline moaned. She wanted Clive to pleasure her and his words had only fuelled her longing. She watched as Clive stood up and walked out of the cell. She did not have long to wait before the hard handle of a whip was inserted into her vagina. She felt his warm breath against her cheek as he manipulated the handle until she was moaning with pleasure.

'My little slave . . . all mine.'

As she neared her climax, Clive withdrew the whip handle and sniffed appreciatively at the wet leather. 'I've had an idea, Caroline. I will whip you until you agree to something. Can you bear such a whipping, my love?'

Caroline made desperate noises into her gag, trying to illustrate that she was in no position to agree to anything. Clive's warm laugh reassured her.

'When your divorce from James becomes final, my love, I want to marry you and I want to have your answer tonight. I will whip you until you agree. Do you understand?'

If Clive had been able to look into her face at that moment, he would have seen her smile as she nodded. Caroline decided to submit quietly to the whipping until Clive 'remembered' that she was gagged and therefore unable to answer him verbally, although they both knew that that answer was not in doubt. As the first stroke landed across her bottom, Caroline's clitoris supplied its own answer. As the thrills of pleasure chased up and down her spine, Caroline smiled and leant her face against the cool metal bars. It promised to be a very long night!

NEW BOOKS

Coming up from Nexus and Black Lace

Sherrie and the Initiation of Penny by Evelyn Culber
October 1997   Price £4.99   ISBN: 0 352 33216 6
On her second assignment for her enigmatic master, Sherrie acts as
instructress to the unhappy writer Penny Haig, initiating her into an
enjoyment of the depraved and perverse games the writer has never
before dated to play. Penny soon becomes a fully-fledged enthusiast,
revelling in humiliating ordeals at the skilled hands of expert discipli-
narians.

Candida in Paris by Virginia Lasalle
October 1997   Price £4.99   ISBN: 0 352 33215 8
Naughty Candida has a new mission – one very much in keeping with
her lascivious sensibilities. She is sent to investigate a clandestine
organisation providing unique sexual services for wealthy Parisians,
and soon finds herself caught up in a secret world of orgies and
hedonistic gratification. She cannot resist the temptation of sating her
prodigious lust – but does she underestimate the danger of her task?

Journey from Innocence by Jean-Philippe Aubourg
November 1997   Price £4.99   ISBN: 0 352 33212 3
When shy young Philippa accepts a houseshare with a young couple, little
does she realise the extent of the dark games of bondage and submission
they like to play. Investigating their cries of pleasure one night, she begins
her own initiation into new realms of perversion, being taken to the limits
of her ability to submit – and to the heights of debauchery.

A Chamber of Delights by Katrina Young
November 1997   Price £4.99   ISBN: 0 352 33213 1
Banished from a life of luxury at the opulent Grymwell Hall, the
young and beautiful Gael sets out to create a new and even more
kinky life in the house of her lesbian lover. Recruiting the naughty
housemaid and the raunchy gardener to assist her in acting out the
wild sexual fantasies of her guests, Gael finds herself embroiled in
increasingly bizarre relationships.

There are three Black Lace titles published in October

French Manners by Olivia Christie

October 1997   Price £4.99   ISBN: 0 352 33214 X

Gilles de la Trave persuades Colette, a young and innocent girl from one of his estates, to become his mistress and live the debauched life of a Parisian courtesan. However, it is his son Victor she lusts after and expects to marry. Shocked by the power of her own lascivious desires, Colette loses herself in a life of wild indulgence in Paris; but she needs the protection of one man to help her survive – a man who has so far refused to succumb to her charms.

Artistic Licence by Vivienne LaFay

October 1997   Price £4.99   ISBN: 0 352 33210 7

Renaissance Italy. Carla Buonomi has disguised herself as a man to find work in Florence. All goes well until she is expected to perform bizarre and licentious favours for her employer. Surrounded by a host of desirable young men and women, she finds herself in a quandary of desire. One person knows her true gender, and he and Carla enjoy an increasingly depraved affair – but how long will it be before her secret is revealed?

Invitation to Sin by Charlotte Royal

October 1997   Price £6.99   ISBN: 0 352 33217 4

Beautiful young Justine has been raised in a convent and taught by Father Gabriel to praise the Lord with her body. She is confused when the handsome wanderer Armand offers her the same pleasure without the blessing of the church, and upon sating her powerful lusts is banished in disgrace from the convent and put into a life of servitude. She must plan her escape, and decide whether to accept Armand's invitation to sin. This is the second Black Lace novel to be published in B format.

The Stranger by Portia Da Costa
November 1997   Price £4.99   ISBN: 0 352 33211 5
When a mysterious young man stumbles into the life of the recently
widowed Claudia, he reawakens her sleeping sexuality and introduces
her to a new world of perverse pleasures. Claudia's friends become
involved in trying to decide whether or not he is to be trusted. As an
erotic obsession flowers between Paul and Claudia, and all taboos are
obliterated, his true identity no longer seems to matter.

Elena's Destiny by Lisette Allen
November 1997   Price £4.99   ISBN: 0 352 33218 2
The year is 1073. The gentle, convent-bred Elena has been introduced
to the joys of forbidden passion by the masterful knight, Aimery le
Sabrenn. War breaks out, however, and they are separated. When a
chance quirk of fate brings them together again, things have changed.
Elena finds that she has to contend with two rivals: the wanton and
lascivious Henrietta, and the cunning and sensual Isobel, who enjoys
playing dark and dangerous games.

NEXUS BACKLIST

All books are priced £4.99 unless another price is given. If a date is supplied, the book in question will not be available until that month in 1997.

CONTEMPORARY EROTICA

THE ACADEMY	Arabella Knight	Oct
AGONY AUNT	G. C. Scott	Jul
ALLISON'S AWAKENING	John Angus	Jul
BOUND TO SUBMIT	Amanda Ware	Sep
CANDIDA'S IN PARIS	Virginia LaSalle	Oct
CANDY IN CAPTIVITY	Arabella Knight	
CHALICE OF DELIGHTS	Katrina Young	
A CHAMBER OF DELIGHTS	Katrina Young	Nov
THE CHASTE LEGACY	Susanna Hughes	
CHRISTINA WISHED	Gene Craven	
DARK DESIRES	Maria del Rey	
THE DOMINO TATTOO	Cyrian Amberlake	
THE DOMINO ENIGMA	Cyrian Amberlake	
THE DOMINO QUEEN	Cyrian Amberlake	
EDUCATING ELLA	Stephen Ferris	Aug
ELAINE	Stephen Ferris	
EMMA'S SECRET WORLD	Hilary James	
EMMA'S SECRET DIARIES	Hilary James	
EMMA'S HUMILIATION	Hilary James	
FALLEN ANGELS	Kendal Grahame	
THE TRAINING OF FALLEN ANGELS	Kendal Grahame	Dec
THE FANTASIES OF JOSEPHINE SCOTT	Josephine Scott	
HEART OF DESIRE	Maria del Rey	

HOUSE OF INTRIGUE	Yvonne Strickland	
HOUSE OF TEMPTATIONS	Yvonne Strickland	
THE ISLAND OF MALDONA	Yolanda Celbridge	
THE CASTLE OF MALDONA	Yolanda Celbridge	Apr
THE ICE QUEEN	Stephen Ferris	
THE INSTITUTE	Maria del Rey	
SISTERHOOD OF THE INSTITUTE	Maria del Rey	
JENNIFER'S INSTRUCTION	Cyrian Amberlake	
JOURNEY FROM INNOCENCE	G. C. Scott	Nov
A MATTER OF POSSESSION	G. C. Scott	
MELINDA AND THE MASTER	Susanna Hughes	
MELINDA AND THE COUNTESS	Susanna Hughes	
MELINDA AND SOPHIA	Susanna Hughes	
MELINDA AND ESMERELDA	Susanna Hughes	
THE NEW STORY OF O	Anonymous	
ONE WEEK IN THE PRIVATE HOUSE	Esme Ombreux	
AMANDA IN THE PRIVATE HOUSE	Esme Ombreux	Sep
PARADISE BAY	Maria del Rey	
THE PASSIVE VOICE	G. C. Scott	
THE SCHOOLING OF STELLA	Yolanda Celbridge	Dec
SECRETS OF THE WHIPCORD	Michaela Wallace	Aug
SERVING TIME	Sarah Veitch	
SHERRIE	Evelyn Culber	
SHERRIE AND THE INITIATION OF PENNY	Evelyn Culber	Oct
THE SPANISH SENSUALIST	Josephine Arno	
STEPHANIE'S CASTLE	Susanna Hughes	
STEPHANIE'S REVENGE	Susanna Hughes	
STEPHANIE'S DOMAIN	Susanna Hughes	
STEPHANIE'S TRIAL	Susanna Hughes	
STEPHANIE'S PLEASURE	Susanna Hughes	
SUSIE IN SERVITUDE	Arabella Knight	Mar
THE REWARD OF FAITH	Elizabeth Bruce	Dec
THE TRAINING GROUNDS	Sarah Veitch	
VIRGINIA'S QUEST	Katrina Young	Jun
WEB OF DOMINATION	Yvonne Strickland	May

EROTIC SCIENCE FICTION

RETURN TO THE PLEASUREZONE	Delaney Silver	

ANCIENT & FANTASY SETTINGS

CAPTIVES OF ARGAN	Stephen Ferris	Mar
CITADEL OF SERVITUDE	Aran Ashe	Jun
THE CLOAK OF APHRODITE	Kendal Grahame	
DEMONIA	Kendal Grahame	
NYMPHS OF DIONYSUS	Susan Tinoff	Apr
PYRAMID OF DELIGHTS	Kendal Grahame	
THE SLAVE OF LIDIR	Aran Ashe	
THE DUNGEONS OF LIDIR	Aran Ashe	
THE FOREST OF BONDAGE	Aran Ashe	
WARRIOR WOMEN	Stephen Ferris	
WITCH QUEEN OF VIXANIA	Morgana Baron	
SLAVE-MISTRESS OF VIXANIA	Morgana Baron	

EDWARDIAN, VICTORIAN & OLDER EROTICA

ANNIE AND THE SOCIETY	Evelyn Culber	
BEATRICE	Anonymous	
CHOOSING LOVERS FOR JUSTINE	Aran Ashe	
DEAR FANNY	Aran Ashe	
LYDIA IN THE BORDELLO	Philippa Masters	
MADAM LYDIA	Philippa Masters	
MAN WITH A MAID 3	Anonymous	
MEMOIRS OF A CORNISH GOVERNESS	Yolanda Celbridge	
THE GOVERNESS AT ST AGATHA'S	Yolanda Celbridge	
THE GOVERNESS ABROAD	Yolanda Celbridge	
PLEASING THEM	William Doughty	

Please send me the books I have ticked above.

Name ....

Address ....

....

....

.... Post code ....

Send to: **Cash Sales, Nexus Books, 332 Ladbroke Grove, London W10 5AH**

Please enclose a cheque or postal order, made payable to Virgin Publishing, to the value of the books you have ordered plus postage and packing costs as follows:

UK and BFPO – £1.00 for the first book, 50p for each subsequent book.

Overseas (including Republic of Ireland) – £2.00 for the first book, £1.00 for each subsequent book.

If you would prefer to pay by VISA or ACCESS/MASTER-CARD, please write your card number and expiry date here:

....

Please allow up to 28 days for delivery.

Signature ....